A RIVER OF FORTUNE

Paula Welch

ISBN: 978-0-6487655-2-3 (paperback)

National Library of Australia reference no. NED97514

Illustrations by Artist. S Lebeuf
Cover Designer: Donika Mishineva | www.artofdonika.com
Typesetting and e-book design: Amit Dey

Email: pjwelch.author@bigpond.com
Website: www.paulawelch.com.au

I DEDICATE THIS BOOK TO

Mum and Dad – for being there
And to four special ladies
Alyson, Alisha, Emma and Sophie
Thanks for all your help

CONTENTS

Prologue – Maggie Malloy ix

Bridget's Plan 1

Club 26 4

Best Laid Plans 6

The Betrayal 10

The Whys and Wherefores 15

Unforeseen Circumstances 20

The Van 27

The Senior Analyst 33

The Butterfly Effect 38

In for a Penny, In for a Pound 43

GCHQ – November 49

Eve 54

Bleak Times 62

A Taste of Rebellion 68

First the Bulb, Then the Tulip 75

Rebel, Rebel 81

Maggie's Plan 86

The Confession 88

GCHQ – March 102

United We All Stand .111

Best Laid Plans 120

The Deposit Gang 125

GCHQ – May 131

The Art of Politics 134

The Ding Dong Brigade 140

All in a Day's Work 143

The Ritz 150

The Rivoli Bar 152

'Tis the Season 163

Friendships 168

A Most Private Dick 175

The Barn Swallow 182

A Fly on the Wall 190

Skulduggery 196

The Devil You Know 200

I Solemnly Swear 201

Never a Dull Moment 209

Club 26 220

Running Out Of Time 221

Cards on the Table. 230

I'll Huff and I'll Puff 243

No Turning Back 250

A Stitch in Time. 268

Hedging Your Bets 277

Cleaning House 279

Come All Ye Faithful 281

Acknowledgments. 285

About the Author 287

Prologue

Maggie Malloy

Maggie Malloy lived her life like it was a neatly folded napkin – orderly and without fanfare.

Don't get me wrong. She wasn't boring. Not in the least. But her life had no ruffled edges to it. She chose comfortability over risk, which didn't leave much room for unconventional behaviour. Caring for her mother until her death afforded her no eccentricities. Maggie felt as if her life was trapped inside a driverless car. She went where she had to go without any input or control over the situation. The sad thing was that Maggie didn't realise she was doing it. If you spoke to Maggie, she would smile and tell you that she was happy.

But that would be a lie. Trapped inside was another Maggie; one filled with hopes and dreams, waiting to burst open and take on the world.

Maggie's problem was that she just hadn't lived. Her job wasn't exciting; far from it. But that could be said for many people. Beggars couldn't be choosers in Friars Meadow, a small town perfectly tucked away into the county of Devon. It was the place where Maggie had been born, had lived most of her life, and probably would die if she didn't open her eyes to let the world in.

Many people in town would say she was luckier than most to have inherited her mother's house on the hill. But that was due only to the cruel nature of cancer.

Her saving grace was her five quirky yet splendid friends. They were her family. They made her laugh when she needed to laugh, and they gave her a shoulder when she needed to cry.

So, you see, Maggie's life hadn't been without hardship and pain. But for some time now, she'd felt like her life was at a crossroads. She didn't know whether to run or jump, cry or scream, sink or swim. So, she simply remained silent. Her cool head prevented her from being anything but sensible.

But let's face it. Everyone needs to be reckless and adventurous at least once in their lives.

Now, as it stood, Maggie's story wasn't very exciting. It would have continued this way if it weren't for a fortunate discovery during a brisk walk on a chilly February day. It was this fortuitous event that dropped fate right into Maggie's lap.

However, life isn't supposed to be neat and orderly, like a practical paper napkin. It's supposed to be like a big, fat, sticky Chelsea bun – messy but rewarding.

Unfortunately, the same couldn't be said for Bridget Monahan. If there were ever two women more different in character and ideology, it was Maggie and Bridget.

It's important that we go back to the beginning, to examine how Maggie's story came about. It all happened with a butterfly effect; Bridget's crime inadvertently led to Maggie's. And so, you must judge for yourself the guilt or innocence of Maggie and her friends. Because by the end of Maggie's story, five people will be dead and many more imprisoned, all because of a little black box called Pandora.

So, let me take you back …

Bridget's Plan

June, Summer

The Navy had taught Bridget Monahan two things: discipline and courage. Unfortunately, that was as far as it went. The Navy's motto was *si vis pacem, para bellum* – Latin for 'if you wish for peace, prepare for war'. Bridget took this to mean: *if you want something bad enough, plan well and take it*. And that's exactly what she did.

Bridget had hated high school and couldn't wait to leave. Up until graduation, her life hadn't been very inspiring. As soon as she matriculated, she left Exeter and joined the Navy. She didn't want to end up like half the girls in her class would – working in a supermarket or factory for minimum wage; living off welfare; or pregnant by eighteen. She wanted better for herself; she deserved better. She wasn't unintelligent – far from it. She had excelled in mathematics but lacked direction. If her teacher had been allowed, she would have written on Bridget's final report card that Bridget had the capacity to either go very far or fall very hard. Even when she was young, Bridget had liked to live life on the razor's edge.

In the Navy, Bridget started her career in communications. From there, she was transferred to naval intelligence. After serving eight years she was recruited into MI5. Unfortunately, Bridget didn't find MI5 very exciting, and hadn't taken to the life of an analyst. So, for two years, she kept her head down and her eyes open.

She hadn't made many friends at work. She didn't need any. Some presented themselves as being above her station, so she took an instant disliking to them. Those below her station could offer her nothing. The only close friend (and part-time lover) she tolerated was Corporal Dillan Andrews, a marine she'd met while serving on board one of Her Majesty's destroyers.

Dillan Andrews now worked for Britain's largest private military contractor and earned three times his original salary. They would meet up whenever he was in London. Casual sex and conversation were all Bridget required of him. She knew that Dillan wanted more, and he knew that she couldn't give it. So, he took what was on offer, and the arrangement worked well for both of them.

Until, one day, Bridget asked Dillan how far he would go to have enough money to live carefree for the rest of his life. His only response was, 'Go on.'

She sat with her legs across Dillan's lap as she outlined her plan. It was a balmy evening in June, and they were lying on the sofa in her apartment.

'You have to admit that it's rather clever.'

Dillan narrowed his eyes. 'Yes, clever. But dangerous, too.'

Bridget went on, ignoring this last part. 'How much would your employer pay for the most sophisticated surveillance software in the world? Do you know someone you could safely approach to make the offer?'

Dillan knew MI5 had the most stringent security measures in the country, along with MI6 and GCHQ – Government Communications Headquarters. Their employees were carefully checked entering and leaving the building each day. No one could conceal any form of data on any form of device without security being alerted to it. Then again, people who worked for the security services wouldn't consider committing treason. They joined to fight the bigger fight. But Dillan knew Bridget well enough to know she wouldn't have suggested the acquisition if she didn't have an exit strategy.

Bridget had always been hungry for something, and Dillan knew it. She knew he found it sexy, too. And now, she'd finally told him what that was.

He grinned at her. 'It could be easy money.'

As Dillan stroked her legs, he pondered Bridget's plan. He knew what she was capable of, but he also knew the type of men she would be dealing with. It was risky and could backfire. If they got caught, it would be treason and life imprisonment. However, the visage of a small smile appeared on Bridget's face, communicating to him that they wouldn't get caught.

'So,' she said. 'Can you do it?'
He said he would make some discreet enquiries.

Club 26

July, Mid-Summer

Archibald Monroe sat quietly smoking his pipe in a private London members club. His eyes betrayed nothing through the haze of smoke that spiralled around him.

'Are you sure this is genuine?' he asked.

'Yes. I've checked her background,' Major James Hamilton replied.

'Make the deal,' said Monroe.

'What about the girl?'

'Take care of her. No loose ends.'

'Understood – what do you want to do about Corporal Andrews?' asked Hamilton.

'If he tows the line, keep him on. If not ...' He left the last sentence hanging in the air like the cigar smoke. Monroe sat back in his chair and inhaled once again.

Major Hamilton knew the answer. He nodded and got up to leave. Corporal Andrews was one of his men. As a soldier, he lived by a certain code and would always protect his men. But if he caused them trouble, well, that was another matter entirely.

When he left the club, the Major dialled Corporal Andrews' mobile.

'Yeah, Dillan here!' he answered.

'You have a deal.'

The line went dead.

Major Hamilton zipped up his jacket as a cold chill ran through him. The sky was as grey as his mood.

*   *   *

'We're on,' Dillan said as he turned over to kiss Bridget on the lips. She gave him a confident smile, then rolled over and lay quietly on her side as she rehearsed her final day at work once again in her head. Plan … Plan … Plan ...

Dillan lay there, thinking. As he did, a shadow briefly crossed his mind, sending a shiver through him. It was a fleeting thing, but it left him feeling like he'd just made the biggest mistake of his life.

For Bridget's plan to work, all she needed was a device on which to upload the software before she exited the building. Her farewell present would be the answer.

Best Laid Plans

August, Summer's End

MI5 – Thames House, Millbank, London

It was Bridget's last day at MI5. She did the usual rounds and thanked everyone for her farewell gift and giant card. She made the obligatory speech while everyone enjoyed her farewell cake. Afterwards, she proceeded to her locker, then to the security office where she handed in her security card and signed all the relevant documents. Bridget Monahan was as calm as the eye of a storm as she exited Thames House for the last time. Bridget had always been a confident woman and as the rest of London spun around her, in the mayhem of everyday life, she showed no fear. She'd done it. She'd stolen the software. No one had suspected a thing.

The idea had come to Bridget four months earlier, when she'd attended the celebratory farewell of a fellow analyst. The MI5 officer was given his farewell gift, cake, and oversized card in the office before being escorted out by security for the final time. One of Bridget's colleagues pointed out to her that at MI5, they did you the courtesy of asking what you would like as a fare-well gift. They usually obliged, as long as it was within budget.

So once Bridget had a buyer, and knew how to steal it, she'd handed in her resignation. For her farewell gift, Bridget had chosen a small electronic pocket notebook. It was compact but would be able to hold the gigabytes she needed. When Bridget's supervisor handed over her farewell gift and card, she feigned open surprise and gratitude to everyone for her generous present.

Bridget was given a regulation cardboard box in which to put all her personal items. She didn't have many; just a plant, mug, and a novel – no photos. No personal mobiles, iPods, iPads, data keys, or any other kind of electronic devices were allowed in the office. They were stored with the bags in the lockers.

After taking a couple of bites of the overly rich chocolate cake, Bridget had walked over to her desk to make one last phone call. In a not-so-quiet voice, she spoke to her mother to let her know what time she would be arriving on the train and asked if there was anything she could get for her before she arrived. As this lengthy conversation took place, Bridget discreetly attached her new electronic notebook cable to the underside of her desk telephone. Once connected, it started to collect the software data Bridget had stored on its memory board the previous day. She knew her security clearance and computer access would be cancelled by mid-morning. But the desk telephone would not. Upon retrieving the data, the file was erased from the phone's memory.

As Bridget gathered up her possessions, she was escorted by security to the locker room, where she collected her handbag before exiting the building. The security guards didn't examine her farewell gift, as they knew she had only just received it at her farewell ceremony.

Once outside, she lifted her head to the sky and smiled deeply while proudly thinking – *I've done it! Thank you, MI5.*

As she walked the seven minutes to Westminster tube station, Bridget texted Dillan to confirm she had the package. Now the game had begun. However, she needed to make one stop before heading home. Then she would head to Exeter to collect her money.

As Bridget exited the bank branch, she smiled the confident smile of a woman who was about to become a millionairess, many times over. She wasn't taking any chances. She had no intention of carrying the notebook around with her until the exchange. She knew the type of men she would be dealing with. So, Bridget had planned ahead.

Two days before, under a pseudonym, Bridget had opened a safety deposit box at the closest bank branch to her office. Inside it, she placed an empty metallic black box that had a six-digit security panel.

Now, after her last day at work, Bridget re-entered the bank and placed her notebook inside the metal box, which she then placed back inside the deposit box. She instructed the branch manager to have the safety deposit box transferred to the Exeter branch by the following morning. For a fee, this could be arranged.

Back outside the bank, Bridget didn't notice the black Range Rover stationed across the street. It didn't follow her as she headed to the tube station, but it would be positioned outside her apartment when she arrived home.

*   *   *

'The bitch just went into a bank. I think she deposited the notebook in a deposit box,' said Sean Butcher, from where he was sitting in the black Range Rover across the street. He and his brother, Chris, had been ordered to follow Bridget and retrieve the notebook for Major Hamilton, who had no intention of paying for it.

'Clever girl,' said Hamilton.

'What do yah want us to do?' asked Sean.

Hamilton thought for a moment. 'There's no point going after her now. We'll have to play it out. Shit! We can track her phone, she's probably going home. She'll have to have it by tomorrow at the exchange. Then, she'll either pick it up on her way to Exeter or have the bank transfer it for her.'

'OK, if she goes back to the bank, do you want us to grab her once she's left the bank?' asked Sean.

'Yes, but if she's as smart as I think she is, she won't carry it on her to Exeter,' said Hamilton.

'Understood,' said Sean.

'If she does go back to the bank, for fuck's sake, be discreet,' said Hamilton, before hanging up.

The Betrayal

Bridget chose Exeter, a city in Devon, because her mother still lived there, and she knew the city well. Besides, London was too hectic and dangerous for the meet. She wanted familiarity at a location of her choosing, away from London's all-seeing eye.

The rendezvous point was agreed to be at the Millennium Bridge over the River Exe at 2 p.m. the following day.

Once Bridget had the money, she planned to leave England – and Dillan. No loose ends.

Bridget arrived home for the last time to gather her luggage and throw the remainder of the fridge's contents in the bin. Her apartment had been furnished when she leased it, so she had minimal personal items to take care of. Since her transfer to London, Bridget had accumulated few personal items; she saw them as unnecessary baggage. Not being a sentimental woman, Bridget could walk away from her life in England and start afresh anywhere she chose, with minimal fuss. Within half an hour of arriving home, she was ready to leave.

She had to say goodbye to her mother, though; she owed her that much. Bridget's mother lived on a council estate just outside Exeter. She would leave her mother something to help her out. It was the least she could do. Not too much, mind you. She didn't want to draw attention to herself. It would be Bridget's last chance to say goodbye; she wasn't planning on coming back.

Bridget called for a taxi to take her to the train station. Her car had been sold two weeks before. As she locked the door to her apartment and walked out onto the street, she didn't once look back on her home or life. But as she climbed into the taxi, she noticed a black Range Rover a few houses down. It had tinted windows, so she couldn't see inside.

It had also been there when she'd arrived home. The next-door neighbours drove a red Ford, and the house next to them drove a ghastly, bright-blue four-wheel drive.

She paused momentarily, then became angry with herself for being paranoid. She sat back in the black cab as it drove her out of the street for the last time.

*   *   *

Hazel Monahan was happy to see her daughter. Being a busy businesswoman kept Bridget in London, and it was rare that they got to spend time together. That night, Hazel was grateful for her daughter's company as she (unknown to Hazel) told lie after lie about her work and life. Hazel was very proud of her daughter.

The following morning, Bridget headed into town. She was relieved that obligation was over. Her mother had reminded her of how her life could have turned out. It frightened her. As she walked out onto the street, Bridget called Dillan.

'It's me. I'm on my way.'

'I'll be there at the bridge. Don't worry, I've got your back,' replied Dillan.

'I know you do. I'll see you there.' Bridget hung up and wrapped her scarf around her neck. Summer was coming to an end. By this time tomorrow she'd be in Rio, basking in the sunshine.

Bridget went by bus into the city centre. She felt optimistic, now that the hard part was over, although she still had a niggling feeling she couldn't shake. Most people would put it down to their conscience, but not Bridget. That black Range Rover kept irritating her.

The bus took Bridget into Exeter. As she walked along its city streets, she realised she'd forgotten how beautiful it was, with its ancient churches, cobbled stone streets, and winding lanes. The modern buildings paled in comparison to the medieval architecture from centuries long past. Bridget did see some beauty in the world, although she'd never valued its true worth.

As she headed towards the bank, Bridget kept looking over her shoulder. For a field agent at MI5, this would be standard procedure. But not for an analyst. Her work had consisted of research and surveillance from the security of her desk at Thames House.

When Bridget arrived at the bank, she showed her false identification. The branch manager introduced himself as Nicholas Wickham. He eyed her up and down. She immediately felt uneasy. A weasel came to mind as Bridget accompanied him to the vault. He reassured her that her box had arrived safely. Once

Bridget signed the relevant documents, he handed her a new safety deposit box key.

Bridget examined the box's contents. Once reassured, she left the notebook where it was and exited the branch with only the key. The exchange wouldn't be for a few hours. The agreement was simple; once the data was verified, the money would be transferred. All this would be done in a public place.

Feeling more confident now that the device was safely tucked away, she walked across the square. She was hungry and decided to get an early lunch. As the rain drizzled down it whipped across her face. Bridget walked with her head down. She didn't notice the black Range Rover until she stopped at a set of traffic lights. As she looked up and down the road, it caught her eye as it crawled along the road towards her.

Her heart started to race. She quickly walked across the road when the light went green and then ran as fast as she could towards the River Exe. Bridget was angry. The agreement was simple, money in exchange for technology. What was Archibald Monroe playing at?

She cut through side streets and lanes, mindful not to be seen by any street cameras. As she made her way down to the river, she kept looking over her shoulder. She ran down Friars Gate and into Collection Crescent. Bridget pulled out her mobile to call Dillan. She needed him to meet her now. Something had gone wrong. When Bridget looked down at her mobile, there was a text message already waiting for her. Bridget slowed her pace to read the message. Before she could reply, a searing pain shot through her body. Bridget was propelled through the air and slammed into a wall across the narrow street. She collapsed onto the cobbled road, her body mangled, unable to comprehend what had just happened.

The car stopped, footsteps approached her, hands felt over her. The car sped off. As she lay on the street, dying, tiny droplets of rain washed away any evidence that Bridget may have provided.

The text read: *DON'T BE LATE ... DILLAN.*

*   *   *

To her shocked mother and former colleagues, she was the unfortunate victim of a tragic hit and run. The police would do everything they could to investigate, but the narrow street had no cameras.

The only witness to the incident was in shock. He had been looking out of his office window when the car hit the pedestrian at the other end of the street. The witness told the police the woman was looking down at her mobile before the car hit her. The driver had stopped and checked on the injured woman but didn't wait or call an ambulance. He'd just ran back to his car and sped off again. Unfortunately, the man hadn't gotten the licence plate. But he was sure it was a black Range Rover.

As Bridget had no will, her mother was her next of kin. But that was of little comfort to Hazel, who regretted the waste of such a brilliant mind and the flourishing future her daughter had been robbed of.

Bridget Monahan had multiple broken bones and severe head injuries. She never regained consciousness and died on the pavement at the scene.

The Whys and Wherefores

August, End of Summer

Maggie Malloy stepped out onto her porch, holding her teacup in both hands. Steam rose in a spiral pattern as the wind tugged it away. Cradling its warmth, she looked out upon the countryside as the morning sun cast shadows over the trees and valley below. Maggie never tired of the view from her porch. She believed there was no truer green than nature's own.

Summer was coming to an abrupt end. Maggie hated summer's end. It depressed her. She felt as though summer were leaving her behind as it continued on its journey around the world. It would be an eternity before she felt the golden warmth of the sun again. She would miss summer's everlasting days. Autumn would slowly take away what warmth was left.

Her demeanour changed as she moved further down the porch and looked upon the undistinguished town of Friars Meadow.

Friars Meadow was situated close to the Dartmoor National Park, with a dwindling population of fewer than 3,000. It was less than two kilometres from the beautiful River Dart, which snaked its way from Totnes down to the sea at Dartmouth.

But on this crisp new autumn morning, Maggie saw no beauty in it. Nor had she for many years. The town's life force deteriorated as the people abandoned her.

Friars Meadow was once a beautiful country town, with shops and houses circling a tranquil botanical garden. The pond inside the garden was built to attract the town's wildlife of birds, ducks, swans and fish.

But even the wildlife had packed up and left. The garden was now overgrown with giant hog weed and Japanese knotweed alongside other nettlesome plants. The garden's dull and lifeless state epitomised the town's lack of *joie de vivre*.

When Maggie was a child, she would sit with her mother, Beth, on their porch and watch the sun's afternoon rays touch the rooftops and emit a sparkling, heavenly glow. Now, at twenty-seven, she viewed it alone and saw no beauty in it.

Maggie's mother had died of cancer over a year ago. That summer had been the hardest Maggie had ever endured. But thanks to her friends, Beth was able to remain at home and enjoy the last of the summer sun. Two of these friends were Eve, a life-long friend of her mother – and also Maggie's godmother – and Anaya, the regional area nurse, who had remained a wonderful friend to Maggie after her mother died. Remembering the good times didn't stop Maggie from feeling like an orphan. But her close friendships made her luckier than most. That's what she kept reminding herself.

Her anxious thoughts were often more pronounced when glimpsed alone in the dark, as most scary things are. Her vitality felt as rundown as Friars Meadow. Shops and homes were dilapidated and needed an injection of life. She wanted to scream out loud at all the unfairness, but she would be screaming to the masses. She was tired of feeling helpless. Nothing ever changed.

As Maggie finished her cup of tea, the rain started to drizzle. She sighed and walked back into the house. She picked up her bag and lunch and left for work. She didn't want to be late.

Maggie worked for Provincial Financial Solutions, which sat just outside Friars Meadow. The company was responsible for the sorting, inspecting, and re-distributing of England's used currency. Provincial had twelve branches around the United Kingdom. But thanks to modern technology, machines were doing the work that was once delegated to mere humans.

Maggie's job was to sort through and inspect by hand the banknotes that were deemed unusable. She would decide if they were fit to be re-circulated or sent in for destruction. It wasn't glamourous, but it was a job.

When the mill closed, many jobs and families went with it, and when the shoe factory closed down, it had sealed the town's fate. Then down fell the housing prices. Those who sold early sold for a respectable loss. But for those who remained, they could no longer afford to sell. Unemployment was at an all-time high and there was no sign of improvement in sight. Not just in and around Friar's Meadow, but in the surrounding towns of Totnes as well.

At least Maggie and her friends still had their jobs. There had been rumours at work about cutbacks. But there were always rumours.

Maggie had inherited her mother's house with a small mortgage she could handle. Her friends were another matter. They had families and commitments, whereas Maggie had no husband or children. That wasn't a regret, just a fact. The problem was that there weren't many eligible bachelors left in and around town. Sometimes she wondered if she wasn't meant for love. Wholeheartedly, Maggie believed that if she met the right man, she would know it instantly. She would feel it. He didn't need to be rich or powerful, handsome, or debonair. He simply needed to be kind and to have a strong, confident character. She would know all this by his smile. Without these attributes, the elusive 'Mr Right' wouldn't stand a chance.

She knew that these kinds of naïve standards made her seem like a dreamer. But what was there, if not hope? Besides, she had always been a shy woman. Maggie was pretty but not sexy. At least, she didn't feel it. At about five and a half feet tall, she had a slim figure. The thing she liked most about herself was her long hair, a velvety auburn colour, which was the envy of her friends. It always bounced when she walked with purpose.

Living alone in her cottage on the hill might seem reclusive to some, but her home was her private sanctuary. The cottage was filled with cherished memories from her childhood. For Maggie and her mother, it had been their refuge through the good and bad times. These memories resonated in every room she walked into and in many objects. They were in the aromatic smells of scented candles, and the perfume from the flowers in the living room and garden. Even the books sitting on their shelves in the conservatory breathed an air of old woody decay that reminded her of times gone by, cracking and stiffening whenever she opened them. The wooden chimes blowing in the wind, which Beth had made, played hypnotic tunes. Her home was her sanctum and it protected her from the harsh world outside. It provided her with constant familiarity, in a world of uncertainty.

In happier times before Beth's death, she and Maggie would hike through the countryside, especially along the river systems. Maggie and her mother would find the smallest of brooks or streams and follow them for miles as they grew and grew in size. These tributaries would eventually become part of the River Dart. Now, when Maggie sat by the river alone, she imagined herself on a boat or barge, floating along the water, or lying down beside the river with the sun in her face, watching the clouds go by.

Within that small but pleasant-enough existence, as far as company was concerned, her friends were the type anyone would wish for. Maybe it was solidarity that kept them together. Dependable, funny, understanding and with a strength any weightlifter would envy, they were her five-pointed star: earth, air, water, fire, and spirit. They would always be there for her, emotionally and physically. Eve, Chloe, Morwenna, Julie, and Anaya were the reason Maggie could face getting up each morning.

If her mother hadn't been diagnosed with cancer, maybe Maggie's life would have taken a different turn. Maybe she would have moved away, travelled abroad, gone to university, or been married with children by now. Maggie had learned to accept the here and now and not to worry about all the 'what ifs' in life. The future hadn't yet been written, and the past was written only by how people interpreted it. All Maggie knew for sure was the loyalty of her friends. There was nothing she wouldn't do for them and vice versa.

Unforeseen Circumstances

Corporal Dillan Andrews met Major Hamilton on the Medieval Exe Bridge to discuss their predicament a few days after the incident.

'What the fuck was she doing? Wasn't she taught to look left, right, then fucking left again?' asked Major Hamilton, his straight-back, lean physique belied his years.

Dillan couldn't believe that Bridget was dead. Only minutes before her death he'd sent her a text message. Was she reading that message when she'd stepped out onto the road? This thought kept going over in Dillan's mind, again and again. What had distracted her?

When Bridget had left the Navy two years ago, they'd lost touch for a while. It was by chance that they'd met again, although it didn't take them long to pick up where they'd left off. He'd felt comfortable around her, at ease. She'd been beautiful, intelligent, and extremely confident. He hadn't realised how much he loved her. Dillan had never told Bridget how he truly felt about her, he'd known it would spook her.

After the exchange they'd planned to take separate flights out the country and meet up in Mexico to have a romantic holiday in the Riviera. Bridget had given Dillan his ticket four days ago. He had the contacts and she the opportunity – a perfect match.

Major Hamilton had made Dillan a very generous offer for Bridget's technology. He couldn't believe she had died because of a stupid hit and run... Her death was not only painful but also inconvenient for everyone involved, and Dillan knew Major Hamilton was not a tolerant man.

'I know it's a setback, but we can still get the key for the safety deposit box,' said Dillan.

'How?' inquired Hamilton.

'We can get if off Bridget's mother. As next of kin, she'll receive all her personal possessions. We'll spin a yarn and say it's for work.'

'It won't work, she registered the box under a false name.'

'We could bribe the branch manager,' said Dillan.

'We have a better plan,' said Hamilton. 'We've set the wheels in motion already. The branch manager, Nicholas Wickham, is the brother-in-law of Malcolm Barker-Smith, the Conservative MP for Totnes.'

'Do you think they'll cooperate?'

'Barker-Smith is hungry for power like all the rest of them. Monroe will make sure he's rewarded come the next general election. Then we'll have another one of them under our thumb.'

'Do you want me to retrieve the key?' asked Dillan.

'Leave it with me, I'll organise the retrieval of the key. I don't want any more fuck-ups.'

'Yes, sir.'

Hamilton seemed to see the pain in Andrews's expression. He wasn't completely unsympathetic. 'I know you cared about her. Take a week off. I'll call you when I need you again. I want you to keep a low profile for a while until we need your services again. And for God's sake, don't go to her funeral. Her colleagues will be there. I don't want you associated with her.'

'Yes, sir,' replied Dillan. He walked off with his head down.

* * *

Once Andrews was out of earshot, Major Hamilton dialled a secure number. His superior, Archibald Monroe, did not tolerate mistakes. This was why he ran the largest and most profitable private military firm in Britain. Major Hamilton saw himself in Monroe's chair. Monroe had never served in the British military, and Hamilton loathed taking orders from him. But for now, he bided his time.

The tone rang briefly before being answered in silence by Sean Butcher. 'Once I've confirmed Barker-Smith's co-operation, give the safety deposit box key to him. Make sure he knows what to do. Our employer wants the notebook out of the vault by the end of the week,' Hamilton commanded.

'He'll get it, don't worry,' assured Sean.

'Were there any witnesses?' asked Hamilton.

'No, the street was deserted.'

'Good, and as far as Andrews is concerned, you broke into the morgue and stole her key from her belongings. Got it?'

'Yeah,' said Sean.

'If he suspects anything, you know what to do,' said Hamilton.

'Yeah.'

'Be careful, he's as well trained as you are.'

'We'll handle him.'

'Just get that notebook out of the vault,' said Hamilton, who was not accustomed to failed missions.

*   *   *

All would have gone to plan if Nicholas Wickham hadn't panicked.

Nicholas Wickham reluctantly agreed to his brother-in-law's request. He was told it was government business – top secret. He knew that was bullshit, but his brother-in-law could be very intimidating when he needed to be. He was also promised a cash settlement once the transfer was completed.

He didn't really like his brother-in-law, Malcolm Barker-Smith MP. He was too high and mighty for his taste, but if he became an influential MP, some of his good fortune would rub off on him.

*   *   *

Two days after Barker-Smith handed his brother-in-law the deposit box key, Nicolas Wickham went to the vault and opened the safety deposit box. However, he saw no notebook but instead a black steel case, nearly as big as the deposit box. He could hide a small device in his pocket, and no one would be the wiser, but not a bloody great big metal box. It was too conspicuous to conceal.

Wickham was angry he'd ever let his brother-in-law talk him into this. Easy money, he'd said. *Bullshit*, he thought. He'd had a bad feeling from the onset, but he'd put it away as being his conscience.

Wickham tried to open the box, but it was locked by a security panel. He took a photo of the device and placed it back in the deposit box, then left the vault quickly. His brother-in-law wasn't going to be happy. He called Malcolm and explained his dilemma.

*   *   *

Afterwards, Malcolm Barker-Smith reluctantly passed on the news to Major Hamilton. His verbal response was not one a mellow person could repeat. They had not foreseen Bridget putting the notebook into a locked encryption box. Malcolm's brother-in-law was not willing to get caught leaving the vault with someone else's property. Malcolm told him to hold fast and wait for further instructions.

Malcolm Barker-Smith did as he was told. He didn't want his idiot brother-in-law messing this up for him. He knew Archibald Munroe could open doors at Whitehall that he had been unable to open previously. This was his chance to make a name for himself. No-one was going to get in his way.

*   *   *

. Monroe told Hamilton there was potentially hundreds of millions of pounds sitting in that safe. He wanted it out. The technology would be worth billions in the long term. There would be nothing he couldn't do with that technology.

Wickham wanted these people out of his life. He offered up an alternative plan to Malcolm. When the Provincial security van next arrived to collect the bank's cash, he could slip the steel box inside the Provincial security case before locking it. Wickham's branch was the last branch visited on the security van's rounds. The case could be left open in the vault while the money was stacked inside by a staff member. Wickham would offer to do this task on that specific day. He would text Malcolm the serial number of the security case in question. The rest would be up to them.

Then all they needed to do was stop the van on its way to the plant and retrieve the case. Simple.

*   *   *

A week later, Corporal Dillan Andrews studied the route to the Provincial plant. The country roads were quiet, it would be doable. They would just need to pull the van over and take the case – or cases – when the opportunity presented itself.

Corporal Andrews was ordered to work with the Butcher brothers for this job. He'd known them by reputation; all three worked for the same employer. The brothers were planning on going into business for themselves, as freelance contractors. Dillan still couldn't tell them apart. He knew they were dangerous, but he had given his word he would see the job through. They were all professionals, and Dillan always kept his word. He still needed to be paid.

Corporal Andrews believed three armed men would be ample muscle to rob the Provincial van.

*   *   *

In early September, Malcolm Barker-Smith received a text message from his brother-in-law containing a long series of numbers and a thumbs-up emoji. The idiot used his personal mobile instead of the pay-as-you-go he was given. Barker-Smith regretted getting him involved. He had always thought him spineless, and now he could add stupid to the mix.

Malcolm passed on the message to Major Hamilton. That should have been the end of it. But when do schemes ever go according to plan?

The Van

Early Autumn

The black, non-descript van drove down the country road within the speed limit. Its occupants were two nondescript men in their forties. Their uniforms were slightly smaller than their waists, implying that they'd been doing their job for many years. Their appearances could be described as those of two wholesome, contented middle-aged men, if it weren't for the handguns holstered to their belts. For security reasons, their employer's logo was not embossed on the side of the van.

On this average Tuesday, their journey had started out as unremarkable as their van. They were heading to the Provincial Financial Solutions branch near Friars Meadow, in Devon. The van was carrying six large security suitcases with a little over one million pounds in each case. They had collected them without fanfare from bank branches around Exeter earlier that morning. The bank notes were locked inside the suitcases and secured inside cages in the van, which was equipped with GPS tracking.

It was Jonas's turn to drive, so Angus was playing the passenger on this trip. They had settled down for their leisurely drive back to base. It was always picturesque along Devon's country roads, especially when the weather was good.

However, on this particular day, things didn't quite turn out the way they expected.

The closer they drove to Friars Meadow, the less traffic they encountered. The road became curvy and hilly, and approximately two metres below, running alongside the road, was a small stream. As they grew closer to Friars Meadow, the stream grew into a fast-flowing river.

After a sharp bend, they came upon a car blocking the road. Its driver's-side door was open, and someone was lying on the road. Jonas slowed their speed, but the hairs on the back of his neck began to prickle. Instinct kicked in. They were not allowed out of the van under any circumstances.

Angus picked up the radio and called Despatch. This was cut short when two men appeared from their right with shotguns pointed directly at their heads. The assailants wore balaclavas, hiding any expression of fear on their part. However, the glass was bullet-proof, so Angus and Jonas were safe inside the van. Yet Jonas momentarily forgot this, in the heat of the moment.

Jonas slammed his foot on the accelerator and drove right through them. The gunmen leaped out of the way. Once they regained their composure, they got to their feet in time to see the van speed past them and swipe their get-away car in the process.

Undeterred, the Butcher brothers jumped into their car and made chase. The brothers leant out of their windows and started shooting at the van, while Andrews drove the four-wheel drive. The van swerved back and forth to avoid the bullets. As it approached an old bridge, one of the van's tyres was shot out and the van veered from left to right. It hit the side of the bridge, causing it to swerve even more abruptly to the other side. The van ran up onto the small footpath, hitting the bridge's wooden railing with such force that the barricade was demolished. The van flipped over and slid down into the river below. The back doors burst open before it descended into the water, sending its contents spewing over the road and into the river.

The river, no longer a pleasant stream, took the cases, guards, and the van along with it for a ride. When the van snagged on some rocks on the riverbed, water started to fill the van's cabin. Jonas and Angus frantically unwound their windows and unbuckled their seatbelts, escaping into the bitterly cold water.

They couldn't swim to the side as the current was too strong. Consequently, they had to content themselves with floating down the river until it widened and slowed enough for them to scrummage to the embankment. Luckily, Angus managed to grab one of the cases as it floated past him. He held on long enough to grope an overhanging branch on the side of the river.

Andrews and the Butcher brothers cared nothing for the security guards' dilemma as they scavenged the remaining suitcases left on the bridge before making their escape.

The police later confirmed they'd stolen nearly £6 million pounds. This was news to Andrews and the brothers, as they only counted £4 million pounds, not that they were in a position to argue. Their employer wouldn't be happy. Major Hamilton had stipulated that one case in particular had to be retrieved. The serial number they were given was not included in the four cases they collected from the bridge.

They were two cases short.

Once they had secured themselves at the old farmhouse that Major Hamilton had rented for them, they confirmed they didn't have the case their employer was after. They had failed their mission. Andrews and the Butcher brothers didn't give a fuck what was in the black box, but they did care that they'd failed the Major. They owed him, and debts must be paid. They reassured Major Hamilton that they wouldn't stop until they found the two remaining cases.

The Butcher brothers accepted their setback. They would see the job done. Life had thrown them many challenges, but they always managed to come out on top.

However, looking for the cases at present would be too risky. If the cases were handed in, there was nothing they could do. Their only hope was if the cases flowed further downstream and remained undisturbed on the river. They would search the river system until they found them. A drone would suit their purpose.

Major Hamilton said they would have one within twenty-four hours once his sources confirmed whether or not the police had found the last two cases.

Surprisingly, Angus and Jonas didn't contradict the police statement when they informed the press how much the robbers had stolen. Angus decided to keep quiet about the suitcase he held on to down the river.

The suitcases were airtight. They had a two-key security system. These keys were safely locked away in the manager's office at each Provincial distribution centre. If opened without them, anti-theft mechanisms inside the cases would release a dye, leaving the notes worthless. But although the security van had the latest GPS tracking, the cases carrying the bank notes did not.

Major Hamilton had provided Andrews with two such identical keys. The cash inside the cases would have been their payment. Now, they would have to stay in this backwater hole in Devon until they found the two missing cases. The Butcher brothers knew that if they wanted to work as freelance contractors, they had to finish the job.

Had the suitcases arrived safely at the Provincial depot in Friars Meadow, things might have turned out differently for Maggie. But as luck would have it, the armed robbery became the pivotal turning point in Maggie's life. Only, she wouldn't feel its effect until Christmas.

As it stood, on this carefully scripted Tuesday in September, two air-tight security cases were bobbing along a tributary of the River Dart. Within a few days they would make their way downriver to within three miles of their original location of Friars Meadow. Their journey would be constantly interrupted by rocks, currents, and weather.

The police released another statement. They were making progress. Reporters asked the standard questions: was it an inside job? The police only said that they were following up all leads. Employees at the Provincial site – and at the respective bank branches – who were visited that day by the security van would be interviewed. And yet, after eliminating their usual suspects, the police had no clue who had robbed the van. By the end of the week, they were instructed to enlist the help of Britain's communications experts, GCHQ.

The Senior Analyst

October, Mid-Autumn

GCHQ – Government Communications Headquarters

Jonathan Swift, a senior analyst at GCHQ, was sitting at his desk in the Doughnut, situated in Benhall in Cheltenham, Gloucestershire. He was five hours into his shift when he was handed a new file – the Provincial robbery. GCHQ had finally intercepted a communication pertaining to the robbery. These requests were usually assigned to a junior analyst. He was unsure why he had been handed the folder. Jonathan rose from his desk and headed to the office of the Chief of staff, Max Evans.

He walked down The Street, as it was known to everyone who worked there. He tapped on Max's door before entering. Max waved at him to sit down while he finished his phone conversation.

When he finally hung up, he turned to Johnathan and said, 'Augh, Jonathan, you're here about the Provincial file, aren't you?'

'Yes. Why did it land on my desk? We have many capable junior analysts who can handle this.'

'True, but I want someone more senior. The Provincial robbery has taken an unusual turn. The braggards who stole the money aren't your garden-variety bank robbers. One has been identified as ex-army. Lance Corporal Sean Butcher. He left the army over two years ago – dishonourably discharged, it would appear. He also has a twin brother who was also honourably discharged over a year ago. Since then, both have been working for a private security firm in Iraq and Afghanistan.'

'And you believe all the robbers were ex-military?' asked Jonathan.

'Possibly,' answered Max. 'The Army has sent over the Butcher brothers' military records.' Max handed them over to Jonathan. 'The Army is concerned they may be looking for capital to start up their own firm. They're happy for us and Special Branch to run with it.'

'What was Sean Butcher dishonourably discharged for?' asked Jonathan.

'He punched a senior officer. The assault was racially motivated, as the officer in question was Black, and Sean Butcher was proudly quoted as saying, "I hated the Black bastard". He spent six months in prison before being released nearly two years ago. Since then, he's been freelancing for one of our military contractors, along with his brother Chris. We can assume his brother was one of the other crew members, especially now that the police can't find either of them.'

'Have you identified the second contact on the intercept?' asked Jonathan.

'Not yet. We had Sean Butcher's voice on file, but not the other contact. They used burners, so we have no identification, only the time and their location. I'll need you to check CCTV cameras in the area during the time of the call,' said Max.

'OK, I'll organise a team to find the other contact,' said Jonathan.

'Augh, but wait, there's more,' said Max. 'The Butcher brothers are still looking for the two remaining cases.'

'What!'

'They only stole four of the cases.'

'Why not just disappear with the funds they have?' asked Jonathan. 'It's risky returning to the scene of a crime. Why risk it?'

'My thoughts exactly – there has to be more to this robbery, Jonathan. Find out what it is. It won't take you long to positively identify the final robber, and the unidentified caller. If these men are working for a third party, we need to know who. The Army and Home Office want these men found before they do any more damage.'

'If they're going into business for themselves, they'll need weapons, which means they'll be looking for a buyer,' said Jonathan.

'Correct,' said Max. 'But we still have two cases floating down a Devonshire river. Find them before they do, Jonathan. Devon, a beautiful county, went there once for a picnic. Caught a fish this big,' boasted Max with outstretched arms.

'Really?' Jonathan said, producing a sarcastic grin. 'I'll look into it, and I'll organise a timeline of their military history to see if we can identify the third man.'

'By the way,' said Max. 'It appears our security guards withheld some important information from the police. They might be stupid enough to be searching for the remaining two million pounds, if they haven't already found it. Have another word with them. If our mercenaries are also out there looking, it won't be pretty if those soldiers find them first.'

'I'll re-assign some junior analysts for this one. It'll be good training for them.'

'Good, you'll be working alongside Special Branch – they'll provide the leg work while your analysts provide the intelligence.'

'Great, thanks Max.'

'You know, to get that cash, they'd need a way to open the cases without the dye going off,' said Max.

'Yeah, the same thought crossed my mind.'

'Treat these brothers as extremely dangerous, until proven otherwise,' were Max's final words.

'Don't worry. We'll find the cases and the Butcher brothers,' said Jonathan, and he rose and left the room.

*   *   *

Jonathan Swift walked confidently down The Street with the files under his arm. He had graduated from Oxford with honours in computer science and information technology. First in his class, he was swiftly picked up by GCHQ before MI5 could grab him.

At thirty, he excelled as predicted. He was taller than average and with sandy blond hair and brown eyes, he displayed a warm, confident intelligence. He was well-liked and respected in the Doughnut. With a wonderful quality for patience, Jonathan had a great track record when training new recruits.

But work was not everything to Jonathan. In his precious spare time, he loved to row and run. Recently, he had taken up dragon boating. He was determined to give the Australians a run for their money if he made the national team next year. He also enjoyed going to his family home in Kent at least once a month to visit his parents.

He was still unmarried. Not because of a strange affliction, but simply because he hadn't found that one woman he wanted to spend the rest of his life with yet. In Cheltenham and London, there were far too many pretty women to choose from. Until he found that one special woman, he was simply going to enjoy himself.

After all, life was far too short and unpredictable.

The Butterfly Effect

October, Friars Meadow

Thank God it was Friday.

But Maggie's euphoria didn't last long. As the clock struck 4.15 p.m., the Provincial staff, who were hanging out for the weekend, were called into the cafeteria for an urgent meeting. Bob Simpson, the branch manager, was centre stage. There was another man in attendance who Mr Simpson introduced as the national finance manager from the London office.

'Ladies and Gentlemen,' announced Bob. 'Thank you for your prompt attendance today. But unfortunately, I have some upsetting news. This branch will be closing.'

Bob Simpson couldn't have been less subtle if he'd punched everyone in the face. Murmurings and gasps began to rise as he tried to continue. He raised his arms in the air, in that mock silent gesture, to quiet the crowd.

'Please, please, settle down, people. I know this is a shock. But due to the unfortunate events in September, senior management have decided to relocate our branch to a new site in North Devon.'

He waited for the noise to quiet down again.

'Our branch will begin redundancies in the next few weeks while the Barnstaple branch gets up to speed. Our branch will close once all the machinery and equipment has been transferred. Up until then it will be business as usual for those who remain. Within two months, this site will be completely closed.'

Every employee stood their ground, only because they were too shocked to move. Maggie heard someone yell, 'Why can't we relocate to Barnstaple?' To which the national finance manager said the positions had already been filled. Maggie felt her familiar anxiety return. Not just for herself, but for her friends and colleagues, too. They would suffer more than she due to the closure.

Over the next few days, the Provincial employees were called into the manager's office and told their finish date. They were given a redundancy package that failed to reflect their years of loyal service. Each employee left the manager's office with the same pauperised expression on their faces, along with a thousand unanswered questions. The unease felt by many was not exclusive. Their fears were the same. How long will my redundancy last? What will I do this Christmas? Where will I find another job? Will I have to move? Can I afford to move?

There were no dreams of a week in Ibiza with their redundancy; no shopping sprees and no new car, either. Unemployment benefits were around seventy-three pounds a week for individuals, and more, of course, for families. But no one wanted handouts. They wanted to work. They may have lost their jobs, but they didn't want to lose their pride as well.

Upon leaving work that Friday, there was no jovial banter. Instead, it was replaced by a sombre silence.

Bob Simpson appeared to be the only person not overly grief-stricken by the closure. As one of Maggie's close friends, Morwenna, pointed out as they left that Friday afternoon, 'He did say your work will taper down.'

Maggie asked her friends if they wanted to go to the pub and drown their sorrows. No one spoke up, until Eve suggested giving it a miss tonight. As they walked outside into the dark, cold afternoon, the clouds opened up and soaked them until they reached their cars. They knew that, for several of them, cars would be a luxury they could no longer afford.

Unfortunately, their dampened spirits carried over into Christmas and the New Year. Only, for Eve, it became more difficult when she received a letter from the bank. Being a private person, Eve kept her problems to herself. If she had shared them with her goddaughter Maggie, both their lives may have taken a different path.

*   *   *

The first of Maggie's dear friends was Eve.

At sixty-one, Eve Merriweather had been a presence in Maggie's life since childhood. As her mother's best friend, Eve had been a loving and constant figure in Maggie's life. But Eve had seen too much sadness in hers. She and her husband George had lost their son James in a motorcycle accident over ten years ago.

George had worked at the old shoe factory making Brogues and Derbies until it closed. Unemployment had been humiliating and depressing for George. He worked odd jobs here and there, but nothing remotely suiting his qualifications. As Eve worked at the Provincial plant alongside Maggie, the extra income had been a blessing. However, George was never quite the same after losing his son. He suffered a heart attack six years ago and succumbed a year later. Time never wearied Eve's memory of him. A tear would appear down Eve's cheek from time to time. Her friends always knew who it was for.

Maybe George died of a broken heart. That's what Eve believed.

Eve had been by Maggie's side through the long days and nights during Beth's illness. Cancer was a cruel killer. Maggie wouldn't have come through it if it wasn't for Eve. Eve never accepted Maggie's thanks; she only said, 'That's what friends are for.' Just as Beth had been there for Eve when her son and husband had died. Eve was simply returning the compassion that she herself had been given.

Regrettably, Maggie would never be able to repay that debt.

Eve's heart was broken by the death of her son. But it almost stopped beating when George died. He was the love of her life. As time went by, Eve's pain of losing George had eased, but the emptiness never had.

*   *   *

We don't always know why things turn out the way they do. Is there such a thing as the butterfly effect? When tragedy strikes, we always ask ourselves – why me?

Maggie knew there were two types of people in this world: those who were intimidated by fear, like she was, and then there was those who were energised by it, and so would fight through it. But for Maggie, her fear was always of the unknown. Subsequently, she believed she would collapse under it. Eve would tell her to seize the day, but that would imply that Maggie should be spontaneous. Unfortunately, she had never been a risk-taker.

When the butterfly landed on Maggie's shoulder, she had two options. Let the weight of change drag her down into depression or grab it by the horns and ride it for all she was worth.

Well, she finally chose the latter.

Unfortunately, that wasn't the case for Angus and Jonas.

In for a Penny, In for a Pound

Late October

Angus and Jonas had been searching for nearly a month for the missing cases. If anyone passed them along the river, they were simply hikers out for a walk. They took it in turns to search the river and its tributaries. They had to wait until the initial police investigation wound down before they could start searching. The police still hadn't arrested anyone in connection to the robbery. Angus reassured Jonas that the robbers would have taken the money they'd stolen and legged it. That would be the smartest thing to do.

There was no telling where the cases would end up, as the rivers waxed and waned in size and speed each month depending on the rainfall. But they knew at least two cases had gone into the river, because Angus had been hanging onto one of them.

Their map was marked into sections, and they marked off each grid before conducting a new search. They had synchronized their witness statements at the hospital, while they were being checked over after the robbery. They said they had been fighting for their lives and hadn't seen any cases floating down the river.

With the arrival of the Special Branch officers last week – who asked them to go over their testimony again – Jonas and Angus had wondered if the cases had been found, or if the police suspected anything. But they stuck to their original story and reassured the officers that they didn't see anything.

Angus and Jonas were fortunate that no one else knew about the missing cases. Otherwise, every man and his dog would be out looking for them. The police had finished their investigation weeks before. Angus and Jonas only saw the usual dog walkers and hikers. Relieved, they continued their search along the river system in earnest.

Jonas was still concerned. How would the authorities know if any of the cases fell in the river if they hadn't made any arrests? Angus told him not to look a gift horse in the mouth.

Their lie, once said, could not be unsaid. They both agreed to stick to their original story. Angus estimated there was at least two million pounds somewhere along the river. Once the coast was clear, they resumed their search.

Out of habit, they always turned their mobiles off while searching. There was no respect for people's privacy nowadays.

Regrettably for Angus, it was his turn to search the river.

On a drizzly Tuesday afternoon in late October, Angus checked his map and started along a new tributary of the river. There had been a lot of rain the last few days, and the river was fuller in parts. He had been walking for approximately one hour and was ready to give up and go to the pub, where it would be warm, when he noticed something in the water.

It was surreal, seeing it just lying there, wedged up against a large rock on the edge of the riverbank. He'd never really expected to find anything. But Angus had told Jonas they had a better chance of finding a case than of winning the lottery. The odds were on their side.

He raced across the shallow water and hoisted the case up onto the riverbank. He'd forgotten how heavy these bastards could be with all that lovely money in them. His smile was as big as the moon. He started to laugh. Then he just stared at it for some time.

Eventually, he pulled out his mobile and turned it on. He went into his contacts to call Jonas but paused momentarily before pressing the number. He couldn't help pondering the idea of not telling his friend. After all, they were only work mates. What if Jonas had found a case. Would he own up to it? Had he already found one and not told him? *The sneaky bastard.*

His mind was racing with indecision when he felt something hot with a powerful sting rip through his body. A searing ice-cold pain erupted through his chest. He looked down and saw a red stain grow across his jumper. His wife had knitted it for him last Christmas. She was always on at him about keeping it clean. This thought was Angus' last as he fell on to the shallow riverbed. His blood slowly flowed away downstream on its long journey to the sea. He was dead before the Butcher brothers reached his body. He never knew what happened to him.

Chris Butcher stepped over Angus' body and retrieved the case from the riverbank.

'One down, one to go,' said Sean Butcher. 'Check the serial number on the case. Let's fucking hope it's the right one.'

Chris bent down to read the serial number. He shook his head, signalling to his brother that it wasn't the one they needed.

'Fuck.'

'Do you think his idiot partner has already found it?' asked Chris.

'I dunno. Mind you, they've been out 'ere looking for nearly a month.'

The Butcher brothers had kept a low profile, but the drone Hamilton had given them searched on their behalf. They had spotted Angus and Jonas out searching on numerous occasions. The crafty bastards.

'I think we should pay 'im a visit, just to be on the safe side,' said Chris.

'Call Hamilton and let 'im know. It'll be his decision if we question the second guard. We don't wanna draw too much attention,' said Sean.

'Well, you should have thought of that before you shot 'im,' said Chris.

'Yeah, fair point, shove 'im in the bushes over there. I don't think anyone will discover 'im anytime soon,' said Sean.

As they walked off with the case, Angus's mobile remained lying on the riverbed. Signal lost.

Lance Corporal Sean Butcher called Major Hamilton to inform him of their discovery, despite it not being the correct case. If they found this one, there was a high probability the final one was still on the river.

Major Hamilton told Sean to leave the area. They retrieved Angus' map that outlined their search pattern. Waving it at his brother, Sean said, 'Very considerate of 'im.'

Angus' body may not have been found for some time if GCHQ hadn't picked up his mobile signal for the briefest moment. It was logged, but no action was taken as they were not suspects in the robbery. GCHQ were only monitoring Angus and Jonas' mobiles as they had lied in their witness statements. But GCHQ hadn't ruled out the security guards misappropriating one of the cases for themselves. Once Angus' mobile was turned on, GCHQ triangulated its position.

It only became a matter of urgency when Mrs Cynthia McPherson reported to the police station the following morning that her husband Angus was missing. His name was flagged along with Jonas Chapman's by GCHQ. The police immediately notified Special Branch. They dispatched officers to the last recorded location of Angus' mobile and found Angus' body shoved into some brambles alongside the river – with a bullet hole through his back.

*   *   *

Corporal Dillan Andrews was technically in charge of the operation, as he outranked both the Butcher brothers. Even though Andrews took his orders from Major Hamilton, Major Hamilton was discreetly giving separate orders to the Butcher brothers. Because of Andrews' infatuation with Bridget Monahan, he had been deemed a liability by Hamilton. But he was a good soldier. The Butcher brothers didn't dislike Andrews. He was a brother, military of a kind. They had a code when they chose to use it. But Hamilton didn't like loose ends. If Andrews found out what they'd done to Bridget, it would be a case of another name being added to their ever-increasing hit list.

Hamilton had recruited the Butcher brothers after seeing first-hand Lance Corporal Sean Butcher's skill with his rifle while serving overseas.

Sean and his brother Chris were rough, foul-mouthed, ruthless hooligans. Hamilton knew their kind well. Men like the Butcher brothers were usually drawn to the military. They hated the establishment and everything the government stood for, but the military gave them a purpose and a skill.

Once the job was done, they would be in a position to start up on their own. Whether they were called private contractors or mercenaries-for-hire made no difference to them. With four million pounds in cash, they could do whatever they liked.

The Butcher brothers were tempted to offer Andrews a job in their new enterprise, now that he wasn't going to Mexico. They were surprised Andrews hadn't realised the kind of people he was working for. The Butcher brothers knew, as soon as Dillan contacted Hamilton with Bridget's proposal, that he had sealed her fate.

Once they completed this assignment, they would be guaranteed lucrative contracts. They didn't need to know the whys and wherefores of what they were looking for, just as long as they got paid.

GCHQ

November, Autumn's End

England's problems didn't stop because of an armoured van robbery and a murder. The Provincial robbery was one of many operations that GCHQ was involved in. Jonathan's team had set up a situation room in the Doughnut. As new intelligence was uncovered it would be dissected and analysed by Jonathan's team. At present, they were looking into the Butcher brothers and all their known associates.

Their last registered employer was Phoenix Security, who confirmed the Butcher brothers had resigned three months earlier and hadn't been in contact since. All intelligence gathered was uploaded into GCHQ's software programs to search for patterns. Faces, places, phone interceptions, forensics at the robbery, and now Angus's murder would all be analysed and dissected. During their daily briefings, Jonathan expected his team to express their opinions and ideas. Nothing was ever deemed irrelevant.

Over the last month, communications had stopped. GCHQ believed that the gunmen had gone underground or possibly left the country. However, with the sudden death of Angus McPherson down by the river, alarm bells sounded: they hadn't realised the extent these men would go to in order to find the final two cases. GCHQ had to accept that Angus had found one of the cases, and then the Butcher brothers or their accomplice killed him for it.

Jonathan's team had to assume that the Butcher brothers had been watching Angus and Jonas the entire month. Whether they staked out their homes or had other means of surveillance, the signs told Jonathan that something bigger was going on in the background.

Jonathan believed he'd made a mistake by not putting Angus and Jonas under surveillance. He cursed himself for being careless. But, as the security guards were cleared of any involvement in the robbery, Jonathan couldn't justify the expense. That was one mistake he couldn't afford to make again.

By the end of November, GCHQ had confidently identified the Butcher brothers' accomplice as Corporal Dillan Andrews. Alas, he was nowhere to be found.

GCHQ and Special Branch set up operational surveillance on the suspects' closest family members, known friends, and associates. The only common denominator was that all three men worked for Phoenix Security or had done until they resigned a few months ago. Jonathan believed they were acting under orders. Whether they still worked for Phoenix Security or were working for themselves, there was still an unidentified caller that they needed to identify. They knew the caller wasn't Corporal Andrews – there was still another player out there.

*   *   *

A week later, GCHQ finally intercepted a phone conversation between Andrews and a Major Hamilton – ex-army, retired honourably five years ago, and now working as a military advisor for Phoenix Security. GCHQ finally had their link. But this didn't prove categorically that the Butcher brothers and Andrews were still working for Phoenix. If the robbery and murder were on behalf of Phoenix, then Jonathan would have to tread carefully. He updated Max on their latest intercept. Max was on the phone to the Home Office within five minutes.

The Home Office wanted discretion. Phoenix was a powerful organisation and had a lot of clout in Whitehall and Downing Street. They couldn't afford to stomp on any influential toes without proof. Max was given carte blanche to deal with the situation and to uncover what they were up to. Jonathan and Max knew that a couple of million pounds was nothing to a military contractor like Phoenix.

GCHQ had to consider that the Butcher brothers and Andrews were working independently with Hamilton.. If so, he would be in a position to acquire weapons from Phoenix's stockpile. GCHQ would have to open up a second line of enquiry into Major Hamilton and all known arms dealers. Luckily, the list wasn't a long one. With the evidence they had so far, they couldn't yet link Phoenix directly to the robbery.

Whitehall allowed GCHQ to run with the operation but reiterated that they needed to be discreet. The Home Secretary echoed his concern to Max that they couldn't bring down a company as big as Phoenix without concrete evidence. Frankly, did they really want to?

Jonathan's team was meticulous. It didn't take long to discover Phoenix Security owned 20% of Provincial Financial Solutions. If they needed keys to open the cases, it wouldn't be difficult to obtain a set. More lines of enquiry were opened up to investigate Provincial's involvement. Being a large company, it would take time to investigate each employee.

When Special Branch had interviewed Angus and Jonas the month before, they had pleaded ignorance of the missing cases. Unfortunately, the opportunity for easy money had been too tempting for them. Money was always a tempting compromise to one's moral compass. Angus and Jonas were no exception.

Special Branch swiftly collected Jonas after Angus' body was discovered. Once the shock wore off, Jonas finally confessed to knowing about the missing cases in the river. He admitted they had been out looking, but only for the reward, of course. The only part of Jonas' story that Special Branch believed was that he hadn't found any of the cases yet. Jonas was released but would be watched by Special Branch. The police hadn't decided whether to charge him for misleading an investigation. He reluctantly agreed to wear an ankle bracelet for his own protection. Special Branch wanted to know his whereabouts at all times. At least until their suspects had been apprehended. He was warned to stay away from the river. This, he swiftly agreed to.

The Provincial van carried front and rear cameras, but these hadn't helped with the identification of the hijackers, as they wore balaclavas. They were athletic and of the same build. GCHQ was confident they were the Butcher brothers, which left Dillan Andrews as the getaway driver. But the cameras did provide GCHQ with a timeline of the van's route that day. Jonathan assigned an analyst to retrace the van's journey and to check all street cameras in case anything suspicious appeared.

If the hijackers were after something other than the money, it would have to have come from within one of the bank branches that day.

If that was a correct assumption, Jonathan's team needed to know which bank branch, and who had access to the cases while in those branches. An all-agencies alert had already been sent out for the arrest of the Butcher brothers and Andrews. But Major Hamilton was not included in this arrest warrant. Jonathan's team needed to investigate him further without drawing attention to Phoenix Security. Police priority now rested on finding these men before they killed again.

Jonathan asked Angela Milford, a senior analyst on his team, to open up an unobtrusive line of enquiry into Phoenix Security's senior management. Angela Milford was indispensable to Jonathan. She'd started working at GCHQ three years ago and had proven herself time and again under pressure.

Jonathan didn't believe in coincidences. He believed, as Max Evans did, that all three men still worked for Phoenix. Proving something like this was what they were good at. Like Jonathan, Angela's analytical skills had saved many lives throughout her career. The stakes were always too high for errors. Jonathan and Angela prided themselves on having the best team of analysts in the country.

GCHQ still didn't have all the pieces of the puzzle, but they would eventually. If they were good at anything, it was solving puzzles. They never allowed any question to go unanswered.

Eve

By Late November

Wednesday night poker became the highlight of the girls' week. Morwenna, Julie, and Eve couldn't afford anything else. They only ever played with one, two, five, and ten pences, which they kept in jars at Maggie's home. Morwenna told them that if she were any harder up, she would have to start using Monopoly money, if she didn't use it for kindling first.

As Maggie was one of only a handful of people still left at Provincial, she felt guilty about her predicament. Her friends brushed off her guilt. They were glad Maggie still had a job, if only for a few more weeks. It was taking longer than expected for the Barnstaple branch to come online.

Anaya was able to pick up Eve, Jules, and Morwenna in her car. Being an area nurse, her car expenses were subsidized by National Health. Chloe drove herself and the kids in the mobile library van, along with all its precious literary contents stacked on the shelves. She had driven the mobile library van for nearly twenty years. With no town library, it was her way of providing knowledge to the young and old in her community.

When they arrived, the kids were ceremoniously marched into the sitting room, where their popcorn and chips were waiting for them. It was Fin's turn to control the remote. At least it wasn't Jeremy's; otherwise, they'd be watching documentaries all night. They didn't like democracy until it was their turn to control the remote.

Maggie was like an aunt to her friends' young children. She adored them all. Julie's son, Jeremy, was methodically complicated while Morwenna's mischievous, exasperating brood often left her exhausted. She loved them all. Maggie had always admired Morwenna's strength and courageous attitude towards life, especially after her husband left. She never allowed the weight of the world to drag her down.

*   *   *

The second of Maggie's friends was Morwenna Stewart. She was thirty-five, although at times she felt fifty-three. A divorcee with four children, Morwenna never knew if she was coming or going. Thanks to Chloe and her contacts, she'd managed to secure a part-time job as a cleaner at the local primary school. It wasn't much, but it was something. Morwenna learned to stretch every penny through every meal. Clothes were mended, not discarded. Toys were passed down, not thrown away. Morwenna's new job caused great mortification for her twin boys when their friends found out where she was working. All three had had to visit the principal's office on more than one occasion.

Sarah, the oldest at fifteen, would collect her younger siblings from school and take them home each night so that Morwenna could clean the school after hours. Sarah had grown up fast. She helped her mother more than she needed to and did it without complaining. She was old enough to understand her mother's predicament.

The twins, Finnegan – Fin – and Alfie were eight, and oblivious to anything that didn't concern them. They were like two freight trains on a collision course. Morwenna went through more plasters, bandages, and bottles of antiseptic than the Totnes hospital, which she had visited on more than one occasion. She was surprised no one had called Child Services.

At six, Harriet, her youngest, lived in a world of her own making, always surrounded by her favourite things and blissfully ignorant of her mother's predicament, as she should be.

Morwenna didn't suffer fools, and unfortunately her husband had grown into one. Her wanker of a husband – as she called him now – was kicked out after Morwenna discovered he was cheating on her. Speaking openly through a mouthful of Jaffa Cakes at poker one Wednesday night, she'd informed the girls: 'The idiot texted his girlfriend using my mobile – he signed us up for a two-for-one offer. The mobiles were identical, the thrifty bastard.' Morwenna gave him his marching orders. She received alimony regularly, but her wanker of a husband now complained about the cost, as he had a new family to support – to which Morwenna pointed out, on each occasion, was not her problem.

Morwenna and her lovingly chaotic family resided in a rented house in Friars Meadow, one of many subsequently owned by the bank. She worked from dawn to dusk and skated skittishly close to the poverty line. But she had a wicked dry sense of humour and always tried to see the good in everything, except her wanker of a cheating husband. In Maggie's group of friends, she was the one who could always make Maggie laugh, even if Morwenna didn't have much to laugh about.

*   *   *

So, during their poker nights, they laughed and played the night away; they discussed their families, politics, and work.

Tonight, while shuffling a new deal, Morwenna mentioned reading about a security van driver being found dead in the river.

'It was only a few miles from Friars Meadow. Rumour has it he was shot.'

They all voiced their opinions, as most of them had known Angus from his deliveries to their Provincial site. They felt bad for his poor wife.

'Fancy surviving a horrific hijacking only to be killed while out fishing,' said Morwenna. 'What are the odds?'

'Yeah, but was he really fishing?' asked Chloe, suggestively.

Chloe then asked Maggie and Eve to be careful when they went out on their walks. If the rumours were true, a killer could still be out there. Anaya asked if they thought he had something to do with the robbery. Nobody could answer that question, as they didn't know him well enough. They sat quietly for a moment, contemplating the same thought. Had he really had something to do with the robbery in August?

As their evening continued, the talk became playful as they finished off the wine and Jaffa Cakes. Eve had been unusually quiet for most of the evening. Maggie asked if she was all right, but she only smiled and said she was feeling a bit under the weather.

*   *   *

Pride is a solitary adversary. Eve's pride had prevented her from speaking to Maggie about her financial problems. She knew what Maggie would say: 'Come and live with me, it'll be OK.' But she couldn't bring herself to mention it.

Eve was becoming more depressed and reclusive since her retrenchment. She still hadn't found a job. To be honest, her heart wasn't in it. At sixty-one, she was never going to be anyone's first choice. Eve was struggling to meet her mortgage payments. The bank was threatening foreclosure. During her husband's illness, Eve had drawn down on her mortgage to help with the extra medical bills. If there were buyers for the house, it would have been sold at auction, but nobody wanted to move to a town with no job prospects. Especially into homes desperately in need of repair.

The bank had all the time in the world. Eve did not. She couldn't bear to rent her own home back from the bank. She told herself it was too big to live in alone, anyway. Eve's biggest regret would be losing her beautiful garden. It was Eve's pride and joy, and it was the loveliest garden in town. It was her sanctuary during spring and summertime. But winter was approaching quickly, and everything felt bleak to Eve. When she asked the bank manager if she could still tend the garden, he refused, stating that the bank couldn't risk an accident and potential lawsuit. If the bank rented it out, it would be up to the new tenants to care for the garden. She was told she would be trespassing.

Eve moved into a bedsit in town owned by Mrs McGuigan, a widower who was grateful for the company.

Maggie reluctantly helped Eve move her belongings. When Eve offered Maggie some of her personal possessions, Maggie initially refused. But Eve told Maggie she didn't have room for them in her bedsit and she didn't want them gathering dust, boxed away somewhere. Maggie could see it was painful for Eve. But as hard as she tried, she couldn't get Eve to talk about it. Eve would simply touch Maggie's face and decline the offer, saying only that she needed to downsize. The house was too much for her to clean and maintain. Maggie knew it was a lie but couldn't press Eve any further on the matter.

Eve had lost everything she loved in her life: her son and husband, her job, and now her home and garden. Bit by bit, what little self-respect and will she had were slowly wilting away, along with the uncared-for flowers in her garden.

To forget about it all, Eve would take herself out walking. She walked through the fields and along the river, hoping to find some reassurance. She would sit and imagine herself falling into the water and being taken away on the current on an endless journey to nowhere – anywhere but here.

*   *   *

Two weeks later ...

Mrs McGuigan was knocking on Eve's door. She had a cup of tea in her hand. Eve had not come down for breakfast. 'Eve, dear, are you there?' Knowing she hadn't left the house all morning, she decided to get the spare key and let herself in.

Justifying this to herself, she imagined that Eve might be under the weather. She hadn't spoken much during her stay, and she had eaten very little.

As she unlocked the door, she tentatively tapped on it, so as not to startle her tenant. But upon moving the door aside, she looked up at a woman hanging in mid-air with a stocking stretched tight around her neck. Mrs McGuigan barely recognised Eve Merriweather with her face a strangled colour of blue and her lips swollen and misshapen. The stocking was tied around the ceiling light, and she could see where pieces of broken plaster hung loosely around the ceiling fixture. If only Eve had weighed more. The fixture might have collapsed. This was the thought that stayed with Mrs McGuigan for many months to come.

Mrs McGuigan's body turned stiff and cold. The teacup had slipped from the saucer and smashed on the floor. Not that she noticed. A feeling of hopelessness swept over her; a surrendering to despair. She quickly closed the door, walked down the corridor, picked up the telephone, and called an ambulance.

Mrs McGuigan sat cradling a cushion, rocking herself back and forth, waiting for the ambulance and police to arrive. She didn't want to go back into that room. Not ever. If only Eve had said something. They could have talked; she would have helped her. To give up on life is a last resort. She had been lonely and felt inconsequential enough times herself, but she'd always found a reason to remain. Hadn't she?

The police asked Mrs McGuigan who Eve's nearest relative was, to which she sadly replied she didn't know. She knew of two friends who collected her sometimes – one drove a mobile library van. The other had come to the door once and introduced herself as Maggie Malloy.

The police examined the bedroom. Eve's suitcase was neatly packed on the bed with a picture of her husband and son regally placed on top. On the table by her bed, the police found two envelopes. One was her will and testament, and the other a letter addressed to Maggie Malloy. Written on the envelope was a note requesting the letter not be opened until after her funeral.

The police handed both letters to Eve's solicitor, Ernie Chandler, who confirmed that the handwriting on both envelopes and the letters themselves were Eve's. Ernie agreed to hand the letter to Maggie after the funeral.

Maggie was the only beneficiary in Eve's will.

Bleak Times

A Cold December

Maggie closed the door on the police and collapsed to the floor.

Why did Eve do it? Why didn't she say something? Why? Why? Why? Maggie knew Eve hadn't been herself lately. But she thought she would bounce back like she always had.

As Maggie sat on the floor, crying, she kept thinking: *I should have insisted Eve move in with me*. At least until she'd found a new home. Maggie had offered to help Eve search. Eve had told Maggie she didn't want to start looking until after Christmas. All the while, she had no intention of looking. Until this moment, Maggie hadn't understood why. Now she did. If only Eve had confided in Maggie about how she felt, she would still be alive.

Maggie curled up in a foetal position on the floor in the hall and sobbed. Why? Why? Why? This one word would repeat itself in Maggie's thoughts over and over again. She had let Eve down when she'd needed her most. She was so consumed by her own worries that she hadn't noticed Eve's.

Chloe arrived later that day to comfort Maggie. There wasn't anything she could say. Instead, she sat quietly beside Maggie and would be there to console her when she was ready.

Maggie spent the rest of the week in a daze. Bob Simpson gave Maggie a week's compassionate leave. She carried out errands in preparation for Eve's funeral. She spent time with Eve's solicitor Ernie Chandler, who was visibly hurt by Eve's death. He solemnly admitted to Maggie how much he'd cared for Eve. But a long time ago, she'd chosen the other guy.

Maggie wanted to know why the bank foreclosed so quickly. Weren't they supposed to give due notice and financial support?

Ernie told her they should have and probably did. But without seeing all of Eve's papers, he couldn't say what had transpired.

Ernie went through the contents of Eve's will with Maggie. He informed her that the funeral arrangements had already been organised and paid for. Eve would be buried next to her husband and son. As the bank had foreclosed on Eve, they had paid her what the house was currently worth, less her debt, plus their standard fees and charges. Once the funeral was paid for, the balance of her estate would go to Maggie. Ernie informed Maggie that the estate would total approximately 140,000 pounds, plus Eve's personal assets.

Maggie's sadness turned to anger. She needed to know what had happened. So, she went to see Eve's bank manager, Thomas Carlyle, but he refused to discuss Eve's foreclosure with her, only offering his condolences. Maggie wanted to smack him. She left more frustrated than when she'd arrived.

Her familiar anxiety had once again become her constant companion.

During that week, Maggie paid a visit to Mrs McGuigan. She needed to know what Eve's state of mind had been leading up to her death. But, on seeing how distraught Mrs McGuigan was in the wake of Eve's death, she turned her attention instead to comforting her. Mrs McGuigan shouldn't have had to witness such a tragedy. That was cruel and unfair. But when is suicide ever fair?

Mrs McGuigan assured Maggie that she was built of sterner stuff. They spent a number of hours getting to know each other. Maggie liked Mrs McGuigan instantly. She was sharp tongued and witty, especially when she expressed her loathing for the banks and government. 'Lazy good-for-nothings' kept coming up. Eve realised that while Mrs McGuigan may be retired and downgraded to a senior citizen, she was still as sharp as anyone half her age.

Maggie's friends were by her side throughout that week. They would be there for her, even when Maggie needed to scream and rage. They understood, even if no one else cared to listen. Maggie's friends had no answers to give her. They could only provide comfort and support, as all good friends do.

*   *   *

The funeral was a sombre and depressing affair. It brought back memories of Maggie's mother's funeral. Chloe had organised a wake at the pub, and many of Eve's friends turned out to pay their respects. They couldn't condone what she'd done, but they understood why she'd done it. Eve's friends from the W.I. came, even though their branch had stopped functioning years ago, they all rallied together in solidarity. Many of Eve's co-workers from the Provincial plant were present, as were her neighbours, to say their farewells.

If only Eve could see how well she was loved.

During the wake at the pub, Ernie Chandler gave Maggie Eve's letter. He thought it would be best to give it to her while she was surrounded by her friends. She carefully opened the envelope, afraid of what she would find. Maggie unfolded the letter inside. Her voice was brittle and coarse, she couldn't read it aloud. Instead, she read it solemnly to herself.

My dearest Maggie,

Please do not be angry with me, it was a conscious decision, and not one made lightly. I have loved and been loved but have lost those I've loved in my life, except for you, dear Maggie. Losing my home was my breaking point. I'm tired of fighting for happiness. Life shouldn't be such a struggle. Please don't think my act selfish. I'm with those I love. I hope you can believe that, because I do.

I have named you as my beneficiary. It is my gift to you. Do not feel any guilt in accepting it. I want you to live, love, and laugh again. You deserve it, my dear Maggie. Travel, study – do with it as you wish. I ask only one condition. Be extraordinary, Maggie. Don't hold back like you always do.

I'm sorry I did this at Christmas, but I couldn't endure another cold and bleak Christmas without them.

My love is with you always,
Eve

Maggie put the letter down on the table and wiped her eyes. She was still surrounded by her friends: Chloe, Morwenna, Anaya, and Julie. They remained silent. No words were needed between them. Maggie's eyes burned as red as Morwenna's lipstick – Morwenna saw no reason to be dull and morbid at funerals, it should be a celebration of the life lived, she believed. Anaya suggested taking her home to get some sleep, assuring Maggie that she would feel better in the morning.

Chloe drove her home and saw her to bed. Although Maggie said she was fine, Chloe didn't leave, and would be there when she woke in the morning.

*   *   *

The third of Maggie's friends was Chloe Silverton, who always denied her fifty-three years, because she felt like thirty-five. She worked part-time at the local primary school, as a class-room helper and reader. She also drove the mobile library van and worked part-time in the only pub left in town, called The Two Swallows. Sam Frobisher, the proprietor, had been a sailor in the Royal Navy prior to owning the pub. Seeing Chloe with her son in uniform one day unquestionably got her the job, or so she thought. Always opinionated to whomever cared to listen, Chloe was a proud feminist. This trait, however, didn't stop her from being a true romantic. She was ever the contradiction, which made her always entertaining.

The one true love of her life was her son, Matthew, a lieutenant in the Royal Navy. As a proud single mum, Chloe had raised Matthew alone, and whatever her opinions were of men, they didn't extend to her son – who undoubtedly was the best man in her life. No girl would ever be good enough for him.

Chloe's life was full, and if she ever needed a cuddle, she had Heathcliff, her cat, who always loved his cuddles. Being vivacious, outspoken, and full of confidence, she was the strength that glued the group of friends together.

*   *   *

Two days later ...

After the funeral, Maggie found herself standing beside Eve's grave. The newly turned earth was a startling reminder of the rawness of what Eve had done. Beside her lay her husband and son. A rage was still burning in Maggie, and she didn't know how to extinguish it. They were all to blame – the government, the banks, big business; every one of them had a hand in Eve's death according to Maggie. None of them would ever know or care how their decisions affected everyone else. Not for people like Eve.

Maggie felt such helplessness as she looked down at the grave. She needed to grab those responsible and shake them, yell at them. She wanted them to pay attention. But she doubted anyone would ever care to listen.

Maggie spoke to her friend's grave. 'Damned if you can't have everything you loved in life beside you for eternity.'

The next day, Maggie salvaged some flowers from Eve's greenhouse, without permission from the bank. Come spring, she would replant them on Eve's grave. As Maggie stole away from Eve's house with the incriminating pot plants, she felt a small tinge of rebelliousness.

A Taste of Rebellion

December

Provincial had become depressing, as staff numbers had been continually dwindling since the announcement in September. Maggie was finally given her finish date. She would be one of the last to leave.

The branch would close in less than two weeks. On her return to work, Maggie was run off her feet. Bob Simpson relied on her extensively. He was taking numerous hours off work, supposedly looking for another job.

*   *   *

Bob Simpson was only thinking of his family when he handed the security case keys to Major Hamilton. He hadn't needed much persuading, though. He had been paid well, and when he was told that the Friars Meadow branch would close, he was guaranteed a transfer. All he had to do was give the keys to Major Hamilton, who had them duplicated. It was simple. He was assured no-one would get hurt. Now, with the death of Angus McPherson, he knew they were after something much more valuable than just the money. He didn't understand the importance of the missing cases, and he didn't want to.

Bob Simpson regretted ever getting into bed with these men. All he had to do now was keep his mouth shut.

*   *   *

Maggie was tasked with overseeing the relocation of the plant equipment, as well as finishing up her usual duties. With less staff, this took longer than expected. Maggie was one of only three women left at the plant during that final week.

The last of the suitcases were shipped out with the sorting machines. The last of the currency deemed unusable for circulation was shipped off for disposal. Maggie found herself running all over the site. She was overseeing shipments, supervising the dismantling of equipment, and overseeing their transfer to other sites.

Although she was run-off her feet, Maggie was grateful for the distraction. Soon, the last of the sorting machines had finally been dismantled and were headed for their new home in Barnstaple.

To open the security cases required two keys. They were both kept locked in the safe in the manager's office. This was strict protocol. Although, since the retrenchments started, certain protocols had fallen far short of that.

As Bob Simpson was out of the office on most days, he gave Maggie the access code to the safe. He told her he trusted her completely. Bob Simpson had made Maggie his new acting supervisor for the remainder of her time at the plant – an honorary title only.

Maggie didn't really care. Being busy kept her mind off Eve. In a week, she would have no job. She'd own her home, but without a job she would have to travel far to look for another one. What skills did she have? Selling her home was not an option. Who would buy it anyway? It was currently worth half its true value. Keeping busy allowed her to keep her muddled and anxious thoughts at bay, if only for another week.

During that last week, Bob Simpson barely made an appearance. He eventually phoned Maggie to thank her for the smooth transition. He was pleased to announce he had been offered a new job up north. He had much to do with his relocation and trusted that Maggie would take care of the final incidentals at the plant.

On her final day, Maggie was running around hectically. Trucks were arriving hourly to take the final equipment away. Maggie followed Provincial's strict protocols right up until the end – except for one little mishap.

After emptying her locker, she gathered up the last of her belongings in a small cardboard box and walked to the security exit. Tired after her final day, Maggie was still wearing her white Provincial work coat and hair net. Company regulations stated that no employee was allowed to remove company property off the premises.

As she walked to the security door, she handed over her card to Simon, the only security guard left on site. He checked Maggie's bags and gave her a gentle peck on the cheek, wishing her all the best for the future. Maggie returned the compliment. They said goodbye for the last time. Simon was going to make one last sweep around the barren site before locking the doors and gates for the final time.

As Maggie walked off, she realised through her exhaustion that she was still wearing her coat and hair net. She pulled the hair net off and threw it into the wind. Then, she ran her hand through her hair to let it bounce freely in the fresh air. As for the coat, she turned at her car and extended her hands.

Simon just smiled from his place at the security door and fanned his arm in the air. 'Keep it as a memento, Maggie, it won't break the bank.' She smiled and waved goodbye, got in her car, and drove out of the lonely, deserted carpark for the last time.

This small oversight was the first crime Maggie ever committed.

On arriving home, exhausted, Maggie flung her dirty clothes in the laundry basket. She drew on her casual clothes and decided to worry about the washing in the morning. She put on her hiking boots and went for a long walk along the river to clear her head.

As she started off on her walk, a slight drizzle matched her mood. The wind whipped the droplets across her face. However, it was refreshing to be outside. As she walked along one of the brooks that started near her house, the tiny rain droplets danced on the water. God, she loved the rain. It always washed away all that was wrong in the world. It was a force no one had control over.

*   *   *

It wasn't until the following day, when she tossed her clothes into the washing machine, that she heard a clanking noise. She opened the lid and felt around for the conspicuous item causing the racket. Maggie squeezed out all her clothes to find the culprit. Finally, she caught sight of her work coat, and unsure why she was washing it anyway, she pulled it out to throw it away. It was then that she felt something hard in the pocket.

Maggie reached into the pocket and pulled out two identical keys.

Shit! Her heart skipped a beat – fear, anxiety, adrenaline. This was the first serious code violation Maggie had ever committed. This infringement would have cost Maggie her job – if she still had one. That was Maggie's first crime, albeit unintentional.

In all the mayhem of the last week, she had forgotten to put the security keys back in the safe. When Maggie had left through the security door, the scanners had already been requisitioned three days earlier by the South Shields branch. There wasn't even a metal detector or hand-held scanner left on site. Simon could only check her bags by hand when she left.

Maggie began to panic. She imagined the police bursting through her door at any moment to arrest her. But with all the chaos of the last week, Maggie had simply forgotten about them. They were the only items left at the branch that hadn't been siphoned off. Maggie realised Barnstaple must have their own set of keys for the cases. Otherwise, they would have asked for them days ago.

Maggie thought of driving up to Barnstaple to deliver the keys in person with an apology. She grabbed her handbag and jumped into her car, then started the engine and put it into gear.

Only, she couldn't drive away. Her foot wouldn't press down on the accelerator. She sat in her car in the driveway for a long ten minutes. With the engine running, she held the keys in her hand. For Maggie, these two simple keys symbolised a crossroads in her life. It was hard for Maggie to later describe what she felt in words to her friends. This moment epitomised a bridge, which she was standing in the middle of. If she took them back, it would be to her old life – her neatly folded napkin life. If she kept the keys, it symbolised a new rebellious side to herself, one in which she could take risks and be spontaneous.

Maggie turned off the engine. She went back inside and dropped the keys into the bottom of the flour tin. She placed the tin back on the shelf and turned her back on them to leave the kitchen, smiling to herself for the first time in a long while. She'd made a stand and now there was no looking back. Rebellious it was.

*   *   *

Maggie's walks became more frequent and lengthier over the next few months. She would wrap herself up warmly, take her hiking stick and her granddad's backpack, and hike miles along Devon's beautiful countryside and waterways. With each new walk, she became more invigorated. She found new spots along the river to sit down and watch the water flow past.

Christmas had been a sombre affair. It passed quietly for Maggie without any fanfare. Her friends did what they could to cheer her up. They missed Eve, too. Maggie spent the day with Chloe and her son, Matthew, who was home on leave. In the evening, everyone gathered at The Two Swallows. Even though

Maggie didn't feel like celebrating, her spirits were lifted by her friends' robust and diligent singing. She was rewarded with hugs from her friend's children for their Christmas gifts. This affection alone lifted her spirits.

Maggie's thoughts were mostly preoccupied by Eve and the prospect of finding a new job. But occasionally, a small smile would appear on her face, and her friends were grateful for this.

To some, Maggie's act of rebellion might not have seemed like much of a risk. But to her, it was an awakening. It was the beginning of something new and wonderful.

Maggie allowed her mind to wander – she was heading into an unknown future. For some people, that was a scary thought. But when these scary thoughts hit, Maggie would just wrap herself up against the coldness of winter and walk for miles. Her least favourite season wouldn't intimidate her as it used to. She was shielded from it.

First the Bulb, Then the Tulip

February

Jonathan Swift's team had been busy over the last few months. Their surveillance of Major Hamilton had been fruitful. Special Branch had captured CCTV footage of Major Hamilton in conversation with an unidentified man in Hyde Park. Through facial recognition, he was identified as Malcolm Barker-Smith, an MP who was also the current Conservative Minister for the seat of Totnes in Devon. With this information, it didn't take GCHQ long to identify Barker-Smith as the mystery voice in the conversation they had recorded with Sean Butcher back in October.

The only known connection that Major Hamilton and Barker-Smith had in common was their membership at a private members club in London, called Club 26, to which Barker-Smith had only recently been offered membership. Archibald Monroe, the managing director of Phoenix Security, was a founding member. GCHQ had been authorised to start a full surveillance package on Barker-Smith, monitoring and listening.

As their investigation grew daily, Jonathan's team extended its examination to Barker-Smith and Monroe's families and acquaintances. This led GCHQ to their first important link –the last bank in Exeter that the security van had visited that day was managed by Nicholas Wickham, Barker-Smith's brother-in-law.

Jonathan's team began a surveillance package on Nicholas Wickham. They accessed all of his computer and phone correspondences, as per protocol.

By the end of the day, GCHQ discovered a deleted text on Wickham's mobile, which had been sent to his brother-in-law one hour before the van robbery. It was a twelve-digit serial number, which GCHQ matched to one of the stolen security cases. This confirmed Jonathan's suspicions. The hijackers were after a specific case, and the only person who could tell them which one was Nicholas Wickham.

Jonathan presented Max Evans with his latest report, stipulating that they should bring Wickham and Barker-Smith in for questioning.

'We have proof that Wickham was involved. He'll crack and tell us who put him up to it,' said Jonathan, as he sat down in front of Max in his office. Max's office was considerably larger than Jonathan's, with a mahogany desk that was at least one-hundred-and-fifty years old, if not a day. On his desk, he lovingly positioned pictures of his wife, Alyson, and their three children. A cricket ball in a glass case sat proudly in the middle, which had been the winning ball for England in the 2013 Ashes at Lords.

'Barker-Smith will deny the text, stating he received it in error,' said Max as he perused the file. 'It's not unfathomable, since he's his brother-in-law.' He looked up at Jonathan before continuing. 'Without the suitcase, the CPS would have trouble getting convictions. We don't have the Butcher brothers or Andrews in custody. If we go in too soon, Hamilton and Barker-Smith could walk. Hamilton can afford the best QCs in London, and the conservatives will close rank to protect one of their own. If Phoenix Security is up to something, we need to know what it is, and until you have all the players lined up, they're not to be touched.'

'Yes, you're right, but I've got a bad feeling about this one.'

Max told Jonathan to look into Club 26 and to find out who its members were. He was reminded to tread carefully, as the members were high-valued VIPs and could ruffle feathers in Whitehall and Downing Street.

Max stipulated that if other members of the club were involved, it would be a tight-knit group. If Barker-Smith was meeting Monroe or Hamilton in the club, they needed to get eyes inside. Club 26 was characterised as a very discreet private members club. The club invited you to be a member, not the other way around. Jonathan had assigned a junior analyst to head up the investigation into Club 26 and its members.

Once GCHQ obtained the members list, Jonathan received authorisation to put surveillance inside the club, which they did as a waiter and cleaner. Phone and room taps were also placed inside the club and at the head office of Phoenix Security. Special Branch put a tail on Wickham. Within a week, Jonathan's team had full surveillance on all their suspects. He hoped one of them would lead them to Andrews and the Butcher brothers. But he knew they were too professional for that – all except Wickham.

Jonathan's frustration with bureaucracy was clearly showing. Only a few people would have known the time and route of the security van and had access to the keys and the serial number for each case. Their link was Nicholas Wickham. But Max's cooler head kept Jonathan's impulses at bay, which was why Max was the head of staff, and he was the senior analyst.

'Money can buy many things but at a terrible cost. If they're prepared to kill for this case, then whatever's in it must be important to them,' said Max.

However, without the case, GCHQ still had no idea what was so valuable. Max told Jonathan to use his head, not his heart. As Max watched Jonathan leave his office, looking despondent, he said:

'Solve the puzzle, Jonathan, and follow the breadcrumbs, that's what you're good at.'

'Great, now you're Obi-Wan Kenobi,' said Jonathan, smiling.

'Listen, my little Padawan. Don't get tied down in frustration for what you can't do. Our politicians won't make a move against a giant of a company like Phoenix without unequivocal proof. Find it.'

Jonathan walked back to his office. He needed to sit quietly and think. Max was right – follow the breadcrumbs. He made himself a coffee, then sat back in his chair and recounted what had taken place that day. If the case remained in the vault, then whatever was put inside it had to have come from inside the vault. It would stand to reason that it had come from inside one of the safety deposit boxes, which meant that they needed to find out whose deposit box that was.

Jonathan conceded to not bringing Barker-Smith or Nicholas Wickham in for questioning. It would be a fruitless activity and would only draw undue attention to their investigation. Whatever upper hand GCHQ might gain, it would be for nothing if their suspects went into the shadows.

After studying Nicholas Wickham for some time and listening to his phone conversations, Angela Milford believed him to be the weak link in the group. She stated that if they were going to question anyone, it should be him. Wickham's phone conversations with his brother-in-law showed him to be clearly intimidated by Barker-Smith. But, unfortunately, there was nothing in their conversations so far that would prove helpful to their investigation.

GCHQ obtained a list of names for the safety deposit boxes at Wickham's branch. They painstakingly investigated each owner until satisfied that their boxes were of no interest to them. Once they had gone through the entire list, GCHQ were left with seven suspicious owners. Using false names to hide their true identities, Jonathan was surprised to find that there were only seven.

At a briefing in March, Jonathan presented his findings to his superiors, with Special Branch and a representative from the Home Office in attendance. They all agreed that arresting Barker-Smith now – on snippets of conversations – might see him arrested but not convicted. Not without hard evidence.

With that in mind, and with the evidence so far, it was agreed that Special Branch would bring Nicholas Wickham in for questioning. They had his direct involvement in the robbery, and if he was truly the weak link, he would break and turn on his brother-in-law and his associates. They had permission to offer a plea bargain, but only on the strict condition that he didn't mislead or withhold any information.

'Well Jonathan, you've got what you wanted,' stated Max, after leaving the meeting. 'Bring in Wickham and see what he has to say for himself.'

'Thanks, Max. Angela is right, he's our weakest link. We need to know why that particular case is so important to Hamilton.'

'Good work. Now go home and get some rest, will you? You look like the cat's dinner.' Jonathan drove home, relieved he would finally get some answers. He hoped Wickham would tell them what was so important about the security case.

Rebel, Rebel

Winter's End, Early February

There was still no scent of spring in the air, although daylight was slowly stealing darkness from the day. Maggie had been looking for work for over two months now but had so far found nothing. To be fair, she hadn't tried very hard. Her heart just wasn't in it. Her long walks were her only respite from her discouraging thoughts.

Her qualifications weren't much to speak of. 'What did you do in your last job?' 'I examined the worthiness of old banknotes.' Becoming a bank teller was an option. But since Eve's death, her respect for banks was at an all-time low. She had her retrenchment payout now, plus the inheritance from Eve. Apart from paying off her mortgage, she hadn't touched the rest.

Maggie knew she wasn't being very extraordinary. She had to sort herself out; she was still restless. She'd lost the two women she cared most about in her life. Her friends kept reiterating that it wasn't healthy to spend all her time alone, but she needed time to recover from Eve's death.

It made Maggie's blood boil when she heard that Bob Simpson was appointed branch manager at the new Barnstaple site.

Eve lost everything because of Provincial; many lives had been turned upside down because of their decision to close the branch. But Bob Simpson had just walked straight into a new version of his old job.

All Maggie could think was: if that van hadn't been robbed last September, maybe the site wouldn't have closed. Maybe Eve would still be alive.

Maggie couldn't shake off the niggling frustration that had been dogging her. She felt the need to strike out, to do something, but what?

Maggie had thought that after England left the EU, everything would improve. England would prosper again. However, as Britain's politicians continually squabbled and unanimously agreed to disagree, nothing was being accomplished. There was still no job growth. No prosperity.

The wheels of politics turned too slowly for Maggie. She felt she was standing in quicksand, frustrated and unable to move. Anaya suggested seeing a doctor. Maybe some sleeping pills would help. Or getting professional help for her depression. Maggie declined, stating she might get too attached to them. Besides, they'd only sugar-coat her frustration, they wouldn't remedy it.

But on a not-so-extraordinary Sunday morning in early March, Maggie walked over five miles along the River Dart. She had her trusty hiking stick and old backpack (as usual), which she'd filled with sandwiches and a flask of tea.

Her walk that day led her to a rocky stream. She trekked along its snaky contours until she reached the infamous bridge where the van had been hijacked. Maggie couldn't remember if they had even arrested anyone yet. But at least the council had finished repairing the bridge.

Maggie stopped for lunch by the stream and reclined, allowing the sun to gently touch her face. She gazed up and watched the clouds slowly drift by, and then she dozed for a while. After a quick bathroom stop behind a mulberry bush, she picked up her gear and continued on her walk.

Six miles from Friars Meadow, the river turned sharply, narrowed, and began to flow faster. Maggie hiked around a bend. As the sun caught her eye, she noticed an object caught on the edge of the embankment. It was shimmering beneath the water. She hiked over to it and could see it was a submerged container of some kind. Her first thought was that some bastard had dumped an old suitcase in the river.

As she moved closer, she started to feel a sense of familiarity. She climbed down the embankment to get a better look. It was wedged against some rocks and a fallen tree branch. The branch was overhanging the river, which partially protected the case from view.

She couldn't believe her eyes. It was surreal to look at, just sitting there under the water, partially concealed, just waiting for someone to discover it.

A Provincial security case.

The hijackers hadn't stolen all of the cases after all. Here was one, wedged in tightly from view.

Maggie reached in and hauled the case out of the water. It was heavier than she remembered. Although, from memory, she knew there were over a million pounds in each case.

Maggie needed to call the authorities. She reached into her backpack for her mobile, but there was no signal. She swore.

She would have to hightail it towards Friars Meadow to get better reception. The denser the population was, the more cell towers, so Friars Meadow had far fewer than most towns. *Cheapskates*, she thought, swearing again. There was no other alternative – she stowed the case under a tree branch and headed on foot back to Friars Meadow.

She walked briskly for over an hour. Her first thought was one of amazement at her discovery. Then her thoughts drifted to a possible reward. Eventually, her pace started to slow, but not out of exhaustion. During her march, her mind had started to clear. The hazy fog that had surrounded her thoughts these last few months was evaporating. Her mind was free to imagine all sorts of exciting ideas.

When she arrived on the outskirts of town, she still hadn't called the police, which she could have done twenty minutes earlier, when her phone regained a signal. It hadn't slipped her mind – the phone call, that is.

Maggie walked up to the edge of the overgrown botanical gardens in the centre of town. She took in all of the dilapidated houses and shops around her. How drab and dreary everything was. She thought how much her town would benefit from all that money.

Her mind was racing with one idea after another. Before she realised what she'd done, Maggie was standing on her patio. She could see everything clearly, and not just because it was turning into a beautiful day. A smile started to curl at the corner of her mouth.

For once in her life, Maggie decided to act in an extraordinary manner.

Then, a chill gripped her. She realised it was nearly 4 p.m. She ran inside and grabbed her car keys. Then, she ran into her mother's derelict workshop, acquiring a few items before she jumped into her car and drove back to the river.

Maggie secured the rope she'd brought with her to the bull bar on the back of her car. Making her way down to the riverbed, she tied the rope threw the handle of the case. She then drove her car forward, brought the case up onto the roadside, and without hesitation, hauled it into the trunk of her car.

As she drove home, she could hear her heart beating out of her chest. Guilt or adrenalin – she didn't know which and she no longer cared.

Sitting in her conservatory that evening, Maggie stared down at the contents of the case. She wiped flour off her fingers as she started to formulate a plan.

Maggie's Plan

The Rest of February

Maggie was a woman possessed! For the whole of February, Maggie became more reclusive than ever. Her friends were becoming concerned by her behaviour. But when she assured them that she was fine, they had to accept her word. Their Wednesday night poker games continued as always and by the end of the month, her friends had seen a vast improvement in Maggie, even though she still hadn't found a job. Her outward appearance seemed upbeat, and she appeared driven, even if they couldn't account for it.

For twenty days, Maggie researched, Googled, and visited the library in Torquay. On a number of occasions, she visited her new solicitor, Ernie Chandler. She also used the services of a retired accountant. She visited the lands registry office and the local council offices in Totnes. She was having the time of her life. She couldn't afford to leave one stone unturned.

During that month, Maggie allocated a portion of her time to re-decorating her garden. She built a fountain featuring a centrepiece of a petite cupid holding a bow and carrying a pouch full of arrows on his back. Water was supposed to spew forth from his penis, but it wasn't working. In fact, it would never work. That was not its purpose.

Maggie planted an array of colourful flowers, which she seconded from Eve's garden, around the fountain and then filled it with water from the tap. It was an eyeful to behold, but it concealed a great deal.

On the first Wednesday in March, it was finally time to present her plan to her friends. She had been so excited and obsessed by her plan that she hadn't thought of how it would affect them.

However, Maggie couldn't carry out her plan alone. She needed her friends' help. But she had been so consumed by her preparations that she hadn't considered how her friends would react, either. They had a lot to lose if they were caught.

Yes, they were going to commit a crime. Okay, more than one. But for Maggie, it would be more of a crime to do nothing. The only person who could technically be charged with theft was Maggie. She would take the blame alone. But it was still a risk. A big one, which she was prepared to make. Only, she couldn't expect that of her friends. They needed to understand the whys and wherefores before they made their decision.

Maggie believed everything that had happened to her since Eve's death was fate. An extraordinary twist of fate.

The Confession

The First Wednesday in March

Maggie felt sick – and excited!

It was 6 p.m. and Maggie was getting the snacks and drinks ready for their weekly poker game. Her nerves were a jumble of excitement, anxiety, and apprehension – hence the nausea. She prayed that everything would go as planned. It couldn't all be for nothing. Maggie needed her friends to understand what she was going to do and why. Nothing was going to stop her. Notwithstanding that, she still needed their help.

*   *   *

Maggie's fourth friend was Julie – or Jules – Hart. Maggie and Julie had been at school together, and she was the last of Maggie's friends to remain in town. She'd stayed not to care for a sick mother but instead for a young son. Julie had also been struggling to find another job since the processing plant had closed. She couldn't move away, as she had Jeremy's needs to think about.

Julie's parents had offered to help, but she was reluctant to move back in with them. Her independence was not something she wanted to give up. Her parents meant well, but she knew that if she moved back in with them, they would start up again about university.

It wasn't just because of Jeremy that Julie had remained in town. Julie loved living in Friars Meadow. Yes, it was going to the dogs, but her life was here; it was her home and she had good friends here. So, she rented one of the dilapidated houses across from the botanical gardens. It had been owned by the bank, on the back of another foreclosure, but it was now privately owned and rented.

Julie's relationship with her parents had been on shaky ground since her pregnancy. They didn't want her to throw her future away. Only, Julie never saw it that way. She'd been very bright at school, but her one transgression had produced Jeremy. Her parents had offered to raise Jeremy as their own so she could continue her studies. It was an idea she contemplated, up until the moment when she held Jeremy in her arms. Besides, Julie wasn't too worried about her education. At twenty-seven, she knew she would go to university one day

Her parents would help her if she needed money, of course. But she couldn't accept money from them indefinitely. She was her own woman now, and she enjoyed her freedom.

*   *   *

The cars arrived and the children came running inside. They all gave Maggie her customary kiss on the cheek and ran directly into the living room where the popcorn, chips, and soft drinks were waiting for them. It was Alfie's turn to control the remote, to Jeremy's displeasure, and everyone else's relief. Jeremy had once told his mum that if they combined the twins' intelligence, he would still be far more intelligent then both of them. No one disputed this – not even Morwenna.

Chloe, Morwenna, Julie, and Anaya walked through the door and into the conservatory. It was an oval-shaped room at the back of Maggie's house, with glass walls that offered sweeping views of the countryside to the north. They all settled down in their customary seats. They acknowledged, as always, the empty chair that was Eve's. Her place was always set at the table.

Maggie glided into the room, carrying the drinks and snacks. She had an unusual air about her. She was wearing a floral, slim-lined dress that flared from the waist to below her knee. Her hair bobbed about her head more profusely than usual. They all took in her decisive walk – it was all very unusual for their Wednesday night poker. Her friends looked at each other quizzically.

'If I didn't know any better, I'd say Maggie has a lover,' teased Morwenna.

'Yes, I agree,' Chloe said, smiling. 'C'mon, Maggie, what's going on?'

'I'm fine. Truly, I'm feeling great. Spring is in the air, and I feel alive for the first time in a long time.' Maggie sat down and started to shuffle the cards. As she did, shesaid, 'I have something I want to talk to you all about after we've finish our poker tonight.'.

Maggie smiled as she dealt the first hand. Her curious friends knew that they would have to wait until afterwards to find out what it was. Nothing interrupted poker.

Maggie's friends eyed each other. Had she found a new job? Was she planning a trip? *Did* she have a lover? But she could have told her friends her news at any time. Judging by Maggie's appearance and behaviour, something else was afoot.

By 10 p.m. – three bottles of wine, countless teas and coffees, a packet of Jaffa Cakes, and a sponge cake later – it was time to wrap up.

Everyone was about to help Maggie tidy the room of dirty plates and glasses when she said: 'No. Leave everything! I want you to stay seated. I have something to show you, and I want you all seated when I come back.'

'Now you're sounding very mysterious,' yelled Chloe as Maggie walked out of the room. They exchanged looks while they waited for the punch line.

'What have you done?' asked Julie, as Maggie walked back in.

'Nothing, yet. It's what I'm about to do, Jules.'

As she sat down, she placed a tin of biscuits on the table, which was in the shape of a red double-decker bus.

'Is that it?' cried Morwenna. 'You wanted to show us your biscuit tin?'

'No,' Maggie said, smiling. 'It's what's inside the tin.'

'More Jaffa Cakes, I hope,' said Morwenna.

'Are you sure you haven't given her anything?' Chloe asked Anaya. 'She's not acting like herself.'

'Maybe she is, and we just haven't seen this side of her yet. Let's just see where she's going with it,' reasoned Anaya.

* * *

The last of Maggie's friends was Anaya Patel who, at forty-one, was an optimist. She lived just outside of Friars Meadow with her devoted husband and two spoilt, self-absorbed children. It didn't take Anaya long to realise she had got that backwards. Her husband had returned to India to visit his family over a year ago and had failed to return. Strangely, she wasn't overly distraught about it. Anaya simply had one less child to look after, and her daughters showed honest maturity during that year.

Anaya relied on her routinely dependable life. Predictability was very important to her. As the area nurse, her work could be hectic and challenging at times. She needed order and routine to keep all the balls in the air at once. The only times Anaya ever let her long black hair down was when she watched the cricket or rugby, her two passions in life.

During Beth's illness, Anaya had been a godsend to Maggie and Eve. Their friendship had evolved during and after Beth's death. Soon after their friendship started, Anaya discovered her third passion – poker – and never missed a Wednesday night game. Anaya was the rational and dependable friend in their group.

* * *

'I want you to understand something first,' began Maggie. 'I'm not crazy or angry anymore. I was deeply hurt when Eve died. I was in a dark place for a long while. So, I did what I loved to do most – I walked, a lot. It helped me to find myself again.'

'We all felt regret and anger over Eve, Maggie,' said Chloe in a soft voice. 'But I'm glad you're feeling better now.'

'I know you did,' said Maggie. 'But a few months ago, a strange twist of fate changed everything. I've a purpose now, but I need your help to achieve it. However, you will need to think long and hard before you decide. With the reward comes risk. Please don't try to change my mind, as I'm resolved in this matter. I'm doing it with or without you. I've thought of nothing else this last month. You're either in or out. Either way, your friendship means more to me than anything. I love each of you and I'll understand if you say no.'

'You're scaring me, Maggie,' cut in Chloe.

'What have you done?' repeated Julie.

'OK … There are three parts to this story.' Maggie took a deep breath and began. 'Fate fell in my lap twice. Firstly, as you know, I was one of the last people to leave Provincial. The place had been fleeced of just about everything by the time I left. I was so busy that last week. You remember me telling you that Bob Simpson was barely there? I was so tired by the time I finished up that I walked out still wearing my work coat and hair net. Simon, bless him, just looked in my bag and wished me good luck. He didn't even have a hand-held scanner anymore. The next day, when I was doing the laundry, I heard a clanking sound in the washing machine, and when I searched the pockets of my work coat, I found two security case keys.'

'What … You didn't,' said Julie.

'Holy shit,' exclaimed Morwenna. 'But why in God's name would you wash your work coat?'

'What did they say when you returned them?' asked Julie, getting uneasy.

'I didn't,' said Maggie, placing the two security case keys on the table in front of everyone. She wiped a little bit of self-rising flour off them as she did.

Their reactions were to be expected: a mix of curse words, shocked silence, and wide eyes.

'Fucking hell,' said Morwenna.

'Haven't they come looking?' asked Julie.

'No … It appears to have slipped everyone's mind,' said Maggie. 'I was going to take them to the Barnstaple branch. I got in my car, but I just couldn't do it. This happened before Christmas. Then something else happened that sealed my fate.'

'Oh, God, what?' asked Julie.

'Last month, I was out hiking along the river. I was a few kilometres west of Friars Meadow when I saw something wedged between some rocks, partially submerged in the river. It just presented itself to me.'

'What did?' asked Chloe, cautiously waiting for the answer.

'A Provincial security case,' Maggie paused. She knew what was coming.

'Holy fuck,' said Morwenna.

'Oh my God,' said Julie.

'*Pavitr bakavaas*,' said Anaya. 'Holy shit.'

'Um, what did you do with it, Maggie?' asked Chloe.

'Well now, that's the second part of my story.'

Maggie opened the tin of biscuits and showed them eight wads of bank notes.

Everyone looked downwards, then upwards at Maggie. Then they erupted all at once, this time coming out of their chairs, gesturing absurdly. Maggie waited until the noise settled down. Then she hit them with her third bombshell.

'I'm keeping it.'

Julie and Morwenna erupted again. Anaya whistled while Chloe sat quietly in contemplation of Maggie's next move, for she knew something else was coming.

'Quiet, please. Listen. I was going to call the police when I found it, honestly. But I had no mobile coverage.'

'Well, that's convenient, now you're blaming B.T.,' said Morwenna.

'I had to get nearer to town to make the call. But by the time I was in range, I'd had time to think about what it meant to find the case – especially since I had a set of keys to open it. It felt like destiny,' said Maggie. 'I had to keep it.'

'No, it means you need to turn it in,' said Chloe.

'I disagree. Finding it was a sign. I'm meant to do something good with it,' said Maggie.

'Yeah, hand it back,' said Morwenna. 'You may even get a reward.'

'It's blind, stupid luck, that's all, Maggie. And it's a crime,' said Chloe.

'No, it isn't. OK, yes, it is. Look, maybe the police think the robbers have all the cases. I haven't seen anything in the news to say otherwise, have you? Nobody knows I found it or that it's even missing,' said Maggie.

'Unless the police do know and they're keeping shtum about it for some reason,' said Anaya.

'*Please* just listen to my plan,' pleaded Maggie. 'I'm doing it with or without you.'

'OK, let her speak. Once we know what she's planning, we'll have a better chance of talking her out of it,' said Chloe.

Maggie looked around the table at her friends. She had gone over this moment a thousand times in her head, but now that actual emotion was involved, she was having trouble voicing the words correctly. She didn't want to sound crazy.

But before she could speak, Jeremy walked in and said: 'Hi, Mum. It's past 10 o'clock. We should have left already.'

'No, it's only 9.45,' said Morwenna. 'You're getting mixed up with daylight savings, sweetie, go back and watch some telly, there's a good boy.'

'No, it isn't, daylight saving doesn't commence until 1 a.m. on Sunday the twenty-fifth of March,' said Jeremy, precise as always.

Julie had often worried about Jeremy. Those closest to her thought he might have bi-polar disorder or some form of autism. He was always so precise about everything. He had the neatest bedroom in England. It wasn't normal. He had trouble concentrating on remedial tasks and found it hard to socialise with other children at school. It wasn't until he was seven that his teachers had put his aloofness down to his intelligence. His mind was always filled with irrelevant facts, which he liked to share with anyone who cared to listen. Julie's friends found him slightly odd but extremely loveable.

'Mummy is having a very important discussion with her friends. We won't be long, so please give us a few more minutes, thanks love,' said Julie.

'Why didn't you just say that?' said Jeremy. He squinted at Morwenna before leaving the room.

Maggie smiled at Jeremy's directness. Now she needed to find that in herself.

'I've spent the last month going over and over my plan. I'm not being vindictive or greedy. I could've handed it in for the reward, but I want to change lives – as many as possible. Not just for Eve's sake but for everyone else in this dilapidated town.'

Maggie's friends were listening intently. 'I want to transform the town back to the way it was. You all remember how beautiful it once was. We've been waiting for the economy to reinvigorate our town along with the rest of the county, but it hasn't. Where are all the new jobs? The politicians are more concerned about their own jobs and taking swipes at each other than about helping their people find work.'

Maggie paused for a moment. She took a deep breath before continuing.

'I'm going to start a trust – the Charitable Trust. I'm using the balance of the money Eve left me for the initial start-up trust – fifty thousand pounds. There's no crime in that. Then, throughout the year, small amounts of money will be deposited into the trust through bank branches all around Devon and beyond. This will be done at random times each week, using the night safe and ATMs.'

Everyone remained quiet as they listened to their friend. Maggie couldn't read from their expressions if she was getting through to them.

'As far as anyone is concerned, they'll be classed as anonymous donations. That's where you come in. I'll need your help depositing the money over the year. Large deposits are flagged and will draw attention from the banks and government. Small amounts will not.'

'The trust needs three people to be its trustees, who would be the three of you – Anaya, Julie, and Morwenna. Anaya, I know your work as area nurse comes first, so I just need you to be a trustee. Morwenna and Jules, trustees don't normally receive a salary. But you'll be doing more than just assessing claims. It will mean a full-time job. Chloe, I want you to run for Councillor of Friars Meadow at next year's local election in May. With you in the council, we could expedite our plans, without drawing undue attention from the council in Totnes. Just think, Chloe, one day you might even become Mayor of Totnes. Everyone knows you and respects you around town. We'd all help with your campaign.'

Maggie stopped to take a breather. She hadn't realised how fast she was talking. The silence in the room was excruciating. But Maggie had momentum, so she continued.

'Our local Councillor in Friars Meadow is Larry Morecombe. Susan McBride is the Totnes Council Mayor. Our MP for Totnes at the moment is Malcolm Barker-Smith. He's a Conservative. I don't know much about them, but I'm sure we can learn before the election.'

'Maggie, I haven't voted for donkey's years,' said Chloe.

'Who cares? You can run as an independent,' she replied.

'What exactly do you want to do with the money, Maggie?' asked Julie.

'I want us to invest it back into the town,' continued Maggie, 'I want to give it to those who need it. Not just immediate relief, but long-term investments. The trust would buy the old shoe factory site back off the bank and re-open it. The workers from the Provincial plant – still out of work – would be offered employment once it re-opens. We could search out some of the skilled workers who once worked there, if they're still around. We'd restore the botanical gardens and breathe life back into this town again. We'd re-open the community centre. I've spoken to

Father Michael about buying it from the church. He's been trying to raise money to repair the roof of the church for years. Through the community centre, we could offer many benefits and social events to help anyone in need.'

Maggie's friends hadn't seen her this wound up in years. She had excitement in her eyes. This was clearly not a whimsical, thoughtless idea. It was like looking at a completely different person.

'I managed to get into the old shoe factory site a few weeks ago. All the old filing cabinets with the employee files are still there. I'm going to do what the politicians should have done. I'm getting our economy moving again, if only for the people in our little town again.'

Maggie continued on for some time. She spoke coherently and rationally. All the profit from the shoe factory would go back into the trust to re-invest in other businesses and ventures. The money would earn interest while at the bank. As more jobs were created in Friars Meadow, the shops in town would generate profit and in time hire more staff.

Maggie's friends saw in her only the good that could be achieved in finding the money. She had ignored the elephant in the room. What if they were caught?

Chloe downed the last of her white wine. She needed red for this.

'I've called it the "Eve Merriweather Trust". None of you have technically stolen anything, and if anyone asks, you should simply say that you applied for the job and were hired by the trust's solicitor, which by the way is Ernie Chandler, who's behind me one hundred percent. He knows what I'm doing and has agreed to act as the trust's solicitor. I've also found an accountant. I've spent a lot of time with her – fascinating woman. She's retired but has agreed to help with financial advice.' She glanced over her friends. 'I know it's a risk. I know what's at stake. I need to do it for Eve and for myself. But I can't do it alone,' said Maggie, pleading for their support.

'I'm not sure, Maggie,' Chloe said. 'You're asking a lot.'

'I know, but when these two gifts fell in my lap, I knew in my heart and head that I had to do something good with them. Eve told me in her letter to be extraordinary, don't hold back – remember?'

'She didn't mean for you to commit a crime, Maggie,' said Morwenna.

'Do I sound irrational? No. All I'm asking is for you to go away and think about what I've said. If you want to help me, meet back here on Friday at 7 p.m. Then I'll explain in more detail what I've got planned for each of you.'

Maggie stood up and looked imploringly at her friends. Was she asking too much? She wouldn't hold it against them if they turned her down. They had responsibilities, far more than she did. Her only fear was that she would have to do it alone, which would make it more complicated but not impossible. For the first time in a month, Maggie had doubts.

And so, her friends agreed to think about it. Chloe, Morwenna, Anaya, and Julie gathered their phones, jackets, umbrellas, and kids, and left.

GCHQ

Springtime, March

GCHQ's investigation was back in swing. The approval to bring Nicholas Wickham in for questioning had been extremely beneficial. Angela's assessment of him had been correct, he sang like a bird. To earn immunity against prosecution, he was prepared to name names – even his own brother-in-law, Malcolm Barker Smith.

Wickham told GCHQ that Barker-Smith needed an electronic notebook out of a safety deposit box. However, when he had gone to retrieve it, he'd found a large metal box instead.

'I couldn't open it – it had a six-digit security locking panel. I couldn't risk being seen leaving the vault with it, so I left it where it was.'

Wickham continued his story, stating that his brother-in-law had come up with an alternative plan. He was to put the metal box into a Provincial security case and have the drivers take it away with them.

'I recorded the serial number on the security case and texted Malcolm the number. That was all I had to do. Nothing more. I swear.'

Angela showed him a list of the bank's deposit box holders and asked him to identify which customer owned the deposit box in question. Wickham did this without hesitation – it belonged to one of seven unidentified box holders. Wickham gave GCHQ what information he could of the woman's description.

'However,' he informed them, 'the woman was apparently killed while crossing a road, the same day she opened the deposit box.'

Explaining yet again why he had to retrieve the box for his brother-in-law, Jonathan thanked him for his compliance.

Jonathan's team studied all CCTV cameras around the bank on the day the unidentified woman had opened the deposit box. They also requested the police file on the hit and run victim in Exeter that day. Once Angela had the police report, she showed it to Wickham, who positively identified her as the same woman who'd opened the box. GCHQ now had a name for their mystery woman: Bridget Monahan.

Jonathan didn't believe in coincidences, and he knew the hit and run was no accident. Whether Wickham knew this or not would be difficult to prove. But when Jonathan was told who Bridget Monahan had worked for up until the day before her death, alarm bells started ringing.

Jonathan raced into Max's office.

'Her name was Bridget Monahan and she resigned from MI5 the day before she was killed.'

'Fuck,' was Max's reply.

'I'll obtain the bank application form that was used to open the box, and cross-reference any fingerprints found on it with Bridget Monahan's.'

On that queue, Jonathan left Max's office in a hurry.

*　　*　　*

The police had investigated Bridget's death, but in the end had put it down to a tragic hit and run accident. They'd never found the car. The only witness had confirmed that she was looking down at her mobile when she stepped out onto the road.

Bridget Monahan's security vetting and profiling showed no indication of criminal activity. She didn't fit the profile of a traitor. MI5 had her down as a high achiever.

The Home Office stipulated that GCHQ were in charge of the investigation, as MI5 could have been compromised. The Home Office ordered a thorough review of everything Bridget had worked on leading up to her resignation. If she'd concealed something in a safety deposit box under a pseudonym, she was obviously hiding something of value.

Angela headed up the review of Bridget's work colleagues and confirmed that the electronic notebook Wickham spoke of was Bridget's farewell gift from MI5. She'd had no access to her computer from 10 a.m. on the day she'd finished up. Security confirmed they'd escorted her to her locker, then to the security office where she'd handed in her key card and ID. From there, she'd exited the building, carrying only her personal belongings.

The only piece of information that Angela thought noteworthy was a phone call Bridget had made at her desk to her mother. This call lasted approximately four minutes. Angela organised for technicians to get access to Bridget's home and work computers. She also needed to speak with Bridget's mother. As next of kin, her mother would possibly have Bridget's phone and laptop.

As for Wickham, his immunity would only be given on the understanding that he revealed everything he knew about the robbery, and the murders of Angus McPherson and Bridget Monahan. But he threw his hands up, swearing blind that he knew nothing more about either murder. He was starting to sweat profusely. Jonathan watched the interview carefully. He could tell that Wickham was telling the truth about the murders, but he had to be lying about the rest. Jonathan made it clear to Wickham that if he withheld anything, he would throw him in the same prison as his accomplices.

Wickham weighed up his choices. He didn't have many, so his answer came quickly.

'Bridget Monahan was in Exeter to sell some software she'd acquired from her employer. She was killed in the hit and run, which is why Malcolm asked me to remove a notebook from her deposit box.'

He swore blind that this was all he knew. Some of Malcolm's friends were buying the software. That's why he'd gotten involved. No, he didn't know who Malcolm's friends were. He pleaded that he only had contact with his brother-in-law. When Wickham was asked about Archibald Monroe or Major James Hamilton, he feigned ignorance of both names.

'It's a pity the young woman died. If she hadn't been in that accident, I wouldn't be in this mess now,' said Wickham.

'How did you get Bridget's security box key?' Angela asked.

'Malcolm gave it to me.'

Jonathan and Angela didn't know if Wickham was thoughtless or just ignorant of the people he had gotten into bed with.

Wickham was happy to shift the blame to his brother-in-law. He continued his repertoire.

'Malcolm would do anything to obtain a cabinet position.' Jonathan believed Wickham would do anything to deflect his own involvement in the heist. He was prepared to send his brother-in-law down the river without a lifejacket.

Jonathan doubted Barker-Smith had known about the serial numbers on the security cases. But they allowed Wickham to continue his farce. Wickham was clearly more scared about going to prison than he was of his brother-in-law and his friends.

The only piece of information that GCHQ found interesting was the fact that Wickham's brother-in-law and his friends were still searching for the missing case.

Wickham was released and allowed to return home. He was under strict instructions and forced to sign a gag order. GCHQ would need him in the future.

He was told to carry on as normal. A sweaty Wickham agreed.

Angela Milford had a junior analyst check every street and shop camera in Exeter on the day of Bridget Monahan's murder.

Luckily, they managed to obtain camera footage from a newly renovated shop. It wasn't open on the day of the hit and run but had installed security cameras in the front and back. GCHQ gathered all the footage from the street cameras and arranged them in chronological order.

Angela watched as the footage captured Bridget leaving the bank. They followed her until she came to a traffic light. While she waited to cross the road, something spooked her, and once the light changed Bridget started to run. They watched as she ran down Friars Gate and into Collection Crescent. Thanks to the newly installed security cameras, GCHQ had footage of Bridget's murder.

Jonathan's team re-lived Bridget Monahan's death over and over again. A car stops. A man gets out — not the driver — and goes up to her mangled body lying in the street. He does not check her pulse, but instead appears to be frisking her for something. Then he stands up and heads back to the car. As he does this, he looks back down the street, his face in clear view of the hidden shop camera.

GCHQ took no time to identify him as either Chris or Sean Butcher. GCHQ still couldn't tell them apart.

Angela's surveillance team searched for the Butcher brothers' car. Using every street camera at their disposal, they followed the car until it reached the outskirts of Exeter. From there they lost it. It wasn't for another week that a police patrol vehicle found the burnt-out car in a field. No evidence was extracted from the wreck of the black Range Rover. It had no plates, no fingerprints, and the engine serial number had been destroyed.

Angela reviewed Bridget's work computer and desk telephone and confirmed that she'd only called her mother the morning she left for work. Once they accessed her mobile records, they found their connection to Dillan Andrews. It didn't reveal anything about what they were planning, but it gave them another piece of the puzzle.

It was coming together well. Only, Jonathan didn't have concrete proof of Archibald Monroe or Phoenix Security's involvement. With the Butcher brothers and Andrews still looking for the final case, it would be a race to see who found it first. GCHQ still didn't know what Bridget was selling.

If they brought Barker-Smith and Hamilton in for questioning, GCHQ would show their hand. They needed to watch and wait, which was what they were good at. Angela suggested using Wickham — to have him get further involved — but Jonathan didn't believe Wickham could be convincing enough to pull it off.

When Angela visited Hazel Monahan to collect Bridget's laptop and phone, Hazel confirmed that her daughter had come to see her the day before she died. She seemed happy but appeared a little uneasy about something. Hazel told the officers that Bridget had resigned from her job and was planning a trip to Mexico with her new boyfriend. Only, he never turned up at her daughter's funeral.

Bridget only stayed the night and was out after breakfast. Hazel said her daughter had claimed to have an errand to run and promised to be back by late afternoon. That was the last time she saw her daughter alive.

Angela asked Hazel if the Special Branch officers could look through Bridget's belongings. Hazel agreed but told them that she'd thrown her daughter's mobile away, as it was broken. It had also reminded her of her daughter's accident. Hazel asked if they had any leads on who'd killed Bridget.

"I'm afraid we can't discuss an ongoing investigation," Angela responded.

To Hazel, the officers appeared more interested in Bridget's personal belongings than in the reason for her death. Hazel knew deep down that something was wrong. She allowed them to take what they wanted of Bridget's. But she also knew that nothing they did now would bring her daughter back.

*   *   *

MI5 was still unsure if anything had been stolen. Bridget could have been running a scam. Their technology in the wrong hands would be devastating to Britain and her allies. MI5 couldn't find any evidence of unauthorised access to any of their sensitive data. Or at least, they hadn't so far. They were disgruntled that GCHQ were in charge of the investigation. For the last few years, rivalry between the two agencies had been at an all-time high.

GCHQ's only priority now was finding the missing case before Hamilton and his men did. Jonathan hated making deals with people like Nicholas Wickham. He saw Wickham as a weasel and coward. He actually hoped that Wickham would let something slip, so his immunity would become null and void. Although, he knew the Home Office was correct to be putting him back in circulation, as he could still be useful to their investigation. Nicholas Wickham would be a means to an end.

Special Branch had been searching the river systems downstream of the hijack since Angus' death. However, their drones had not found the suitcase. They couldn't keep searching indefinitely and had to concede that someone else may have found it. Worst case scenario, it had floated all the way out to sea or was sitting somewhere on the bottom of a Devonshire river.

Jonathan knew the case would sit like a dark cloud over their heads until it was found.

United We All Stand ...

Two days later

Maggie spent the next two days pacing, thinking, and walking. She feared she had asked too much of her friends. Would they gang up on her and insist she hand the money back? Would they turn her in? No, they would never do that.

Maggie went over every aspect of her plan again and again. She re-read reports and brochures. She reviewed government policies, documents, and council procedures. She pasted sticky notes over every fact and point she felt was important. Every time she thought of what could go wrong, she analysed the problem until she knew how to fix it. Every angle was covered. Or was it?

On Friday, at 6.45 p.m., Maggie organised hot savouries. She put out seven wine glasses and seven cups and saucers. Maggie's newly appointed solicitor and semi-retired accountant were already in attendance. It was either going to be an excitingly long night or a sombrely short one.

By five minutes past 7, there had been no glimpse of headlights, no sound of tyres on asphalt, no footsteps up the drive, and no sound of the doorbell.

At ten past 7, Maggie sat quietly in her sitting room. She was fidgeting, feeling dejected. She wouldn't let Eve down.

But could she do it alone? Her solicitor and accountant would step in as trustees. Maggie would have to run for councillor herself. That terrified her more than going to prison. She knew herself to be an introvert. Running for public office was pushing her luck. Her thoughts were spiralling around in her head like a vortex. Her temples were throbbing so loud she didn't hear her accountant call to her.

'Maggie, dear, that's your doorbell,' said Mrs McGuigan.

Maggie jumped up and ran to the door. She opened it to see Chloe standing outside.

'Well, let me in, then,' said Chloe, as she stepped inside. 'This is going to be fabulous, unless we get caught. So, we'll have to work extra hard to make sure we don't.'

Chloe gave Maggie a hug, then walked into the sitting room. Chloe walked straight up to Ernie and gave him a kiss on the cheek. Then she saw Mrs McGuigan. Chloe didn't know if she was pleased or proud, so she offered Mrs McGuigan a hug and a kiss on the cheek. Then she helped herself to a glass of red wine.

Maggie let out a sigh of relief. Well, one out of four wasn't bad. Then she heard Morwenna behind her.

'You better know what you're doing, Maggie, or we're all in the shit-house.'

Maggie turned to see Morwenna, Julie, and Anaya standing side by side, smiling at her. They walked into the room and introduced themselves to Ernie Chandler, and on seeing Mrs McGuigan standing beside Chloe, they knew their team was complete. Then they helped themselves to some wine, too.

They raised their glasses to salute Eve. 'For Eve,' said Chloe. They all drank to her memory.

'I hope you have Jaffa Cakes,' said Morwenna, as she sat down in the armchair.

Mrs McGuigan appeared more refreshed than they remembered her from the funeral. Discovering a suicide was a terrible memory to dispel from one's mind, but it appeared that Mrs McGuigan was built of sterner stuff. She reminded Morwenna of a WWII primary school teacher – without the cane.

Maggie's smile lit up the room. She went into the kitchen to retrieve the savouries she was keeping warm in the oven and a packet of Jaffa Cakes, which she kept in the cupboard especially for Morwenna, who never got any at home. Her children usually devoured everything on sight before she was able to pack the groceries away after each shop.

As Maggie took the savouries out of the oven, she stopped what she was doing and put her hands firmly on the kitchen counter. Then, she slowly brought her head down. She took a deep breath and slowly exhaled, then repeated the action over again. She couldn't believe it was actually happening. Maggie picked up the savouries and gathered herself before calmly walking back into the living room.

She started by handing out all the brochures, booklets, and documentation they would each need to read in order to play their parts. If Chloe was going to be the town Councillor, she needed to promote herself around town. This wouldn't be too difficult, as she was already well known from her shifts at the pub and from running the mobile library.

Chloe would have to run against Larry Morecombe, Friars Meadow's current Councillor. They would need a strategy to beat him in the next election.

Maggie had leased one of the old shops in town, which was currently derelict and in need of a little renovating. It was right in the centre of town and across the road from the botanical gardens.

Maggie, Ernie, and Mrs McGuigan sat down with Anaya, Julie, and Morwenna, and explained how the trust would work and what their responsibilities as trustees would be.

As the pamphlets and trustee documents mounted, Morwenna asked if they could be laminated, so that she could read them in the bath, stating that her baths were the only privacy and spare time she ever got. The trust's aim was to give the money away, but they couldn't be too frivolous about it, or they would run out before they achieved anything. Such a sudden amount of expenditure might also seem suspicious and draw unwanted attention. They needed to be thrifty if they wanted the money to last. Some funds would be given out on a case-by-case basis, but if they wanted to help make everyone's lives better in Friars Meadow, they needed to help the community as a whole.

Ernie Chandler's knowledge of the law was invaluable, as were Mrs McGuigan's financial skills. She explained how much of the 'suitcase' money could be deposited on any given day as not to draw attention to the trust.

Ernie Chandler had all the paperwork ready to set up the trust: business name and number, tax documents, and bank accounts. He didn't have a partner, only a legal secretary, who he trusted explicitly. Alisha Partridge had worked with Ernie for over seven years. Even though Ernie's work had tapered down over the years, he had kept Alisha on part-time. He valued her friendship and loyalty. Ernie confided in Alisha what Maggie was planning and had her full support.

All they needed were the three trustee signatures on the allotted documents to start the ball rolling. Each newly appointed trustee – Anaya, Julie, and Morwenna – took turns in signing the trust's legal documents.

Julie and Morwenna suddenly realised that they were now permanently employed. Morwenna gleefully commented that there would be no more cleaning toilets at her son's primary school. If Morwenna never saw another tiny cistern, it would be too soon. Her boys splashed enough at home.

They all agreed to meet every Monday at Maggie's to discuss any issues or problems that might arise. Then, when the office was ready, they would have their meetings there. However, when discussing Chloe's election, they would meet at Chloe's. The local election would be held the following year, on the first Thursday in May.

But that was a long way off yet. Or so they thought!

Maggie outlined some of the costs that they would incur over the next few months. Renovating the trust's office and the purchase of both the community hall and the old shoe factory

– as well as care packages for those in immediate need – were all noted. Maggie also allocated funds to help with Chloe's campaign. Of course, all of Chloe's donations were within legal limits.

Chloe lifted her eyebrow and told Maggie not to get too far ahead of herself. But Maggie knew that with the right campaign, it was not an unrealistic task. They all agreed that Chloe would make a great councillor, but they needed a strategy to beat Larry Morecombe. Morwenna pointed out that he wasn't called Lazy Larry Morecombe for nothing. Everyone's ears prickled when they heard this. Maggie made a mental note to discuss this little titbit with Morwenna closer to the election.

Within a month, the Eve Merriweather Trust was up and running.

*　　*　　*

By the end of the first month, Morwenna invited Chloe, Ernie, Maggie, and Mrs McGuigan to dinner. She had much gossip to spill about Lazy Larry Morecombe.

By withholding their sugar intake for the day, Morwenna had managed to get the twins upstairs to bed. Well, to her bed, with a DVD playing. Sarah had read Harriet a bedtime story, and she came downstairs soon after to wash up in the kitchen.

'Well,' said Morwenna, as she placed a folder on her lap containing her notes about Larry Morecombe. 'From what Josie Bushall said, Larry promised to have the security fencing fixed and to replace the swings in the park for the kids. He never did – he only had the old swings repaired, which broke again within the month, even though Josie said she heard he was given full funding for new ones.'

'He was supposed to speak with the mayor about new garbage bins. He never has,' said Chloe. 'Carmel told me in the pub the other day.'

'He appears to promise a lot but delivers very little,' said Maggie.

'The church had to close their hall because their funding dried up,' said Ernie. 'I know this because Alisha, my secretary, is a church member and enjoyed helping with the activities at the hall. The W.I. used to hold their meetings there. Whatever Larry Morecombe is doing for Friars Meadow, he isn't sticking his neck out for the townspeople at the council.'

'Yeah, some of the mums complained when the hall closed, as it provided play groups for their little ones. It also gave them a place to meet and talk to other mums, so they didn't feel so isolated,' said Morwenna.

Sarah walked in and everyone hushed up. They all realised that, from the kitchen, she must have overheard everything.

'I'd like to help. Can I help you during your campaign, Chloe? You won't have to pay me. I've been studying the history of British politics at school, and I'm fascinated by it. I would like to learn about modern politics.'

'I would love for you to help me, sweetheart. If your mum says it's OK,' said Chloe, looking over at Morwenna.

'As long as it doesn't affect your schoolwork, I'm OK with it.'

Mrs McGuigan suggested looking into Larry Morecombe's council records to see what he'd been up to.

'All his expenses are recorded and lodged at the Totnes Council,' said Mrs McGuigan. Then added with a wink, 'Always follow the money, my dear.'

*   *   *

Maggie and Ernie spent time with each of the newly appointed trustees that first month, until all three trustees were fully informed and confident about operating a trust. Maggie discussed government policies and procedures with Chloe. It was still a long way off, but Maggie said it was never too early to start.

Firstly, they needed to deposit the money into the trust's bank account. Mrs McGuigan estimated that this would take a little over a year. Their bank didn't have a branch in Friars Meadow. They chose it for that very reason.

Everything had turned out better than Maggie expected. Her conscience was clear – no butterflies, and no regrets. Maggie knew she was doing the right thing. OK, maybe not the *legal* right thing, but definitely the moral right thing.

For the first time in a long time, Maggie fell into a deep and peaceful sleep. This capacity for slumber continued for many months to come.

*   *   *

As the months drifted by, the money slowly but constantly flowed into the trust's bank account and swiftly out again. The trust provided struggling families with financial payments and packages that contained supplies desperately needed to see them through each week. The promise of job growth lifted their spirits.

Once the community centre was up and running again, many activities and social events were re-established to energise and reunite the townspeople. Through these clubs, the trust got to know who needed help the most in town.

It was not long before their care packages spread to the outskirts of Friars Meadow and into neighbouring villages. By May, the trust became a household name around Friars Meadow. Some people were curious as to where all the money came from. Many had known Eve and knew she couldn't have left Maggie that much money. But no one ever questioned Maggie or her friends about the money; they just accepted their help with grace.

Best Laid Plans

March

Major Hamilton didn't like loose ends. He was still fuming. They never should have involved an amateur like Wickham. He'd balked at the job. The Butcher brothers and Andrews would stay the course until the end — they were loyal to him. All three had worked with him in the 'sandpit', as it was known to those who had served in Afghanistan. Although Andrews wasn't made of the same cloth as Sean and Chris, he was still a good marine.

However, if Andrews ever found out what they'd done to Bridget … Well. Andrews was yet another loose end that would need tying up. But for now, he was playing ball, and they needed all hands-on deck to find the missing case.

For the last few months, they'd found nothing. Eventually, they would have to get the Butcher brothers and Andrews out of England.

All Hamilton could do was to watch intently as their fiasco slowly got out of hand. But Hamilton wasn't the type of man who got where he was without always having a back-up plan.

As for the Butcher brothers, they were pissed. Nothing had gone according to plan. It should have been a simple robbery. But now the police had identified all three hijackers. They would have to leave England. With over three million pounds, they had the capital to start their own business. But they had to finish the job.

Since Andrews was playing ball for now, Sean and Chris offered Andrews a partnership. It was also the simplest way to keep an eye on him. He would also be a hell of a soldier to have on their side.

But first, they needed weapons and equipment. Andrews said that he knew someone.

*   *   *

Jonathan was currently being briefed by their newest member of the team, Ned Holland — he had been put inside Club 26 as an intelligence officer, passing on information about club members — when Jonathan received news of Corporal Andrews' arrest.

Andrews had scheduled a rendezvous with an old army mate to purchase weapons. The soldier was working at the Merville Barracks in Colchester, when the military police apprehended the Supply Sergeant, along with Corporal Andrews and a large parcel of cash.

The Butcher brothers were nowhere to be seen.

Corporal Andrews would not talk, other than to tell them to fuck off and get me a lawyer.

Max was concerned; once word got out of Andrews' arrest, the Butcher brothers might try to flee England. An all-agencies alert was sent out again for the imminent departure of their fugitives. But with an employer like Phoenix Security behind them, who had a small military at his disposal, Jonathan knew that the Butcher brothers could get out of the country undetected.

However, Jonathan's gut told him that they were still in England. With a case still missing, they weren't going anywhere. They would simply go dark, as they had done before.

Special Branch officers arrived at the barracks to interview Andrews. The officers went through what they knew with him — the murder of Angus McPherson and the van hijack.

His only responses were 'no comment' and 'fuck off'. They finally asked him if he'd played a part in Bridget Monahan's murder. The shocked look on his face told the officers that he hadn't.

The officers played Dillan the video footage of Bridget's hit and run in Exeter; they knew he wouldn't believe them without seeing the evidence. His face turned red with anger when he saw one of the Butcher brothers exit the car. He couldn't control his temper any longer — he threw his table and chair across the room in a fit of rage. The military police subdued him before they could continue with the interview; his wrists were handcuffed to the arms of his chair.

The interviewers couldn't tell Andrews which brother had run her down, but only that they were both involved in her murder.

'It doesn't matter, they are one and the same,' replied Dillan.

Angry and dejected, Andrews finally spoke.

'Protecting mates is one thing, but killing Bridget is another,' he muttered angrily under his breath. He confirmed what GCHQ already knew about the robbery and murder of Angus McPherson after he'd found one of the cases. Unfortunately, it hadn't been the one they were after.

And so, Dillan Andrews confirmed that all his dealings had been with Major Hamilton, and that yes, they were all still working for Phoenix Security, off the books. And no, they hadn't found the final suitcase.

Special Branch asked if he knew what was on the notebook that Bridget had placed in the deposit box.

Andrews looked up at them, his eyes set. 'Yes.'

When he told the Special Branch Officers what was on the notebooks, they exited them interview room and immediately called GCHQ and MI5. They knew that all hell was about to break loose.

Jonathan knew that Andrews' confession wouldn't be enough for a conviction, against Monroe. But it was a start. He was also concerned about how long Andrews would last in prison once he agreed to testify against the Butcher brothers and Hamilton. Jonathan needed to have him secured somewhere safe.

With that, Andrews was transferred to the Colchester military prison in Essex.

But within a week, he was found dead in his cell. The official verdict from the prison was suicide. He'd strangled himself using a cord.

The prison pointed out that it was quite common in the first few days of incarceration for inmates to attempt suicide.

Jonathan was unconvinced. The only flaw in that assumption was the scratch marks about his neck, and Jonathan didn't believe that Andrew's was the type to take his own life..

*   *   *

Jonathan looked up at the information board on the wall in the situation room. It had grown substantially in the last month; all the players were on the board. Archibald Monroe and Hamilton were now at its centre. They had their instigators, but no direct links to either of them. Losing Andrews had been a blow, but they were not down yet.

GCHQ's drones had searched all the river systems in Devon. If they hoped to find the final case, they would have to start searching from the beginning again. Their drone's AI would scan every pixel of every picture the camera took. It knew exactly what to look for. Their technology was 99.6% fool-proof. It never missed what a human eye could.

But their resources would be futile if the case was no longer on the river.

Jonathan knew that Hamilton's crew hadn't found it either. GCHQ would be listening. But for now, everyone was silent. For Jonathan, it was now a waiting game.

The Deposit Gang

Meanwhile, Maggie and her friends had been hard at work in Friars Meadow, and time was fleeting by.

The deposits began in earnest. To look like anonymous donations, Maggie and her friends needed to deposit the funds all around the county. Discretion was the key; the case contained over one million pounds. More than Maggie had estimated.

Within the first three months, the community centre was up and running. The trust's office was renovated, and they put in an offer for the purchase of the shoe factory site.

So, for the next year, to protect their identities, the friends disguised themselves and travelled near and far, depositing cash into every ATM and night safe they could find. Morwenna liked to go a little bit further, not in distance but in disguise. For one reason only, she was enjoying herself: she felt like Mata Hari.

They would conceal their faces with shawls, hats, wigs, and umbrellas.. They made their deposits dressed in every disguise they could think of. Once, Morwenna even masked herself as an old woman, using a Zimmer frame borrowed from her grandmother – no questions were asked until Maggie had a word with her. Poor little Harriet never knew what to expect when she went shopping with her mother. Mind you, she loved joining in on the dress-ups.

Even Mrs McGuigan took herself out of town for day trips and slipped funds into the bank's ATM. They would travel as far as Cornwell, in the south, and over to Newquay and Truro. They deposited at every bank branch from Plymouth to Lynton, with the occasional visit as far as London. They travelled up north to Bath, Bristol, Newport, and Swansea, then over to Bournemouth and Southampton. They were becoming quite the professionals.

Maggie monitored the trust's bank account as it gradually grew and grew and grew. This was where the money laundering charge would come into effect, if the authorities could positively identify the suspects depositing the funds. Fortunately for the deposit gang, CCTV cameras could never quite capture the identity of the individuals making the deposits.

Once the trust was up and running, the community centre became a hub for the many new activities in town. It provided all forms of information and support, educational classes, and craft classes. The Women's Institute started up their branch again. Headed by Alisha Partridge, it grew in size faster than any other branch in England. The trust offered financial advice and assistance to anyone who needed it, thanks again to Ernie Chandler and Mrs McGuigan.

Through the community centre, they learned what was needed around Friars Meadow. With the combined help of the Red Cross and the church, the community centre thrived. As the jobs started to grow, the town began to revitalise. The trust hired townspeople to rejuvenate the botanical gardens, and builders were hired for the renovation of the old shoe factory in preparation for its grand opening.

The trust opened the community centre once a fortnight on a Monday evening at 7 p.m. so that the townspeople could speak about social, political, and communal needs relating to their town. This was well received and gave the trust, Chloe, and Maggie the opportunity to gauge the topics and issues that were important to the townspeople and brainstorm what could help Chloe in her campaign.

The trust invited Larry Morecombe to attend their first fortnightly meeting. He did turn up, out of curiosity more than anything. But on hearing everyone's problems, his simple and unconvincing response was: 'Yes, that problem will be addressed at the next council meeting.'

Larry's wife, Elle, often volunteered her time. After the meeting, Elle approached Maggie to offer her condolences for Eve. She confessed that she and Eve had been good friends in their earlier years, but they had sadly drifted apart, as people do.

Chloe came to realise, during these meetings, how many issues needed attention. She promised honestly to deal with each of them once elected. Maggie watched Chloe taking notes and smiled at her tenaciousness. She could see that her friend was already becoming a politician.

But Chloe was worried. Would people think the same of her as they had every other politician? Chloe couldn't bear people thinking of her that way. She made herself a silent promise – she would be different. She would honour her promises.

Even though she had not yet been elected, Chloe wanted to help as many people as she could here and now. At night, alone at home, she reviewed what she had learned. Chloe developed a profound sense of responsibility towards the townspeople. She'd always secretly loved the idea of becoming a town councillor. Occasionally, when she was feeling particularly dreamy, she would imagine herself as Mayor of Totnes.

With the backing of the trust, in time, she made her silent pledge a reality.

*   *   *

The old factory site was worth nothing, since the bank couldn't give it away. At a cost of 385,000 pounds, they would have plenty of cash still in reserve for other ventures. They agreed that once the factory started to make money, the profits would be channelled back into the trust to generate more income.

By the beginning of the fourth month, the trust owned the old shoe factory. Contractors were renovating the site and the trust would shortly commence advertising for jobs at the factory.

During that time of transition, Julie and Morwenna spent time contacting the old sales reps and supervisors that had previously worked there, to see if they were interested in coming back to help set up a new factory. Some had retired, some were settled far away. But a few were interested and agreed to come and talk with the trustees about their days at the factory and who their best stockists had been.

They also spent their time with landscape gardeners, obtaining quotes for the town's gardens. They listened as designers and landscapers hummed and tutted their way around the overgrown space. Julie had acquired some old pictures of what the gardens had looked like in their heyday. A number of retired residents in town offered to help with the restoration.

Friars Meadow used to have a small community newspaper; however, it had shut down over eight years ago. This was another project that Julie wanted to re-start.

The whole town was getting involved in the reenergising of Friars Meadow. Maggie and her friends would often be stopped around town by people offering their thanks for what the trust was doing. They were congratulated on bringing the town back to life again. More importantly, they were congratulated on bringing the people back to life. This was all going exactly how Maggie had envisioned.

Maggie had set aside funds for Chloe's campaign; they agreed the funds would come from Maggie's personal funds. Donations for political parties and individuals had to be disclosed if they exceeded six thousand pounds, and so Maggie organised for a number of townspeople to donate small amounts, not exceeding one thousand, toward Chloe's campaign. Chloe's new benefactors were only too happy to oblige, considering they were allowed to keep a small commission for their services.

Everything was going smoothly. Almost too smoothly. It unnerved Maggie, and so, at their weekly trust meeting, she insisted that the group decide on a code word, which would be used in the event of an emergency. Chloe came up with WATERLOO.

They were the Seventh Coalition, the Magnificent Seven – Maggie, Chloe, Julie, Anaya, Morwenna, Mrs McGuigan, and Ernie Chandler. Morwenna pointed out that things hadn't ended too well for some of the Magnificent Seven.

*   *   *

As time passed by, Maggie's anxieties seemed to wane with the season. Her only complaint was for the amount of work she had to do. Her friends had come up with even more ideas for the town, and so Maggie's work kept mounting

Maggie realised this on one particular day when she came home and noticed her hiking boots resting in their basket by the front door. Maggie realised that she hadn't been walking for months. It was now May, and summer was coming up fast. Grabbing a sandwich and a flask of tea, she climbed spontaneously into her walking boots and headed off for a long walk across the countryside, to find a stream to follow.

During her walk, rain started to drizzle, but this did not affect Maggie. She simply pulled her hood over her head and carried on.

Maggie tilted her head towards the sky and felt the cool droplets pat her face. She hadn't realised how much she'd missed it.

GCHQ ... A Few Months Later

May, End of Spring

Jonathan's team had been working around the clock. They had dozens of separate surveillance operations in action on their suspects. Unfortunately, there had been very little traffic to report from their phone taps and surveillance. Since Corporal Dillan Andrews's death, their suspects had grown quiet again.

Since February, Jonathan had had very little time to visit his family. His work monopolised his time in both Cheltenham and London. When in London, he would meet with his Special Branch undercover operatives, who were still actively working inside Club 26. They hadn't picked up anything relating to the notebook, which GCHQ now called 'Pandora'. But they had picked up some other interesting conversations, which they passed on. Ned Holland was good at his job, although getting a little bored. He was inconspicuous, quiet, and knew when to listen and report back.

After a meeting at the Home Office, Jonathan and Max went for drinks in the Rivoli Bar at the Ritz, in London.

'I'm going to pull the Special Branch officers out of Club 26 soon. It's a waste of resources. You'll need new evidence to justify them remaining,' said Max.

'I agree. I can't honestly say we'll ever find that missing case. Not now, anyway,' replied Jonathan, who had grown frustrated at all the inaction. He knew his hands were tied until one of their suspects made a move.

'Well at least Major Hamilton and his team haven't found it either,' responded Max, without much consolation.

'My only regret is not seeing those bastards charged with anything.'

'Their time will come, but for now we need them free and unawares of our investigation. Go home to Kent for the weekend and relax with your family. It will all be here on your return, Jonathan.'

Jonathan knew Max was right. Maybe that was what he needed.

*   *   *

By June, the investigation scaled down dramatically. There was no sign of the Butcher brothers. Barker-Smith was being monitored, but his association with Club 26 had simmered. Now that his usefulness to Hamilton and Monroe had ended. Meanwhile, Barker-Smith had no suspicions about his brother-in-law, who had kept his distance over the last few months. They only met on family occasions, and Wickham cited tiredness and over-work as excuses for avoiding him.

However, on the plus side, since the investigation had smouldered, Jonathan had started taking himself off on the weekends to his parent's home in Kent. He wanted to get back into shape for his dragon boat trials. If he wanted any chance of being chosen for the team, he needed to get back on the river.

Paddling was his way of releasing tension, which he had built up plenty of lately. It was a good remedy for clearing his thoughts as well.

The Art of Politics

As the trust was now well and truly up and running, Maggie spent more time with Chloe. Learning the responsibilities and requirements of a councillor was exhilarating for Chloe. She was also learning how the Totnes Council was run.

Maggie and Ernie gave Chloe mounds of documents to read. And so, she spent many hours in the evenings with a good wine, going over every document and taking extensive notes. She learned how the elections worked and what would be expected of her if she won. During her secluded month of February, Maggie learned what she could about email marketing and blogging, which she was now passing on to Chloe. She also showed Chloe many social media platforms, such as Twitter, Facebook, and LinkedIn, so that she could use them to her advantage when promoting her campaign.

It was really happening for Chloe. She felt a great sense of pride in what she was planning to do. During her shifts at The Two Swallows, she received many endorsements and pledges of support from Sam's customers. Chloe used her shifts with the mobile library to learn what people needed from their councillor.

During their visits around town, Chloe and Maggie heard more than once about the failings of Lazy Larry Morecombe. Chloe listened intently to everyone's problems, through endless cups of tea and coffee and sometimes something stronger. The more Chloe heard about the townspeople's problems, the more determined she was to become the next Councillor of Friars Meadow. But not wanting to wait until the next council elections, Chloe felt she needed to do something now. Chloe was resolved to find a way to knock Lazy Larry Morecombe off his perch.

*   *   *

As luck would have it, during a drink at the pub the following week, Morwenna spoke with Chloe and Maggie about some more recent complaints she picked up on from the mothers' group. Larry's favourite saying was, 'It's in the hands of the Totnes Council now. I did everything I could.'

'As it turns out,' stated Morwenna, 'this woman rang the Totnes Council to find out when her claim would be processed, only to be told that they knew nothing about it.'

'Mrs McGuigan did say to look at Larry's expenses for the last few years,' said Chloe. 'That way we could review what he's claimed compared to what he has actually done.' Maggie said she would speak with Ernie and obtain the relevant paperwork.

Councillors didn't receive a salary, but they did receive a 'member's allowance' in recognition of their time and expenses incurred during their official business with the council. Whether as an independent or with a national party, all councillors received help and support from their respective councils. Unlike Larry Morecombe, Chloe would put the £10,800 pounds to good use.

At their weekly trust meeting, Mrs McGuigan reminded Chloe and Maggie to 'follow the money,' before she spread some pâté on a cracker biscuit and savoured the moment.

Within five days, Ernie Chandler presented Mrs McGuigan with a copy of Larry Morecombe's council expense sheets for the last two years. Mrs McGuigan rolled up her sleeves and meticulously scrutinised every expense that Larry had submitted, claim after claim.

A week later, after a delicious dinner at Mrs McGuigan's, she explained to Maggie, Ernie, and Chloe how Larry was falsely claiming expenses for work he didn't do. Mrs McGuigan suggested to Maggie and Chloe that they should interview some of the people associated with these claims and have them sign an affidavit or statement detailing what had actually taken place.

Chloe and Maggie did just that throughout the following week. Their findings turned out to be auspicious, on more than one occasion. They finally had proof that Larry was claiming money for projects and activities that had never come to fruition.

That evening, in bed, with Heathcliff snuggled beside her, Chloe googled what she was looking for. She typed in the following.

Disqualification criteria for councillors and mayors.

The results brought up exactly what Chloe was looking for. She was getting the hang of Google.

Once Chloe and Maggie had enough evidence against Larry Morecombe, Ernie Chandler presented it to the Totnes Mayor, Susan McBride. Within a week, Larry Morecombe was called into the council and asked to explain himself and his manufactured expenses. He was caught off guard by the accusations and was unable to conjure up adequate explanations. He had no defence and was asked to resign immediately.

Susan McBride was happy to see him go. She'd never taken to him in all the years she had been the Totnes Mayor. Subsequently, the Totnes Council had to prepare itself for a by-election in the town of Friars Meadow.

Within a month, the council announced the election date to fill the casual vacancy of Councillor. This position would be filled temporarily until they held the next council elections were held in in May, next year.

Chloe's campaign was now well and truly up and running.

*   *   *

There were two other people running for councillor. One dropped out after six days, while the other slogged it out until the end.

Chloe ran as an independent. She didn't have much trust or belief in the major parties. Being an independent would allow her to follow her own agenda without scrutiny. This suited Chloe to the nines, as she hadn't voted in a local or general election for over twenty years.

Chloe had never found a reason to vote, up until now. She'd never believed anything could change. But now she wanted to see change more than ever. Listening to the townspeople and their problems, she'd realised hers were minor compared to theirs. Chloe truly believed that Friars Meadow deserved a councillor who would actually help them, and not just help themselves.

Once Chloe was registered to run at the by-election, she FaceTimed her son with the exciting news. He was impressed, not only that she was running for councillor but that she actually knew how to FaceTime.

Chloe had always loved working in the mobile library van. She loved talking with the avid book readers who would come to her van. Now, she would use the van to promote herself as she made her rounds about town. She stayed awake, visualising all the possibilities and changes she could accomplish. This was her time!

*   *   *

Unfortunately, as the by-election marched on, Jonathan's investigation had come to a standstill. They had no new evidence in connection to the robberies and the murders of Angus McPherson, Dillan Andrews, and Bridget Monahan. The Butcher brothers were still in hiding, possibly out of the country by now. Jonathan had to accept that the final case would never be found. If it made its way out to sea, there was no telling where it would end up. He needed to believe it was still lying on the bottom of a riverbed somewhere in Devon.

Max reminded Jonathan that if they took all the players off the chess board, there wouldn't be any more moves left to play. Their operatives at Club 26 had now been recalled. However, on that front, their intelligence had proved most helpful in a number of other ways.

They would still monitor Barker-Smith, Hamilton, and Monroe's phones and movements. The Home Office assured GCHQ that Barker-Smith would never run for office again. But they were to leave him in place for the time being.

Even though their investigation had stalled, their alerts would remain active. GCHQ had plenty of other investigations to keep them busy.

But for now, Pandora was on hold until something new turned up.

The Ding Dong Brigade

Summertime, June

With the sun shining, a bounce in their steps, joggers on their feet and clipboards in hand, Chloe and Maggie marched from one end of Friars Meadow to the other. Through door knocking and bell ringing, Chloe introduced herself as a candidate for town councillor. Sometimes accompanied by young Sarah, they made their way from door to door around town. They were offered more tea, coffee, water, lager, wine and on one occasion, homemade rum. Chloe was really enjoying the art of politics.

For Chloe's birthday, Maggie gave her a diary, so that she could record her political journey. It became a keeper of keys, holding all her thoughts and actions. It quickly became her most valued possession.

This simple gift opened a new chapter in Chloe's life. It signified the direction in which her life was heading. Both professionally and personally, she made promises and plans that needed to be honoured and fulfilled.

During their Wednesday night poker games, the girls had a chance to catch up and hear about each other's activities.

'I have to say, Morwenna, your daughter Sarah is proving very resourceful. I see a future politician in her,' said Chloe.

'I know, she never stops talking about it,' replied Morwenna, before biting into another Jaffa Cake.

'Thanks for pulling a few shifts at The Two Swallows, Julie. I'm run off my feet and Sam relies on me.'

'Happy to help, Chloe,' replied Julie. 'Although, he does ask after you quite a bit.'

'Do tell,' Morwenna chimed in.

'We're old friends, that's all,' said Chloe, giving Morwenna a mischievous look.

Maggie watched on as her friends laughed and bantered the night away. Their lives had been blessed since finding the suitcase. Although, she still had moments of loneliness, they were easily dispelled with an abundance of work to keep her busy.

Maggie and Chloe knew nobody in their right mind would have bought a house in Friars Meadow one year ago. Even at their reduced prices, the houses were in an area without job prospects, and therefore lacked appeal. However, with the prospect of growth, the house prices had stopped falling.

Chloe made a note in her diary to have Ernie Chandler look into who owned all the rental properties in town, and to confirm their responsibilities to the tenants, as she had received a number of complaints regarding the maintenance of rental properties in town. Ernie Chandler was becoming quite indispensable. He was not only the trust's solicitor, but he had become Chloe's legal advisor throughout both her political and personal life. In fact, he'd become everyone's solicitor, as Maggie and her friends were going to need one by this time next year.

With Chloe's sense of achievement came a deluge of anger when she became privy to all the promises and work Larry Morecombe could have done and hadn't.

The Seventh Coalition spent the next month canvassing Friars Meadow and promoting their candidate for Councillor. With children in tow, the friends plastered every lamppost and shopfront with posters of their candidate. With every book taken out from the mobile library, the customer was given a free bookmark with a picture of Chloe on it and a caption below stating, 'A picture tells a thousand words – we only need four. Vote for Chloe Silverton.' Sam put up large posters outside the pub. Morwenna's children received twenty pounds each for their contribution to Chloe's campaign by putting flyers into letterboxes. They were accompanied by Sarah, Morwenna's eldest, who prevented them from putting them in the nearest bin.

By August, Chloe was sworn in as the new councillor for Friars Meadow.

All in a Day's Work

Summer's End, August

Even though summer was drawing to its close, Maggie didn't feel her usual trepidation. If anything, she felt herself brightening. Autumn and winter didn't seem as foreboding as they once did. For the first time in many years, Maggie realised she didn't need to be afraid of change.

The botanical gardens were vastly improved. The trust had built a small greenhouse so that they could re-germinate seedlings for each new spring. People saw a pride in Friars Meadow which had been lost for many years.

Some people may have thought spending the trust's funds on restoring the gardens was frivolous. But to Maggie, it represented the soul of Friars Meadow. Restoring it meant restoring its people. She had been right. They walked with their heads a little higher than they used to, and not just to capture the last of the summer sun.

As Morwenna had given up her cleaning job months ago – much to her sons' relief – her new salary afforded her the opportunity to contemplate buying her own home. Morwenna discussed this option with Ernie and Mrs McGuigan, who provided her with all the legal and financial advice she needed.

She finally had money left in her purse at the end of each week. It was a strange phenomenon. Like most mothers, what little Morwenna earned had always gone to her children. Not feeling the least bit of guilt, Morwenna started to treat herself once a week to something nice, and there were always Jaffa Cakes in the cupboard.

Anaya's time at the trust office was limited. As area nurse, she had plenty to keep her busy. But her knowledge of the most vulnerable in town allowed Chloe and the trust to step up and provide more care and transport for the elderly, especially those who were unable to leave their homes without assistance.

Chloe and Anaya made sure everyone received all their entitled benefits and medical assistance where needed.

Julie absorbed everything there was to know about running the trust. She craved to know more. Do more. Julie realised her parents were right about university. She still had Jeremy to think about, although the idea of studying was becoming more appealing.

There was so much good being done, the friends had become completely blindsided to the risks involved.

*   *   *

The renovations were finally finished at the old shoe factory. Mr Tinkler, the previous supervisor, had agreed to come back, and operations would be up and running shortly.

To Mr Tinkler's surprise, a large number of the stockists agreed to place orders once they'd seen the quality of the merchandise. Mr Tinkler reminded Maggie that there was a lot to be said for patriotism.

Maggie's friends had helped her bring her dream to life. Maggie witnessed this change as she walked through the town. The trustees' lives might have become much more hectic, but they were exhilarating, too. They felt unstoppable.

In quiet moments, Maggie would be reminded of the consequences if they were caught. This thought occasionally niggled at Maggie's conscience. On one hand, her friends were having the time of their lives; they had purpose. But on the other hand, there was always the threat of exposure. Maggie would sit for hours on her patio and wonder why one hand always weighed more than the other. How could she protect her friends – her family?

*   *   *

When the shoe factory was finally up and running, Ernie Chandler expressed concerns to Maggie about the security of the employees' jobs. Over a pint in the pub one evening, he spoke with Maggie about it. He had an idea.

'If we let the staff buy a share of the business, once it's making a profit, then the banks wouldn't be able to touch the shoe factory, even if your enterprise is discovered and the government seizes the trust. It would be owned independently by the workers.'

'That's a good idea. Then we can re-invest the money from the sale of the factory back into the trust, and directly into other projects,' said Maggie.

'Precisely,' smiled Ernie. He took another swig of his beer. They spent the evening discussing how they would do it.

As always, Maggie found Ernie indispensable, and she knew it was a sound idea. Once the business was making a profit, they would discuss it with Mr Tinkler, who could propose the idea to his staff.

*   *   *

Meanwhile, Chloe's visits to the Totnes Council enabled her to learn the responsibilities of her local council. She listened and learned as the councillors discussed and debated all issues brought up during their meetings. If Chloe was ever to run for Mayor of Totnes, she needed to know what her whole region needed – not just Friars Meadow. Susan McBride was the current Mayor of Totnes. She had been elected by its sixteen councillors, and at fifty-eight she had been mayor for over fourteen years. However, she announced at their last meeting that she would be retiring the following year.

This announcement set fireworks off in Chloe's head. Was it really fate, like Maggie had said? Chloe hadn't envisaged her progress happening so quickly. She didn't know if she was ready for the responsibility. But becoming mayor would afford her more authority to carry out her initiatives, for not only the people of Friars Meadow but all in Totnes.

Afterwards, Chloe met up with Maggie at a café, where they discussed the opportunity they had just been handed. They continued their discussion all the way home and the unique possibilities it offered.

'You know, you don't have to run if you don't want to,' said Maggie.

'I know that but think of all we can accomplish!' Chloe was resolute.

Maggie could see how popular Chloe was already in Friars Meadow, but outside their shire, she was practically unknown.

But Chloe pointed out that if she wanted to be Mayor of Totnes, she only had to impress fifteen people. The other councillors of Totnes.

*   *   *

Once Ernie had given Chloe the details of the rental properties around town, she had Sarah ring the occupants to make sure that the properties had been properly maintained.

Chloe was alarmed by the number of houses that needed restoration. She sent the banks a stern letter regarding their responsibilities to their tenants, and within three weeks, repair work had begun. But not all properties were owned by the banks.

After school, Sarah would help Chloe with all her mail and any research she needed. On the weekends she helped Chloe in the mobile library van. Once Sarah received her driver's licence, she would be able to work solo shifts in the van. Chloe loved Sarah dearly and saw in her the making of a great politician. So, she encouraged her in every step she took.

Maggie couldn't help herself envision Chloe's political future. She knew she was allowing her dreams to run away with her – their current MP was a conservative, Malcolm Barker-Smith.

Maggie made some notes from what she could gather on him from the internet. He hadn't done much for Friars Meadow over the years. Maggie doubted he even knew where it was. But she couldn't pass judgement until she looked deeper into his career and reputation.

Maggie started a dossier on Barker-Smith and would add to it over the months ahead. Not knowing the man well or the kind of politician he was, she would need to seek help elsewhere. When the time was right, she would hire a private detective to look a little deeper into his work and life.

*   *   *

As the months continued to roll by, Christmas was once again upon them. Maggie wanted to show her gratitude for all her friends' hard work over the year. So, to thank them properly, she planned a surprise for them.

At their Wednesday night poker game in early December, Maggie announced a night out in London.

'I have tickets for us to see *The Book of Mormon* and we will be staying at the Ritz.' This was her gift to them for helping her keep her promise to Eve.

'Now, it's our turn to have some fun', said Maggie, as she waved the tickets at them.

Once they had stopped screaming, Julie spoke up. 'Don't you know, Maggie, we've had the time of our lives since you started us down this road.'

'It's us that should be thanking *you*,' said Chloe.

They all agreed. But Maggie knew their current jobs were keeping them busy enough, while they were still depositing the remaining cash into the ATMs and night safes. They also had to find time to look after their families and homes. Maggie tried to express what it all meant before she started to cry.

Christmas would be for the kids, but this weekend would be for them. Mrs McGuigan and Ernie Chandler had agreed to look after the children for the weekend.

Mrs McGuigan and Ernie thought they would be in for a challenge with Morwenna's twins, Fin and Alfie, but it was Jeremy who monopolised their time the most. His incessant questions would drive most people up the wall. But Mrs McGuigan had all the time in the world for him. She answered question after question and even threw in some of her own, to which Jeremy had to take a step back before answering.

Mrs McGuigan's life had transformed from one of quiet solitude to one filled with excitement and rebellion since meeting Maggie. It was a shame it was under such unhappy circumstances. Her lonely existence was full again – and, more importantly, she felt needed again. She had forgotten what that was like. Mrs McGuigan had been one of those old, forgotten, incidental citizens for too long. Now, she felt twenty years younger. Even Ernie rose to the challenge when answering Jeremy's questions. They were now part of a very large extended family. Whether they liked it or not – well … the answer to that was clearly in the affirmative.

The Ritz

150 Piccadilly, St. James's,
London W1J 9BR

December

The metropolis of London was its customarily vivid and exciting self. The friends had been jitterbugging ever since Maggie revealed their Christmas gift.

Maggie and her friends had never seen anything so magnificent as the Christmas decorations on display at the Ritz. The real Christmas tree was the star attraction, standing tall under the dome in the foyer. It was adorned with massive decorations and lights, all in shades of red and green and gold. It looked and smelt amazing. Morwenna and Julie both agreed to bring their kids up to London to see it before Christmas.

Anaya, Julie, and Morwenna had never been to the theatre before, let alone the Ritz. They were all ecstatic. They felt like royalty as they walked through the foyer of the famous hotel. Maggie also surprised her friends by announcing a Sunday afternoon tea in the famous Palm Court before heading back home. For the rest of Saturday, Maggie and her friends spent their time shopping for dresses for their evening out.

After their shopping spree, they went to their respective rooms and readied themselves for dinner. Morwenna treated herself to a long bubble bath – something unheard of in her house. She even helped herself to a glass of bubbly and the complimentary chocolates left on her pillow.

Julie climbed into her shower, but not before calling Mrs McGuigan to check on Jeremy. Julie had never left Jeremy with anyone except her parents. Mrs McGuigan told Julie to stop fretting; she only confirmed how exceptional her son was. So, Julie enjoyed a very long hot shower in her inordinately large bathroom.

Chloe checked her emails to make sure there were no pressing matters that needed to be dealt with. Satisfied, she helped herself to a glass of Australian Shiraz.

Once Anaya had checked up on her daughters, she jumped onto the bed in her robe, kicked her legs around with excitement and then flicked through some TV channels while she waited excitedly for an important phone call from a new acquaintance, Dr Theo Sharma.

They agreed to meet in the Rivoli Bar at 6 p.m. They would dine first, then walk to the Prince of Wales Theatre on Coventry Street, less than a mile away.

The Rivoli Bar

5.45 p.m.

Maggie was dressed and ready by half past five. Taking the elevator downstairs, she walked sheepishly into the bar, alone. Her shiny hair, freshly washed, bounced off her shoulders as she entered the room. Her features were subtly enhanced by the minimal makeup she wore. Her new dress accentuated her soft complexion and feminine figure.

When Maggie walked in, she couldn't see her friends. Feeling awkward, she decided to walk up to the bar. As she did, her eyes took in all the grandeur of the room. It was no less breathtaking than the Ritz's foyer. With its dark brown and orange tones, it was very regal. The Christmas decorations were more subdued in the bar but no less beautiful. Made of gold and silver, they added to the room's elegance. She'd forgotten how much she loved Christmas time. When she reached the bar, her attention was drawn to a man on her right. As she passed him, his eyes met hers and they held each other's gaze for a moment.

Maggie sat on one of the stools at the bar. Her shy elegance was unintentionally charming as she fidgeted before making herself comfortable.

'What would you like to drink, madam?' asked the barman.

Maggie wasn't quite sure what to ask for, but when in Rome. 'Could I have a cocktail, please?' replied Maggie.

'What kind would you like?' responded the barman.

'I'm not sure. Do you have a special one?'

Seeing how unsure the young lady was, the barman thought for a moment and said, 'I'll make you a Rob Roy. I think you'll like it.'

'Thank you.'

As Maggie watched the barman make her drink, through the mirror behind the bar, she could see and hear all the conversations around the room. Maggie listened as the soft voices spoke in beautiful exotic languages. She caught French, Spanish, and Italian amongst other tongues.

However, her attention was drawn to two important-looking men (one of whom she had just locked eyes with) sitting across from each other, quietly talking. They appeared to be in a serious conversation. Probably businessmen, only they weren't wearing suits, and there were no briefcases that Maggie could see.

The barman placed Maggie's drink in front of her. She thanked him and gave him her room number for the bill.

While she waited for her friends to arrive, Maggie read the hotel's cocktail list. She could see that they were all named after famous people in history. Winston Churchill used to come to the Ritz to discuss military operations with allied nations during World War II – his cocktail was named 'Churchill's Courage.'

It took twenty-four hours to make and cost around twenty-two pounds.

She wished she had the courage of Churchill.

Maggie took a sip of her Rob Roy. Her face immediately flushed with the alcohol and delicious flavour. She liked it very much. The two gentlemen who had been in a tight conversation stood up and shook hands. Maggie wasn't eavesdropping, but she overheard the shorter of the two wish the taller one a merry Christmas and instructing him to enjoy his leave with his family in Kent.

'And you too, Max. Give Alyson my love.'

As Max walked out, he wrapped his scarf around his neck and buttoned up his coat. The second man didn't leave but came to the bar and nodded to the waiter. While he waited to be served, he smiled back at her, then turned to face the mirror behind the bar.

Maggie felt her face grow flushed; she couldn't tell if it was from the drink.

'Is that a Rob Roy?' the man asked.

It took Maggie a moment to realise he was talking to her. She nodded.

'Yes,' she said.

The gentleman asked the barman for the same. He walked over to her and asked, 'May I?' He pointed to the seat next to her.

'Yes, of course,' said Maggie.

There was an awkward moment of silence, but he gallantly recovered it by extending his hand and saying, 'Hi, my name is Jonathan.'

Maggie put down her glass and offered her hand.

'Hello. I'm Maggie.'

'Well, you're obviously English, by your accent. Do you live in London, or are you just visiting our beautiful metropolis?'

'I'm just visiting for the weekend. I'm here with some friends. We're going to see *The Book of Mormon*. Have you seen it?'

'Yes, I have, it's a great laugh. You'll love it. Unless you don't have a sense of humour,' said Jonathan, smiling. Maggie allowed herself a smile also.

*   *   *

During their conversation, Morwenna walked into the bar and glanced around for her friends. She thought she was the first to arrive until she spotted Maggie, talking to a man at the bar. This prickled Morwenna's attention. Her friend was having a conversation with an unknown man. A handsome one, at that! Morwenna didn't want to spoil the moment, so she ducked into the first seat she could find and laid low while the conversation continued. The chair had its back to them, and so she had to stick her head around it, to peek at what was going on.

*   *   *

'Where are you from?' asked Jonathan.

'I'm from a small town called Friars Meadow, in Devon.'

For some reason, Friars Meadow registered in Jonathan's mind – he knew the name. But at this present moment, he was too fascinated with this beautiful woman to make the connection. Her eyes were filled with a kindness that emanated a warmth and elegance.

Suddenly, he remembered. The heist! Now he recalled the name – the Provincial robbery last year.

Small world. Or then again, maybe not.

'Where do you work, if you don't mind me asking?' enquired Jonathan.

'I work for a small trust in my hometown.' Maggie was getting a little anxious. She'd just realised it was the first time outside of Friars Meadow that she had spoken openly about the trust.

* * *

Just as Morwenna was stretching her head around the chair again, Anaya arrived and looked over at her.

'What the hell are you doing?'

'Shush, she'll hear you, come over here,' said Morwenna, waving her hand at Anaya. 'She's chatting to a handsome man.'

Anaya quickly ducked into the chair in front of Morwenna. She tilted her head to the left to cop a better view. 'He *is* handsome, isn't he?' she gushed.

* * *

Meanwhile, Maggie and Jonathan were still locked in conversation.

'Have you been working at the trust for long?' asked Jonathan.

'No, not very long. I used to work for a money processing plant, but it was shut down over a year ago,' Maggie replied.

'You mean Provincial Financial Solutions?'

Maggie's heart fluttered. 'Yes. How did you know that?' she asked.

'Oh, sorry, didn't mean to be inquisitive. I work for the Chancellor of the Exchequer. I heard about it at work. Your security van was robbed,' said Jonathan, quickly recovering himself.

Jonathan couldn't tell anyone who he actually worked for – unless they had been vetted by the security services. He had a cover that worked quite well, as most people found it slightly boring. This ensured they never asked him too many questions.

It worked every time.

He knew he would only ever reveal the truth about his work if he was serious about someone. His usual flings never warranted such a confession.

But Jonathan was frankly taken aback by this enchanting lady. She gave the room a *Casablanca* feel. Jonathan had been at the Rivoli many times before, but he never appreciated the alluring ambiance of the room quite as he did now.

'They arrested one of the men responsible, didn't they?' asked Maggie.

Still mesmerised, Jonathan shook himself from his thoughts of admiration. 'Sorry, what did you say?' he asked.

'The police arrested one of the men who committed the robbery, right?' repeated Maggie.

'I believe so,' said Jonathan. He wanted to change the subject, as the robbery was still an ongoing operation. Besides, he didn't want to talk shop. Not to this spellbinding young lady.

'Do you go to the theatre often?' he asked, changing the subject.

*   *   *

When Chloe and Julie walked in, Morwenna quickly called them over before they could head to the bar.

All four friends were now seated on the couches by the entrance to the bar. The friends were rhythmically straining their heads around the corners of their chairs for better views of the handsome man. Maggie appeared to be in a close, amorous conversation. Well, that's what it looked like to Morwenna. Or maybe it was just the ambience of the room.

They wanted Maggie to be happy and to find someone to share her life with. She deserved it more than anyone. But her friends had become very protective of her.

As the barman finished making a To Be or Not to Be, an ode to William Shakespeare, he noticed a strange group of women at the other end of the room. They were frequently poking their heads around their seats to watch him. He smiled to himself – he had always seen himself as good looking, but they were barking up the wrong tree. Oh, well, let them look.

*   *   *

'I haven't been since my mother brought me, nearly seven years ago. I'm looking forward to it,' Maggie said.

'You and your friends will have a great time,' said Jonathan.

As he looked up into the mirror behind the bar, he caught a glimpse of a woman poking her head around her chair. She nearly slipped over the side. Was she watching him? If she was, she wasn't being very covert. He had no reason to believe anyone would be watching him. Jonathan's profession kept him always on guard. Then the penny dropped.

'Didn't you say you were here with your friends?' he asked.

'Yes, four of them. It's kind of a ladies' weekend. A friend is looking after the children,' said Maggie.

'Oh,' said Jonathan, a little crestfallen. Although, he didn't see a ring on her left hand.

'How many children do you have?' he asked.

'Oh, no, I don't have any children. I meant my friends' children,' said Maggie. 'They should be coming down soon – we said we would meet here at 6 p.m. I'm not sure what's keeping them.' She looked at her watch.

'Oh, I do,' said Jonathan, smiling. He nodded his head towards the mirror. As Maggie peered into the glass, she saw a reflection of two heads jutting out from behind a couch.

As Maggie spun around, Morwenna and Julie quickly pulled their heads in. A beat too late – they'd been caught. After an awkward moment, they rose from behind their chairs and walked towards the bar with as much dignity as they could muster.

'How long have you all been there?' said Maggie, a little embarrassed.

'Oh, not long,' said Morwenna. 'We didn't want to disturb you.' She turned a mischievous smile towards Jonathan.

Jonathan admired Maggie's friend's openness and affection towards her. Maggie, however, had turned redder than her cocktail.

'Would you care to join us?' asked Jonathan.

'Well, now that you've offered,' said Morwenna.

Maggie hopped off her stool. 'We can't. We'll be late for dinner, and we don't want to be rushed. The show starts at 8 p.m., but thank you, anyway.' As Maggie reached for her purse, Morwenna received a nudge on the arm from Anaya, who gave her a conspiratorial look.

'It was nice talking to you. I hope we'll meet again someday,' Jonathan said, honestly.

'Definitely,' said Morwenna, with a cheeky smile.

'Thank you, that would be nice,' said Maggie, as she put her arm in Morwenna's and guided her out of the bar.

Jonathan watched them walk away and truly hoped he would see her again. He only knew her first name and partial address – Maggie from Friars Meadow.

GCHQ had suspended their investigation until they uncovered new leads. For the government, the missing case felt like unexploded ordnance buried somewhere, just waiting to go off. Where the hell was it? Jonathan still believed it was on the river. If anyone had found it, and opened it, the money would be worthless. Would they discard the black box or try to open it? The expression of 'no news is good news' was not comforting to Jonathan. He hated leaving assignments incomplete.

Jonathan finished his drink and walked to the station to catch the train home. Strangely, he arrived at the platform without realising how he'd gotten there. He hadn't even felt the cold. He spent the whole journey thinking about a beautiful young woman, known only as Maggie from Friars Meadow.

*   *   *

The dinner was delicious, the company great, the show amazing, and the night perfect. This was how the friends described it. They all laughed and danced their way back to the Ritz. When they arrived, they walked into the bar for a night cap; they didn't want the evening to end. They spent the last of the night's hours talking about their fabulous day, the mouth-watering dinner, and the amazing show.

However, Maggie's thoughts kept drifting back to the spot at the bar where she had sat only hours before, talking to the amazing young man she only knew as Jonathan. The Rivoli Bar seemed different to Maggie this time, a little colder. It had lost some of its atmosphere.

A smile crept across her face every now and again. Whenever she thought of him, delirious warmth touched her face. She knew this time it wasn't the cocktail.

They would never have been able to have a trip like this if it hadn't been for Maggie finding the suitcase. Maggie and her friends were swimming in a river of fortune. Eve would've been proud of Maggie and all she had accomplished. They didn't know where it would take them or when it would end, but Maggie wished it would go on forever.

But when did best laid plans ever go according to one's wishful thinking?

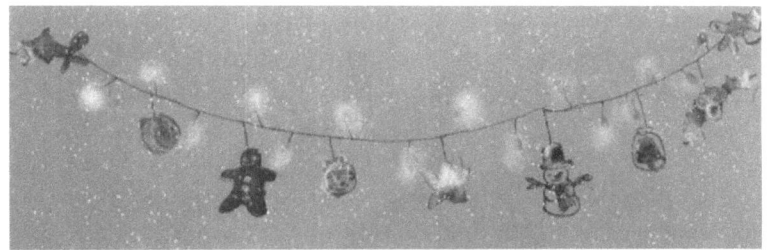

'Tis the Season

Christmas, December

Chloe and the trustees pulled out all stops to light up Friars Meadow for its most splendid Christmas in decades. They had been inspired by their stay at the Ritz. Christmas lights sparkled across the botanical gardens and the townspeople decorated their homes, shops, and street fronts. No one noticed the cold this Christmas. People jollily walked their dogs, and the children around town admired the decorations. People from outside townships actually travelled to Friars Meadow to see the magnificent lights, instead of leaving, for a change.

For Maggie, it was a stark contrast from the previous Christmas, when she'd felt the acute loss of Eve and her mother. She remembered how happiness had been a hard taskmaster back then. But her sadness had slowly disappeared throughout the year, helped by the changes she'd been able to incite through her hidden crime.

Sam Frobisher splashed out on the pub. He was inspired by the pub's largest takings for several years during that Christmas period. He even adorned himself in a Santa suit and handed out gifts for the children.

During the Christmas week, the trust spent every waking moment organising the festivities for their Christmas celebration. On Christmas Eve, the vicar resided over the largest congregation in the town's history. It seemed they all had something to be grateful for. Even the choir improved. Everyone knew it was all thanks to the Eve Merriweather Trust.

When Christmas Day arrived, the church held a second service, once again full to capacity. After the church put on a splendid feast of turkey dinner, gifts were presented to the children and to the volunteers for their help. The wine and spirits were graciously donated by Sam from the pub's cellar. That evening, the choir turned up at the pub and everyone was treated to more Christmas songs as they slowly got sloshed and slurred their words.

Maggie and her friends had spent Christmas Eve in The Two Swallows. On Christmas day, Maggie invited Chloe, Sam, Matthew, and Mrs McGuigan over for a turkey dinner. Ernie had declined, as he'd accepted an offer to spend Christmas Day with Alisha and her daughter. Later that evening, Julie, Jeremy, and Morwenna with her horde arrived to spend the rest of Christmas night together. The kids were delighted at more presents under the tree, and with the candy canes and gingerbread men that Maggie had perched on the tree branches for them to devour.

The only friend not in attendance was Anaya. She and her girls were spending Christmas at the estate of Anaya's new friend and his family. But more on that later …

Bloated, Maggie and her friends sat in the living room and watched the carols on the BBC while their dinner went down.

While they were resting, Harriet spotted snowflakes falling from the sky. All the kids ran to the windows to watch the flurry of flakes. Then they ran outside to feel them on their faces and capture them in their hands, knowing the snow wouldn't be there in the morning. As the children slowly fell asleep one after the other, the friends settled down to watch their annual Christmas film, *Love Actually*, still angry and amazed that a sequel hadn't been made yet. After one too many drinks, Chloe promised to write to the BBC and complain – on council letterhead.

What a year! Maggie lay in bed that night, repeating that thought, over and over, with such a sense of fulfilment that her smile was frozen in place. This was the best Christmas she had had in a long time. As she closed her eyes, her thoughts kept drifting – as they had done so frequently lately – to the Rivoli Bar and the Ritz. Her head was filled with happiness and images of grandeur and excitement, especially for her mysterious man at the bar. His soft voice and kind smile warmed the cockles of Maggie's heart.

Jonathan of London. Would she ever see him again?

Maggie had been tempted to go back to the Rivoli Bar and have a drink on a Saturday afternoon, after a day of Christmas shopping. But that thought was ridiculous. What were the

chances of him being there again? Although, people were crea-
tures of habit. He might visit there often ...

But after these little fancies, she would always come down to
reality and realise how ludicrous the idea was.

*   *   *

One person who didn't have a wonderful Christmas was Larry
Morecombe. The disgraced ex-councillor of Friars Meadow was
the kind of person to hold a grudge. He was fuming. He knew it
was Ernie Chandler who'd grassed on him to the Totnes Mayor,
Susan McBride. *The self-righteous bastard*, he thought. It wasn't
any of his business what he'd done with his councillor allowance, or how he dealt with the town's problems. He'd helped
some people, sometimes ...

His long-suffering wife, Elle, prepared a lovely Christmas
meal, to which he gave no acknowledgement or gratitude.

His mind was preoccupied by his fall from grace. He knew
that Chloe Silverton and Maggie Malloy were behind it – they
were thick as thieves, those two. Larry believed it was all part
of a conspiracy to get rid of him. Chloe, Maggie, Ernie, the old
woman who hung around with them, and her friends at the trust
– they were all in on it. There was something fishy going on
there, and he was determined to find out what it was. He'd spent
the last few months watching them, following them, and making
notes. Only, no one would talk to him about the trust; they would
only say how great it was. Everyone in town was acting cagey.
He knew Eve Merriweather hadn't had that much money when
she'd died.

After Christmas, he met up with his old friend Thomas Carlyle at The Jolly Roger, a pub in a neighbouring town. Larry knew that if anyone could help him regarding the trust it would be Thomas. Thomas couldn't help directly, as the trust didn't do business with his bank, but he said he would look into it and see what he could find out. He had contacts and would see what he could do.

After their discussion, Larry Morecombe finished his pint and drove home. He told his wife that evening that he would get to the bottom of what was going on. He would wipe that smile off that bitch's face. Chloe Silverton's, that was. Elle simply nodded. 'That's nice, dear,' she said, before retiring to bed. Secretly, she knew that Chloe Silverton had done more in four months than her selfish husband had done in three years.

Friendships

February

Throughout one's life, you might be fortunate enough to know someone who could truly be called a friend; someone who would be there for you when you needed them the most, and vice versa. Maggie was fortunate to have more than one, and her friends could say the same. They had become a very close-knit group, whether through secrecy or kinship, Maggie knew she was privileged to know them all.

The beginning of a new year saw a new vitality in Maggie. She had dusted off her old lingering anxieties, and she took in the new year with fervour. Spring would soon return and with it the wildflowers that adorned the countryside. Life would rejuvenate and the days would grow longer and warmer. It was the colours of spring that she looked forward to the most. None would be spared in the gardens and across the fields this year. The air slowly filled with the fragrances of springtime.

It was also election year.

Maggie spent some of her spare time helping in the botanical gardens with the rest of the volunteers. She loved her own garden, but sometimes she felt alone up on the hill. Even though she was kept busy most days, she had a silent longing that kept interrupting her thoughts.

Memories of her mother and Eve crept back at times, when she was alone. But they didn't make her feel depressed like they used to. Pride was the feeling she felt when thinking of them; pride at what she'd accomplished. Her loyal friends had stuck by her and risked everything, and the authorities still hadn't suspected anything.

Maggie hoped it would remain that way.

The town's gardens weren't as large as most botanical gardens, but what they lacked in size they made up for in character.

During the first few months of the new year, Maggie was rewarded by how much the trust had achieved. Unemployment in Friars Meadow was dropping weekly. The politicians would probably pat themselves on the back for that one.

Her days were spent visiting the shoe factory, overseeing the improvements around town with the trustees, and helping Chloe with her council work.

However busy the friends were, their Wednesday night poker was never missed. They invited Mrs McGuigan to be a member, which they regretted shortly after, as she turned out to be a very good player. 'Ringer' was the word Morwenna used to describe Mrs McGuigan.

As the accountant for The Right Step – the new shoe factory – Mrs McGuigan provided Maggie with financial updates each month. Even though she had the documents she needed, Maggie loved meeting with Mr Tinkler to discuss how the business was going. They were also finalising plans to purchase the business.

In the evenings, Maggie would sit on her patio and look down at the town and its transformation. She had turned into a shrewd businesswoman.

*   *   *

For Julie, the trust had opened her eyes to many who were worse off than herself. She learned to appreciate her own life. But, it also showed her how much more she could achieve if she had a degree. On Saturdays, she would help Sam in the pub, as he was run off his feet. Business was growing steadily for him, and so – as Chloe had many council commitments – Julie had started taking over Chloe's Saturday shift.

Julie and Jeremy moved into a small cottage on the outskirts of town. Julie used the services of Ernie Chandler to procure a loan from the bank to buy the property. For the first time in Julie's life, she was the proud owner of her own home.

Everyone attended the housewarming. Julie's parents were proud of their daughter, only mentioning university a couple of times. Maggie reassured them that Julie had good friends and they would all do their best to encourage Julie to enrol in university.

Julie and her intriguing son, Jeremy, spent the first few weeks painting and decorating their new home. Her nights were no longer filled with worry about Jeremy's future. She knew he would go far in whatever field he chose. People just needed to get past his unorthodox manner. His maths was off the charts at school, and his teacher had suggested he go to a school for gifted children. Jeremy would find their intellect more challenging than the children he associated with each day at the local school. This last insight was directed at Fin and Alfie, who never had a logical reason behind anything they did. The schools would also offer full board and weekly or daily tuition.

Julie knew she needed to make a decision soon, but she hated the thought of Jeremy being out there in the world without her. Subconsciously, Julie had to admit to her friends that she was more worried about her own life. Holding Jeremy back was just an excuse. She knew that Jeremy would thrive. Letting him go would mean she would have to get on with her own life.

One evening, after a long day painting the bedrooms, Julie finally sat Jeremy down and talked to him about his future and where he would like to go. He could start at the new school, after the summer holidays, if that's what he wanted. He said he would review all the schools and what they had to offer and get back to her shortly. Julie gave him the longest hug of his life. For once, he didn't complain.

*   *   *

Anaya's absence at Christmas was due to a handsome Indian doctor who worked at the Totnes Community Hospital. They'd met when she requested a home visit for a patient. Luckily, he was on call that evening. They couldn't keep their eyes off each other, and they'd been close friends ever since. Anaya knew she would have to decide soon about her husband. If they divorced, she would have to give him half of their assets, including the house, and she would need to take out a loan to pay him. The thought of ending it once and for all was worth the investment. Anaya had become closer to her daughters over the last year, and their closeness had not diminished on being introduced to Dr Theo Sharma. She had decided that this was her time to live. She even gave herself a new hairstyle to commemorate her new daring.

Once Christmas and the new year celebrations had happily settled down, Anaya knew she had to move forward with her life. So, in mid-January, she had walked into Ernie Chandler's office and asked him to start the divorce proceedings.

Morwenna had also taken out a loan for a house in town. Her new salary had made her independent and secure. For the first time in a long time, Morwenna didn't have to count her pennies. Her family was thriving. The kids loved their new home and they all spent quality family time redecorating it.

Fin and Alfie were very proud of their mum, especially as she wasn't cleaning the school toilets anymore. Their giant smiles were identical in their admiration. They had gotten into more than one scruff over the matter. Nobody was allowed to make fun of their mum.

As for Sarah, her eldest, she was turning into a bright young lady. Helping Chloe part-time in the mobile library and with her council duties afforded Sarah first-hand knowledge of how the council worked. It also meant first pickings of the best books to read. For the first time in her life, Sarah had her own room and enjoyed her privacy. However, most mornings, Sarah would still wake to find Harriet sleeping snugly beside her.

Morwenna, like the others, felt a proud sense of achievement. If she were religious, her silent prayers would be for their ride to never end.

*   *   *

Chloe's son Matthew came home on two weeks' leave. She always cherished that time with her son.

He liked to help her around the house, fixing this and that. Although, there wasn't much to fix, as Sam had proudly taken on that responsibility. Matthew was delighted that his mother was running for re-election as councillor and would campaign for Mayor of Totnes. The election for councillor was now only a few months away.

Mathew had heard on the grapevine that his mother might run for MP of Totnes one day. Chloe laughed and brushed it off, knowing he had heard it from Maggie or one of the girls at the trust.

However, Matthew was slightly concerned about the origin of the trust. 'The council might start snooping around the trust's financial records,' said Matthew one evening. 'Especially if they think you're a part of it. People play dirty if it gets them what they want.'

Chloe knew Matthew was right. She couldn't afford to lose her job. She still had so much to achieve. If people started making allegations about her and the trust, how much would actually be true?

*   *   *

Even though Jonathan's work was keeping him busy, the 'Pandora' case had given GCHQ no new leads, and so he managed the odd weekend in Kent with his family. Their lives always seemed so carefree. It was refreshing to be around normality for a while.

During his long drives back to Cheltenham, his mind would sometimes drift to a small town in Devon. What if he just happened to be driving through – despite it being completely out of his way? Jonathan decided to look up the trust that Maggie worked for.

He read that it was in honour of a woman called Eve Merriweather, who'd committed suicide. He had no business in Friars Meadow, and even if he did drive past the trust's office, he doubted he would see her. If he did, what would she think of him? She'd probably think him a stalker.

The thought was ridiculous, so to clear his mind he put on a CD and listened to Hunters & Collectors for the rest of his journey home from work.

A Most Private Dick

Springtime, March

The trust was cruising along smoothly, no ripples or snags. Chloe's campaign for councillor and mayor was taking shape, and Maggie's future plans for Chloe to run for MP were still on the back burner for now. However, on the few occasions she had seen their elected Member of Parliament, Malcolm Barker-Smith, she hadn't thought much of him. He had airs and graces Maggie had no time for. If Chloe became Mayor of Totnes, however, she would be dealing with him more frequently, and it would be beneficial to know a little more about him.

Enter: Havelock McIntyre, private detective, ex-policeman. Maybe it was his name that won her over. As Maggie didn't know anything about private investigators, she thought she could trust an ex-policeman. They arranged to meet in London, at the Rivoli Bar. She couldn't help herself.

Maggie took to him quickly. He had a bushel of red hair, and from his size to his smile, he was Scottish through and through. He was upfront about his fees and services, and about what he could and couldn't do.

Maggie outlined what she needed from him. A friend could possibly be running for MP of Totnes at the next general election; all she wanted was a background check on their current MP, Malcolm Barker-Smith. He currently held the seat with an 8% majority. Maggie summarised what she had already ascertained from his public profile online. She was hoping a private detective might find something more interesting in his past or present.

Havelock McIntyre agreed to take on the contract and would be in touch within two weeks.

While Chloe was in council meetings, Maggie spent her time making subtle enquiries about Barker-Smith. She got to know the staff at the council very well. They needed little encouragement when talking about Barker-Smith. He appeared squeaky clean, so Maggie knew he was hiding something.

After a two-week investigation, Havelock was true to his word. He had been digging all around town, finding out what Barker-Smith got up to outside of business hours. Unfortunately, Havelock informed Maggie, Barker-Smith didn't appear to have any secret lovers, gambling debts, or drug habits; he was the most boring politician he had ever come across. He was a member of a private club in London and would frequent it when he was in town, sitting at the House of Commons. Havelock couldn't get in, but he had managed to obtain Barker-Smith's driver's logbook and his expense sheets for the last two years. Maggie passed these on to Mrs McGuigan to do what she did best.

The driver's logbook revealed nothing out of the ordinary. Neither did his expenses. Maggie asked Havelock to make some tactful inquiries into Club 26. Not much came up on the internet about the club when Maggie searched for it. It obviously didn't advertise for members. As Maggie and Havelock had no other leads, it was worth taking a look.

Club 26 turned out to be a very private club, with an influential membership. Havelock provided Maggie with a list of members, no questions asked. It read like a 'who's who' in politics and the wealthy high-end of town.

'Notably, only English dare enter,' said Havelock. 'It's just a rich private member's club, nothing illegal or strange about it.'

'I bet they make multi-million deals in there every day,' said Maggie. 'It would be interesting to be a fly on the wall, though.'

'I'd say, lass. Not many MPs are members, so I don't know why he is.'

Havelock re-assured Maggie that he'd gone through Barker-Smith's routine and there wasn't anything of interest to report. His private life was as boring as his political one. He wasn't a high-flyer in London and wasn't in the Cabinet. Havelock said, sadly, that there was nothing else he could do for her. He felt guilty about taking her money, especially after being paid a visit by Special Branch officers.

Two days earlier, two very serious young gentlemen had escorted him to Special Branch headquarters in London to discuss his investigation into Club 26 and Barker-Smith. They wanted to know what he was doing and who he was working for.

Havelock initially deferred to client privilege, to which the officers counter-offered a charge of interfering in an ongoing investigation relating to national security, to which he gave up Maggie's name. He explained who he was working for and why. Havelock shared with them the information he had given Maggie, excluding the driver's logs and club membership list. That part they didn't need to know.

Special Branch made him sign a gag order. He agreed not to speak about the club or about Malcolm Barker-Smith to anyone. He was instructed to advise Maggie Malloy that there was nothing of interest at the club or in Malcolm Barker-Smith. His investigation must come to an end.

Therefore, by the end of March, Havelock advised Maggie that it was a dead end. He also advised her to dispose of all the documents he'd given her in relation to their enquiry. Maggie nodded and agreed that she would.

Havelock knew that, for Special Branch to be involved, there was obviously something going on at the club. But he would not be the one to sabotage it. The last thing he wanted was to see this lovely young lady caught up in anything illegal.

Maggie thanked him for all his help and conceded to give up. She was disappointed. Could Chloe ever win as an independent against Barker-Smith?

The officers from Special Branch closed their file on Havelock McIntyre and his client and forwarded the details to GCHQ. It was marked 'no further action required' in relation to Maggie Malloy and Chloe Silverton of Friars Meadow, Devon.

*   *   *

Maggie realised that, if Chloe was to ever win a seat in the House of Commons, she would have to prove herself as Mayor of Totnes first. It couldn't just be about digging up dirt on your opponents. Maggie felt ashamed of her actions. Being elected came from earning the trust of the people and providing them with what they needed.

Maggie decided to forget about her investigation, although she still had doubts about Barker-Smith. She didn't believe a politician could be that squeaky clean. On the few occasions she'd met him at the council, he had unnerved her. Maggie believed him to be an ambitious man who lacked any regard for his constituents.

As Maggie waited in the council offices for Chloe, she had time to reflect on what she had done. Was she doing all this out of spite and some personal grievance against the system? Was getting Chloe elected as MP overstretching it? Maggie didn't want to appear bitter. It would diminish everything she had worked for. The last thing she wanted was to put extra pressure on Chloe. Being councillor and possibly mayor should be enough.

*   *   *

As Chloe and Maggie drove back to Friars Meadow that afternoon, they discussed at length their next strategy.

'I just want to ask – are you sure you want to go through with the campaign for mayor?' Maggie probed.

'What's gotten into you?' asked Chloe.

Maggie pulled the car over so that they could talk face to face.

'I just want to make sure you're doing it for you, not for the trust or Eve or me,' said Maggie. 'I've been selfish, haven't I?'

'No, you haven't. You had a dream and you saw it through. Your mum and Eve would be proud of what you've achieved. As for me, for the first time in my life I'm doing something really important. I feel privileged to be doing what I'm doing, and I have you to thank for that,' said Chloe. She touched the side of Maggie's face tenderly.

'I hired a private detective to look into Malcolm Barker-Smith.'

'I thought you were up to something. It's not necessary.'

'Don't worry, it's over. We didn't find anything. Barker-Smith is actually quite boring and squeaky clean,' smiled Maggie. 'I'm afraid, if you ever decide to run, you're going to have to win on your charms and merits alone.'

'You know they might just vote for me because they like me and believe in me.'

'True, you're very likable.'

'You don't need to dig up dirt on Barker-Smith or anyone else. If I ever choose to run for MP, I want to win because people believe I'm the best candidate for the job,' said Chloe seriously.

'Can you imagine if you became MP?' said Maggie. 'Think of everything we could do. You'd be in the House of Commons, scrutinising legislation, debating with other MPs. You'd be on committees. You'd protect and advocate the interests of your constituency at a higher level.'

'God, that was a mouthful,' said Chloe, 'Where did that speech come from?'

'The internet … Where else?' They both started to laugh.

'Listen,' began Chloe. 'There's something I want you to do for me. Look into the rental properties around town. Ernie provided me with a list of rental properties last year, but I think some have changed hands since then. The banks don't own all the properties. Even if they're privately owned, the owners still have a responsibility to their tenants. I'm concerned they're not meeting their obligations. Ernie said he will help with the legal requirements if we run into any trouble. I've had more than one person complain that their rental properties haven't been repaired.'

'Sure, I'll get onto it,' assured Maggie.

They pulled back onto the road and headed home. While Maggie drove, Chloe pulled out a folder from her briefcase and started reading out the slogans the kids had come up with for her re-election as councillor of Friars Meadow and possible nomination for mayor.

'"The best man for the job is a woman" – that was from Sarah,' said Chloe. '"Make me your first choice, I'll be your loudest voice" – that was from Jeremy. I like that one.' She smiled. '"Vote for the local lass; you'll end up with more cash" – that was from one of the twins, I can never tell which one. And lucky last, "I'll go the extra mile to make you smile" – you can guess who wrote that one.'

'Morwenna,' said Maggie. They both started to laugh. As the rain drizzled down, the friends settled in and relaxed for the remainder of their drive home to Friars Meadow.

Being that Maggie's life was so busy, she was remiss in disposing of the documents Havelock McIntyre had given her.

They remained in her desk drawer with the rest of her work papers.

This was Maggie's first mistake.

The Barn Swallow

GCHQ ... Early April

Back at GCHQ, Jonathan had just concluded his daily team meeting. They'd reviewed all of the current operations his team were involved in. The country's problems never stopped. Once his team was fully briefed, he gathered his tablet and walked back to his office.

Pandora was dead in the water. No new leads had arisen in months; everyone was still lying low. With any luck, Hamilton's team may have given up hope of finding the final case, as GCHQ had. Their drone had covered all the waterways to the sea along the River Dart. If it was out there, GCHQ would've found it by now. They would lay charges against Barker-Smith and Hamilton shortly, but the Home Office had extended the deadline until the beginning of May. This allowed Jonathan's team to keep listening, in the hope of intercepting a communique.

Unfortunately, Jonathan's reports to Max were getting thinner by the week. Even so, they went straight to the Home Secretary and senior members of the security services. The Home Office diligently awaited any new leads pertaining to the software that Bridget Monahan had stolen from MI5.

Angela Milford entered Jonathan's office with her tablet. Her work during the investigation had been exceptional – he'd recommended her for promotion. Once Angela had covered the usual updates, she mentioned some additional information relating to a private detective.

'He was hired by a woman to look into Malcolm Barker-Smith. During the detective's investigation, he also looked into Club 26,' informed Angela. 'It seems Barker-Smith might be in for more competition at the next general election. Not that he'll be running, anyway.'

'Are you sure there's no connection?'

'Yes. A Chloe Silverton was a possible candidate running as an independent. She's currently the councillor of Friars Meadow, and will be running for re-election in May, as well as for mayor at the forthcoming election. Her assistant hired the private detective to look into Barker-Smith, which led them to the club. We've spoken with the private detective, and he won't be delving any further into either,' said Angela.

On hearing the town's name, Jonathan's attention was momentarily drawn away from the detective to the Rivoli Bar.

'Did you say Friars Meadow, in Devon?'

'Yes,' said Angela.

Angela continued with the report, stating that she was satisfied this was an isolated incident and confirming that they were not connected to their investigation. She concluded by mentioning that Chloe Silverton and her assistant, Maggie Malloy, had no affiliations with the club or Barker-Smith.

On hearing the name *Maggie*, Jonathan drew slowly to attention.

'Thank you, Angela. If you're satisfied, you can close that line of enquiry. However, I would like to review it before you do. Please forward it to me.'

'Sure.'

'If this Maggie Malloy comes up again in our investigation, I want to know immediately.'

'OK, will do, Jonathan,' said Angela, as she got up to leave.

Once Angela had closed the door, Jonathan brought up the file. It opened with a picture of Havelock McIntyre. Then he saw Chloe Silverton's picture, which he recognised from the Rivoli Bar. He then flicked over to see the woman he'd only been imagining for the last few months staring back at him – Maggie Malloy. He had searched the trust's name and address but didn't dig into its employee records. He would never violate her privacy, and it was against GCHQ procedures, which he would never abuse. But there she was, staring back at him, his Maggie from the Ritz.

Was this a coincidence? He didn't believe in coincidences, not in his line of work.

That night at home, Jonathan couldn't sleep. Instead, he went meticulously through the files on both women. It all appeared straightforward. Still, he spent the night going over it again and again, always being drawn back to Maggie's picture.

That weekend, he decided to drive to Friars Meadow. He programmed his satnav in his 1966 red MG and drove down to Devon. It was over 118 miles, which took him just under two hours. He arrived in Friars Meadow around lunchtime.

He wasn't quite sure what to do, but when he saw the town's botanical gardens, he decided to take a stroll through them. They were just as beautiful as any gardens he'd visited in London, Kent, and Cheltenham – just more compact. He noticed a plaque on a tree. It read: *These gardens were re-established on behalf of the Eve Merriweather Trust.* There were benches situated all around the gardens, and each bench had a plaque on it. Engraved on each one was a dedication to someone who had loved and been loved.

He felt like an intruder here – foolish, even. He wasn't sure what he was looking for. On second thoughts, he decided to leave, but not until after some lunch at the pub. He was starving.

Jonathan walked into The Two Swallows and ordered at the bar. As the publican handed him his beer, Jonathan noticed a tattoo on his arm: an anchor with two barn swallows sitting on the anchor tips. Jonathan's father had a couple of similar tattoos.

He remembered his father's stories. In naval history, each swallow symbolised five thousand miles at sea. If a sailor drowned at sea, the swallows would carry his soul up to heaven. As the publican had two swallows, Jonathan assumed he'd been a sailor for some time. Seamen were known to be very traditional and superstitious. As swallows returned to the same place every year to mate and nest, they would guarantee the sailor would return home safely from sea. Jonathan felt he knew half the man's history before even talking to him.

He smiled to himself, knowing all things had reasoning behind them, if you looked deep enough.

The ex-sailor gave Jonathan his change and suggested eating outside, since it was a beautiful day. Jonathan ordered fish and chips. The barman told him that Julie would bring his lunch out as soon as it was ready. Jonathan thanked him and walked outside. He found a table in the sunshine. He was famished.

Jonathan felt unwise, being here in Maggie's town. He had driven past the trust, knowing it would be closed on Saturday. He was unsure why he'd come, knowing only that he needed to see this place. Generally, Jonathan didn't act on impulse – everything he did was calculated and planned. There were procedures and regulations he worked and lived by, and without them, there would be disorder.

Just as he took another swig of beer, he noticed a woman wiping down one of the outside tables. Soon after, she returned with his fish and chips and smiled knowingly at him. Her face seemed familiar, and every now and then he caught her staring at him as she worked the tables. It was a little unnerving – it was usually him doing the watching. Then he realised where he recognised her from – she was one of Maggie's friends from the Rivoli Bar.

The colour drained from his face. He felt embarrassed. He should have realised that the five women were from the same town.

Jonathan finished up quickly and left. He climbed into his car and started the long drive back to Cheltenham.

*   *   *

Once he was out of sight, Julie pulled out her mobile and rang Maggie.

'Hey, what's up, Jules?'

'Hi, you'll never guess who I just served in the pub …'

As Jonathan drove out of town, he merged onto a quaint country road. His MG snaked its way out of Friars Meadow alongside a winding stream. He crossed over a bridge, and as he turned the car in a northerly direction, he saw a woman on the other side of the shore. She was trekking with a hiking stick alongside the river.

She stopped walking and looked up. Jonathan could see that she was on her mobile. When she turned towards the road, he saw exactly who it was: Maggie.

Jonathan's MG veered onto the other side of the road. He quickly recovered, but by then he had passed her and could only see a glimpse of her through his rear-view mirror.

He wanted to pull the car over and run back along the road, but he couldn't do that. What would he say to her?

'Hi, fancy seeing you here,' or 'Hi, I was just passing.' It wouldn't be romantic like in the movies – it would be creepy.

And so, he drove the 118 miles home thinking about what a fool he'd been. It was the longest two hours he could remember.

*   *   *

As Julie's words sank in, Maggie stopped in her tracks. Her Jonathan was in The Two Swallows eating fish and chips? Julie had to be mistaken, but her friend re-assured her that she wasn't.

Could it be a coincidence? What was he doing here? She remembered telling him that she lived in Friars Meadow. He knew the area because of his work for the Chancellor of the Exchequer. Was that why he was here?

Maggie became a little uneasy. Was he here for work? No – not on a Saturday, surely. Was he here because of the trust? Had the trust been reported to the treasury? Maggie's mind was racing. Just then, she heard the revving of a car engine on the road. When she looked up, she saw a red convertible driving off. Maggie was feeling light-headed. This couldn't all end now.

There was still so much to do. She needed to think; she had to walk. It was the only way to clear her mind.

For the first time in over a year, Maggie feared for her friends and the trust. What did Jonathan's presence symbolise? Did he even remember her? Of course not, why would he? He had known her all of ten minutes, over four months ago.

But Maggie hadn't forgotten him, had she? She felt foolish. She was flushed, and it wasn't from the hiking.

A Fly on the Wall

End of April

Lazy Larry Morecombe hadn't taken to forced retirement. In the last few months, he'd seen the town's fortunes transform. Unfortunately, he was incapable of seeing the good in anything. Instead, he spied and listened for any information on the trust. He decided to make meticulous notes on everything he'd seen and had started taking photos of the trustees' comings and goings. It was a shame he hadn't put in as much effort into being councillor.

The town's fortunes had been reversed. But to Larry, it was because of those women at the trust handing out money like sweets, bribing everyone for Chloe Silverton's vote.

The trust and Chloe were spending far too much money. He knew it wouldn't be included in her councillor expenses; Eve Merriweather had never had that much money, or so his sources informed him.

Money was pouring in from everywhere. The town had been flushed with it. From the pub and the shops' booming trade, the town had gotten itself a face lift. How many were in on it? Larry believed that Chloe was bribing people for their vote. It wasn't very original, but then again, neither was he.

Leading up to Christmas, Larry Morecombe was busier than he had ever been as councillor. If the trust and Chloe Silverton were committing fraud and bribery, he needed evidence.

Larry watched how all the women associated with the trust strutted around town like they owned the place. He wasn't having it, and he was going to get to the bottom of it. The only obstacle in his path was that nobody would speak to him about the trust's finances or the shoe factory's funding. Lately, he'd heard rumours of a furniture factory being opened, too. How were they financing all these new business endeavours?

The trust's business details were in the public records. However, digging into their financials would be harder. His friend Thomas Carlyle had looked into the legitimacy of the trust, to make sure everything was above board. This had proven fruitless; everything was in order.

But that still didn't explain where all the money came from.

Through his snooping and spying, Larry came to realise that Maggie was the one running the show, despite her not being a trustee. Larry had been watching all the trustees – Julie, Morwenna, and Anaya – and he still couldn't understand how they'd come into their roles at the trust. Two single mums and a nurse? It didn't make sense.

Unfortunately, Larry's first mistake was visiting some of his old constituents. His questions were rebuked with scorn. On a few occasions, after being told to piss off, his old constituents phoned Chloe and Maggie to warn them of his snooping.

Maggie should have realised that Larry wouldn't take his dismissal lying down. She had planned to discuss it at the next trust meeting – only, with her hectic schedule, it ended up slipping her mind. Maggie knew that Larry was lazy, but she'd never contemplated the possibility of him being dangerous or vindictive. And so, she didn't prioritise the conversation as much as she should have.

This was Maggie's second mistake.

*   *   *

One day, in mid-spring, Larry decided to tail Morwenna.

She headed out of town on a bus to Newton Abbot, and he followed the bus until it stopped near a bank, where he watched Morwenna alight and deposit something in the night safe before walking off. He stealthily followed to see what else she would do. He captured her on his camera at the bank, but couldn't get a good picture, since her head was down. Morwenna was a trustee, so it would stand to reason that she would deposit funds on behalf of the trust. But why deposit funds so far from home?

Since Thomas Carlyle and Larry were as thick as thieves, he asked his long-time friend, once again, to look into the deposits that had been made by the trust. Thomas said he would make a few discreet phone calls. Their history went back so far that they'd lost count of the favours each owed the other. Plus, Thomas was also curious about the trust's finances. Why would they not bank with his bank, which was in walking distance from the trust's office? He saw no logic in it.

Thomas Carlyle had made a lucrative portfolio for himself over the years. When a number of the town's houses foreclosed on their previous owners, he was able to secure a beneficial loan from the bank – one under his own name and two under his wife's. He'd purchased the houses at rock-bottom prices, but now that the town's prospects were improving, the house prices had started to rise.

It wasn't only him – Larry and a few of his friends had managed to secure cheap loans to buy foreclosed properties. They'd planned to lease the properties out until the housing market grew again, and they'd known it would eventually. Then, they could make a profitable increase on their return.

Even though Thomas agreed to help his old friend Larry, he was secretly delighted that the house prices in Friars Meadow were on the rise, thanks to the trust's investments. Thomas was worried his old friend might shoot himself in the foot with his investigation. He decided he would take his time looking into Maggie and the trust – he didn't want to rock the boat.

But eventually, he handed Larry a printout of the trust's deposits for the month of March. Thomas didn't know what harm it would do, and it got his friend off his back. The deposits seemed legitimate; Thomas told Larry to let it go and get on with his life. But Thomas hadn't realised – just as Maggie hadn't – how vindictive Larry could be.

As time went on, Larry recorded several occasions where Morwenna, Julie, and Maggie deposited envelopes into numerous ATMs around Totnes. He was so consumed by what they were up to that he completely forgot about the council elections in May.

He thought of going to the police but realised he would have to admit where he'd got the financial information from. Larry knew that the ATM deposits would match their cash donations. Maybe it was all legitimate. Maybe people were donating money by posting cheques to the trust ...

But why deposit so far from home?

On one occasion, Larry followed Julie, who drove to Torquay, made her deposit, bought an ice cream, walked along the sea front for half an hour, then drove home. It wasn't a hot day, but she was wearing an overly large sun hat. He took pictures of her at the bank, just as he had with Morwenna, but her face was conveniently obscured by her hat.

Larry knew the trust met every Monday evening. They also met at Maggie's every Wednesday night. If there was any information to be had, it would more likely be discovered in Maggie's home. She was the ringleader.

He decided that he would pay her a visit and present her with what he knew, to see what she had to say for herself.

*   *   *

Young Harriet watched the strange old man who was following them. He had taken her picture, to which she'd stuck out her tongue. Harriet watched closely as he followed her and her mum along the street. She kept tugging her mum's coat, repeating the title that only one designated, privileged person deserved. 'Mum, Mum, Mum!'

'What?' said Morwenna, looking down at her youngest. Harriet was pointing at something.

'He took my picture.'

Morwenna looked to see who her daughter was pointing at. Larry Morecombe quickly darted into a shop.

Morwenna picked up her mobile and texted the group. She used the code word, *Waterloo*.

They all agreed to meet at her house at 7 p.m.

*   *   *

That night, Maggie, Morwenna, Chloe, Anaya, Julie, Mrs McGuigan, and Ernie Chandler gathered for their impromptu meeting. It was agreed that everyone needed to be more diligent. They had nearly finished depositing all the cash from the suitcase, and now money was coming in legitimately from the shoe factory and the coffee shop in the gardens.

Chloe suggested putting a stop to the deposits. They had enough funds in the trust, and they didn't need to take any more chances with Larry Morecombe snooping around. They had no idea how long Larry Morecombe had been investigating them, or what he had already uncovered.

Morwenna stated the obvious. 'He's a sore loser.'

'Yes,' Ernie agreed. 'But we still need to keep an eye on him. It's the devil you don't know that could get you undone.'

The devil was in the detail. If Maggie had realised her earlier mistakes, maybe things would have turned out differently for the friends.

But you can't squabble about hindsight, can you?

Skulduggery

Early May

Larry Morecombe knocked again – still no answer. He slowly walked around the porch, peeping through the windows. The back of the house took in the view of the countryside. Even Larry had to admit it was breathtaking. As he walked further around the house, he came to a conservatory made wholly of glass. He tried the handle; it opened. *Stupid girl, leaving her house unlocked.* He called out to her – no answer.

He stepped inside and had a furtive look around. The room had a table in the centre with six chairs around it, and a deck of cards in the centre. He'd wanted to question Maggie – to catch her off guard. But in retrospect, he was glad she wasn't at home.

He walked through the conservatory and quietly around the house. He entered a small study, which contained a desk, computer, bookshelves, and a filing cabinet – which was locked.

He walked up to the desk and started to flick through the papers on top. Then he rummaged through the desk drawers. He wasn't sure what he was looking for, until he came upon a folder with the name Malcolm Barker-Smith MP on it.

He pulled it out and flicked through it. It was a dossier filled with reports on the MP's comings and goings, and a list of his expenses, going back a couple of years.

Larry was interested. What was Maggie doing prying into Malcolm Barker-Smith? Was she up to her old tricks again? Unless she had other grand ideas ...

Bloody nerve of the woman, he thought. As Larry searched further through the desk, he came across some folders on Chloe. One was full of campaign documents and flyers for Chloe's re-election as councillor. Another file was for her campaign for mayor, and the third file held papers outlining the responsibilities and requirements for becoming an MP. He saw flyers and promotional leaflets for Chloe Silverton – MP for Totnes.

Well, well, well, he thought. What would Malcolm Barker-Smith give for information like this? Maybe they could help each other.

Larry thought it ridiculous that Chloe would think of running for MP. She was a nobody: she worked in the pub and drove the mobile library, for Christ's sake. She hadn't even been in politics for a full two years. This vexed him even more.

Larry took some photos on his mobile phone and quietly left the house. He knew that Barker-Smith would welcome this information. Larry smiled as he quickly walked away from Maggie's home. He believed there might even be a job in it for him, if he played his cards right.

*   *   *

When Maggie arrived home that evening, she felt a strange sense of unease. The house felt cold. She went into each room, looking for changes, but they appeared untouched. That is, until she walked into her study. From a glance, she could see that her desk was not as she'd left it. Checking through the drawers, she knew immediately that documents had been moved. A chill ran down her spine. Maggie walked into the conservatory and moved towards the glass doors. When she turned the handle, it opened. A gush of cold air hit her face. She couldn't believe how foolish she'd been to leave her door unlocked.

Maggie swore to herself as she locked the door, but not before looking outside to see if anyone was still out there. Someone had been in her house. She quickly checked the rest of her home. Nothing appeared to be missing. She was tempted to call the police. But to say what? 'I left the back door open, and I think someone came in, but they didn't take anything.' No, she didn't want to appear even more stupid.

That night, Maggie sat at her computer and googled 'motion sensors' and 'home security cameras'. If anyone came around again when she wasn't home, she wanted to know about it. That night, and each night after, Maggie double-checked the doors and windows before going to bed; she also ensured that she did this every time she left her house.

At the trust's office the next day, Maggie mentioned it to Julie.

'What was kept in your desk drawer?'

'Promotional leaflets for Chloe, for her election as councillor, mayor, and so on.' Then she remembered the other file she'd hidden in the bottom of the drawer … which she'd promised to dispose of and hadn't.

Cursing to herself, Maggie realised her mistake.

The Devil You Know

'It's that Larry Morecombe again for you,' said Melanie, a week later.

'Tell him I'll call him back,' said Malcolm Barker-Smith.

'He's not calling this time – he's here waiting to speak with you.'

'What! Find out what he wants. I'm busy,' said Malcolm.

'I did. He said he has information about Chloe Silverton and a trust in Friars Meadow. He said something about bribery and illegal payments from the trust.'

'Tell him to go to the police,' said Malcolm.

'He said he can't. But you'd be interested, because Chloe Silverton is planning to run as an independent for Totnes at the general election next year.'

This caught Barker-Smith's attention. 'Bring Mr Morecombe in,' he told Melanie. As Larry Morecombe walked confidently into Barker-Smith's office, Melanie was asked to close the door, which she gladly did.

I Solemnly Swear

May

'Deirdre Carr, six … Chloe Silverton, ten! Our new Mayor of Totnes is Chloe Silverton,' said the speaker.

She'd won! Chloe couldn't believe she'd done it. Matthew was there to cheer her to victory. Chloe could see how pleased he was for her. More than she'd ever been for herself.

The other councillors of Totnes had voted for their new mayor. The seats on the council were Conservatives – eight, Labour – two, Liberal Democratic – three, Greens – one, and Independent – two.

Chloe was the second independent on the council, there to represent Friars Meadow. Fran Matters, her fellow independent representative, had followed Chloe's progress over the last year, and marvelled at Friars Meadow's transformation. She wanted to introduce the same initiatives in her own town. Chloe was all too happy to help Fran. When the two candidates came to give their speeches for nomination, it came down to Chloe and Deidre Carr, a Conservative.

In her speech, Chloe shared her achievements for her community and discussed what more of this progress would mean for the whole of Totnes. She spoke of potential unemployment decline and future job prospects. She talked about self-respect and fulfilment in one's personal life, as well as in the community.

Her vision for the future now included the whole of Totnes, not just Friars Meadow. It was an honest speech and one she had been dreading until now. To her fellow councillors, Chloe was a bright star – one that would shine down on all of them. Chloe even managed to secure some of the Conservative councillors' votes. Knowing Chloe as they had this last year, they knew she would undertake everything she set out to do.

Chloe's friends were all present to celebrate her win. For the first time that evening, at the post-election party, Chloe was formally introduced to Malcolm Barker-Smith MP. She had seen him at the council offices from time to time, but he'd never approached Chloe directly to introduce himself. A nod of the head was all she'd ever received in passing.

As he congratulated her on her win, he held her hand a little tighter and longer than expected.

'How long do you plan to hold the position of mayor?' he whispered.

This took Chloe by surprise. 'As long as the people of Totnes will have me,' she replied.

He was standing a little too close for her liking. She didn't want to step back, as that would signify a withdrawal, so she stood her ground.

'Being the Mayor of Totnes is quite different from being the councillor of a small town like Friars Meadow. It will be very demanding,' he said.

'I dare say I'll manage. I have a great team,' said Chloe.

'I'm sure you do,' said Barker-Smith.

At that moment, Matthew walked over and put his arm around his mother's back. 'We're all very proud of her, Mister ...' he said, extending his hand.

'Barker-Smith, MP for Totnes,' Barker-Smith replied, shaking Matthew's firm hand. Then he smiled and walked off, taking a long look in Maggie's direction as he did so.

Another attendant – as proud of Chloe as Matthew – was Sam. After the post-party celebrations were over, everyone ended up at the pub, and Sam gave a memorable speech.

'Raise your glasses to our new Mayor of Totnes. I give you Chloe Silverton – a great woman all round.' At this last remark, he extended a wink to Chloe, who returned his gesture by walking up to him and kissing him squarely on the lips.

The next day, Chloe offered Sarah a permanent position on her staff at the council. Sarah would help Chloe with her councillor duties in Friars Meadow while Maggie was appointed her adviser in her capacity as mayor. Chloe was now able to improve the whole of the South Ham district.

It was now only one year until the general election. Brexit had divided the nation. People had lost faith in the major parties. They wanted the whole fiasco over with. Some were looking to the minor and independent parties for answers, and the nation was expecting a big shift in conservative voting. Some MPs were getting a little nervous.

By June, figures had come in to claim that unemployment was down to an all-time low in Friars Meadow and surrounding towns. The trust had sold the shoe factory to its employees and made a respectable profit, and it was now preparing to rent the old Provincial site. The site would be used for the new furniture factory.

The trust hired consultants to look into the prospect of logging again, as the forests were well and truly endowed and would be a great source of materials for the furniture factory. They would need council permission to log Devon's forests, and with the logging would come substantial re-planting. The jobs alone would tally over a thousand – with loggers, forestry personnel, factory workers, and more, not to mention the shop and trade services that would profit once the site opened.

While this was being looked into, Chloe spoke to the other councillors and asked them to review her plan for future logging and its potential benefits for their area. They would all get a chance to voice their initial interest and concerns at the next council meeting.

*   *   *

Summer was once again upon them. Everything was in bloom and soaking up the sunshine. The countryside was ablaze with colour as all the flowers and bushes basked in the sun. The town was experiencing an upsurge of visitors because of the gardens, and more homes were being leased and bought. Their value was slowly rising as the branch managers had always predicted they would – albeit a little earlier than expected.

As Maggie walked past Eve's old house one day, she came upon a new family in the throes of moving in. They informed her that they'd just bought the property, and that the husband had just started work at the shoe factory.

They asked Maggie if she'd known the previous owner. Maggie told them about Eve and her love for her garden. It was a little overgrown now, but the woman told Maggie she loved gardening and would enjoy restoring it once they were moved in – hopefully before summer's end.

Maggie smiled at the thought of this. Eve would be pleased to know her garden would be looked after again. She apologised for the decay of the garden, explaining that the bank wouldn't let Eve or herself maintain it.

The new owner corrected her. 'It was a private purchase,' she said, confused. 'It wasn't owned by the bank.'

Maggie knew it had been leased for a time last year, but she hadn't known that the bank had sold it. She'd never seen any for sale signs out front. Maggie politely asked the woman who she'd purchased the house from.

The owner smiled. 'His name was Thomas Carlyle.'

On hearing the name, Maggie turned red and had to excuse herself before she swore in front of them.

Thomas Carlyle was the owner of Eve's house. The bastard had foreclosed on Eve, then had the tenacity to buy it from the bank at a bargain basement price. Now he'd sold it at a profit. *The fucking prick!* That was the only way Maggie could describe him. She couldn't stop swearing. He should've helped Eve re-finance her mortgage instead of knocking the chair out from under her and watching her fall.

Maggie headed straight to Ernie Chandler's office with the news. She asked him to look into any malpractice by Thomas Carlyle. Ernie said he would, and he asked Alisha to look into who else had purchased properties around town that fell into foreclosure. He was only interested if there was a connection to any branch managers in the Totnes area.

Maggie wanted to know if it was illegal for a branch manager to buy a property owned by their own bank. Did it have to be advertised for sale? Was it unethical or illegal if Thomas Carlyle didn't give appropriate advice to Eve?

Ernie reminded Maggie that it wasn't illegal to purchase a property after foreclosure, but that the bank manager had an obligation to provide all advice and assistance to the owners before they were foreclosed. Unfortunately, it would be difficult to prove in Eve's case, as she was not here to say if he did or not.

Maggie discussed what she'd uncovered about the sale of Eve's house with Chloe on Wednesday.

'I'll start an investigation into the matter and see if it's more widespread,' Chloe promised. She hadn't seen Maggie so agitated in over a year. Her friend was anxious and pacing around the room. Chloe could see that deep down, she still wanted someone to blame for Eve's death.

*   *   *

'I'm engaged!' yelled out Anaya, later that night at the poker table. She wasn't going to keep it a secret any longer.

Their official announcement would come on the weekend, at her new fiancé's parents' home in Cornwell. Anaya was marrying Dr Theo Sharma. Her girls had taken to him, just like a father, and they were both to be Anaya's bridesmaids.

Dr Theo Sharma had a large estate on the outskirts of Totnes. Actually, it was an eighteenth-century manor house, sitting on ten acres of beautiful countryside. Every time Anaya walked through the giant wooden door, she felt she needed to curtsy. Her girls felt like they were in a fairy tale. The newly married couple would be honeymooning in Spain and Italy.

Anaya's friends were excited for her. They spent the rest of the evening discussing the wedding. The ceremony would be held at her new estate under a marquee.

Meanwhile, Julie was feeling anxious for Jeremy; he had been accepted into the exclusive school for gifted children. He would be away for the school week but would be back home on the weekends. He would start after the summer holidays.

Julie didn't know what she was worried about more – Jeremy trying to fit into a new school, or her living alone in an empty house. Anaya pointed out to her that she'd be too busy to worry, as she'd be studying for her law degree. No more excuses.

Morwenna, as always, had her hands full with the twins and Harriet. Harriet was to be a flower girl and was extremely excited about going to the castle. She was going to wear a beautiful princess dress, with wings on her back. Anaya had to draw a line in the sand when Harriet asked for a wand. The wedding would be a lavish affair – all Morwenna kept thinking was, *please don't let them break anything.*

After letting slip to her twins that she had actually wanted golden retrievers, Fin and Alfie had been working on her for a puppy. They would bark and growl at her whenever she asked them to do anything, and sometimes they would roll on their backs in the living room and wriggle for a belly rub or cock their legs up in the air. They weren't as bright as Sarah, or even Harriet for that matter, but she wouldn't exchange them for anything – even two cute golden retrievers.

However, she eventually relented, now that they were in their own home. She was going to surprise them on their birthday with a golden retriever pup.

Never a Dull Moment

June

'Never a dull moment' was definitely the right descriptor for Chloe's life. Due to implementing her plans for Totnes, dealing with council matters, and investigating the prospect of logging – which was proving harder than she'd thought – Chloe was rushed off her feet. Susan McBride was invaluable in giving Chloe advice on all matters of council. Chloe knew it was Susan's recommendation that had secured her the majority of votes for mayor. Susan warned Chloe that even though her job was rewarding, there was also a vicious side to the game.

Susan described it as two gladiators in the arena fighting to the death. 'Well, that's politics for you,' she said. 'Only one is ever left standing.'

Chloe laughed off her analogy, but it wasn't long before she got a taste of dirty politics for herself.

After arriving home one Thursday night, Chloe kicked off her heels and picked up the post, which was lying on the floor by the front door.

She poured herself a glass of merlot and put the leftovers of yesterday's casserole into the oven to warm. It was always simpler to make more dinner than necessary, although recently Chloe had been dining with Sam on more than one occasion during the week. On Sundays he'd been coming over, and she liked to cook him a roast.

Chloe sat on her sofa and opened her mail. There were some letters from constituents; everyone seemed to know where she lived now. These she briefly scanned, then put aside for Sarah to address. She put a couple of bills aside to pay later, alongside some leaflets to discard. The last letter that she picked up had no postage stamp; it had been put through the letterbox personally. When she read it, the colour from the wine drained from her face.

The message was typed in large, bold letters.

If you run for MP of Totnes, bitch, I'll bring you and the trust down.

For the first time since the start of her campaign, Chloe felt afraid. She had been warned about the press – the deranged stalkers and habitual complainers. She knew she shouldn't always expect sunshine and roses. With praise came contempt ... but this was not an attack on her work as mayor. It was a warning not to run for MP at the next general election. And it threatened the trust.

She hadn't even planned to run. Chloe's work at the council kept her busy enough. There was so much more to learn before she could contemplate running for MP. This note implied, however, that the person who'd written it knew of her connection with the trust and the private conversations she'd had with her friends about her ambitions. Chloe sat for a while, contemplating the idea that some-one might know where the money was coming from. Who knew she was considering running for MP, apart from her close friends?

Chloe didn't want to worry her dear friends so soon, so she called the only other person she felt safe confiding in. Sam arrived within five minutes. Chloe put the letter in a plastic divider with the envelope, and Sam told her she had to hand it in to the police, in case she received more and they escalated. This, she assured him, would be done in the morning.

Sam insisted on staying the night. He could see it had derailed her, and he feared for her safety. Being hated that much by an unidentified person was fear-provoking, which was obviously the note's intent. However, Chloe was more concerned about the impli-cations of the note, rather than the outright threat. Sam knew, as most people did, that the trust had more money than it should have.

Chloe couldn't put if off any longer – she sent out a text mes-sage to the team with the code word: *WATERLOO*. They agreed to meet at Maggie's the following night. Chloe wasn't prone to over-reacting, but she needed everyone to know about the threat.

She had no idea of who might have sent it.

*   *   *

Later that night, before bed, Sam double-checked the doors and windows before retiring to the spare bedroom.

He loved this woman. Nobody was going to hurt her, not on his watch. Sam climbed into bed and was reaching over to turn off the side lamp when he heard a noise outside his bedroom door.

He grabbed one of Matthew's football trophies and slowly crept to the door. He grabbed the door handle and flung it open, raising the trophy high in the air, ready to strike.

Chloe looked startled momentarily. Then she smiled and said, 'Well, are you going to let me pass, or are you protecting your virtue?'

'I thought you'd never ask,' he said, as he stepped aside to let her in.

For the first instance during her time as mayor, Chloe was late to work the next morning.

*   *   *

As agreed, Chloe handed the letter to the police. They ensured that they would send it to forensics but that she should expect hate mail along with the well-wishers from time to time. They earnestly suggested she increase her home security. This Chloe also agreed to. The police said they would check the letter for fingerprints and any DNA, but they doubted there would be any.

Once everyone had arrived at Maggie's, Chloe told them about the threatening letter. Sam was present at their meeting, as Chloe had finally confided in him about the trust. She admitted to her friends that she trusted no one more than Sam. They all looked at him, waiting for some kind of reproach, but none was forthcoming. All Sam said was, 'I hope you know what you're doing.' He knew now that the growth of the town was down to Maggie and the trust. Everyone's lives, including those of his employees and guests at the pub, had flourished because of it.

Maggie mentioned the intrusion at her home in May as a possible connection. She filled them in on the break-in and how – while she couldn't be totally sure – she believed someone had rummaged through her desk. Then she told her friends about the file on Barker-Smith.

They all agreed that the letter was a warning to Chloe not to run. However, they didn't believe for a minute that an MP would be stupid enough to drop a note like *that* in Chloe's letterbox.

'Who do you know that is spiteful enough to send such a stupid message? Someone who has a grudge to settle?' asked Sam.

'Oh, my god, Larry Morecombe!' Maggie suddenly exclaimed. 'He's been nosing around for months. If he got into my house and saw the contents in the drawer, it's possible he's malicious enough to want payback.'

This piece of information actually made Chloe sigh with relief. The thought of the note been written by Larry Morecombe made sense now. They all knew him to be a lazy bastard, but nevertheless, they considered him harmless.

They had to presume he knew something about the trust. What evidence did he actually have?

'It would fit. He may even have told Barker-Smith about the campaign brochures he found in your drawer, Maggie. He could be hoping to benefit in some way,' said Ernie.

'Yes. If he couldn't find anything on the trust, he could be trying another way to cause trouble – especially now we've stopped depositing the money,' said Julie.

'Spiteful old dip-shit,' cut in Morwenna.

'If the police get too involved, they might start snooping around the trust,' said Mrs McGuigan. 'Maybe that's what he wants. If he hasn't found anything himself, he may try to get the police involved.'

'True, but he could just tell the police or the Treasury to look into the trust if he wanted to cause trouble,' added Anaya.

'They won't be able to prove where the money came from. The deposits just look like anonymous donations – he would simply look vindictive. Either way, we need to be careful,' said Julie.

'He could have told Barker-Smith with the prospect of working for him in mind. You know, quid pro quo,' said Anaya.

Everyone had an opinion, and they were all valid. Sam asked Maggie to increase her security. She nodded and explained that she'd installed motion sensors and cameras around her home.

As the meeting came to a close, and everyone started getting ready to head home, Maggie took Chloe aside.

'I'm sorry this has happened. I don't want you hurt. You're doing so much as mayor, and that's enough,' said Maggie.

'Don't worry, Maggie. It could all amount to nothing. He could just be blowing off steam. I'm just angry about being intimidated. This is twenty-first-century England, not the bloody Dark Ages. It makes me want to run for MP just out of spite.' Chloe smiled.

'Just as long as you know what you're doing, Chloe, my love,' said Sam, overhearing their conversation.

'I do,' said Chloe.

'Did he just call you "my love"?' asked Maggie.

'Not another word,' said Chloe, pointing her finger at Maggie.

'My lips are sealed,' smiled Maggie.

'When we're ready, we'll tell everyone. I haven't told Matthew yet,' said Chloe.

*   *   *

Security measures were put in place at Chloe's home. The trust also installed security measures inside their office and on the street outside. Maggie's motion sensors would trigger an alarm on her mobile if someone came snooping around. The footage would also be recorded and downloaded to her computer.

No one expected the threats to continue, but this didn't stop Chloe from being concerned by the threat. She finally understood Maggie's earlier frustration at how nothing ever changed. She was achieving so much, and she was afraid it would all come to an end. Chloe had no intention of resigning as Mayor of Totnes or Councillor of Friars Meadow. If it was a fight he wanted, it was a fight he would get. Her work was too important.

Chloe sat quietly on her couch, stroking Heathcliff. She hoped it would all blow over. Should she back down? If she pushed, he might push back. Chloe hadn't planned to run for MP of Totnes anyway. If she made this known, maybe they'd back off. Then again, maybe they'd come after her and the trust regardless.

A week later, during an interview, a reporter asked Chloe about her political ambitions for Totnes and the district of South

Hams. The reporter could sense a change in the air. Totnes was coming alive, and the reporter wanted to know what Chloe's ambitions for her future were. Why had she chosen to run as an independent?

'I believe I can make a significant difference to the lives of all the people living in Totnes,' said Chloe. 'But right now, I'm happy doing my work as mayor ...'

'What about the rumours that you're thinking of running for MP of Totnes?'

Chloe feigned surprise. 'Where did you hear that?'

'Just a rumour going around the council.'

'I have enough on my plate as mayor without the added pressure of running for MP.'

The reporter ended her article with a footnote: *Silverton for MP*.

Chloe was mad. The journalist was reckless to add in such a thing. She reiterated to anyone who cared to listen that she still had no intention of running in the next general election in May.

Still, the note she'd received still vexed her. Chloe chastised herself – she didn't want to draw any undue attention to herself or the trust.

*　　*　　*

'I don't think the warning worked,' said Malcolm Barker-Smith into his mobile. 'I think we should take it up a notch.'

'Send me the details you received about the trust, and I'll have my people look into it. If Silverton has accepted any funds for her campaign illegally, we'll find out what they are,' said Hamilton.

'I know she's up to something with that trust. I was told they've been throwing large amounts of money around for over a year,' said Barker-Smith.

Hamilton frowned. 'This is our last favour to you. We owe you nothing else. Understood?'

Barker-Smith understood, he didn't want to push is luck with Major Hamilton. 'Yes.'

*   *   *

Five days later, Chloe arrived home to find a package on her doorstep. She hadn't ordered anything online and felt unsure about opening it. She phoned Sam, who came around within four minutes. He approached the package and asked her to step back.

When he saw what was inside, he quickly closed the box.

'Chloe, go inside,' he instructed her grimly. When she was out of sight, he read the note that was attached to the inside of the box's lid.

If you run for MP, you will be as dead as your cat.

And then, below those words, was another menacing line, underlined and written in capitals.

WE KNOW.

Sam never allowed Chloe to glimpse the body inside the box. He took Heathcliff away and buried him in a beautiful spot in the garden.

Maggie arrived within the hour. She had never seen Chloe so distraught. Sam stressed to Maggie the seriousness of what had been done to Heathcliff. Who would go to such extremes to frighten Chloe? The cruelty of the person alarmed him.

Sam couldn't believe that Larry would do something like this. He was selfish and vindictive, but not cruel. The only other person to benefit from Chloe's not running would be Barker-Smith. He had more to lose than anyone else.

They had to assume it was Larry who had entered Maggie's house and then told Barker-Smith of her intentions. Sam couldn't believe an MP would do something like this. He may have hired someone to scare Chloe, but even so, he'd gone too far.

'On the day of the election, when he congratulated me on winning mayor, he made my flesh crawl,' said Chloe. 'Larry must have already told him about what he found in your house, Maggie.'

'The note said, "we know",' added Sam. 'What do they really know? Do they know where the money came from regarding the trust? Or only what Larry told him, which could be circumstantial at best?'

'I don't know,' said Maggie. 'My filing cabinet was locked. He only saw what was in my desk drawer.'

Chloe wanted to hurt the bastard. All she could think about was poor Heathcliff, to have died like that, frightened and in pain.

Chloe wanted payback. Nothing would stop her now. This she told Maggie with wet eyes when Maggie suggested dropping the whole idea now and in the future.

'If I quit now because I'm afraid, I don't deserve to be an MP, let alone a mayor,' Chloe sniffled.

Sam checked the CCTV cameras at Chloe's home and sent the video footage to the police. He also told them to check the cameras outside the trust's office and at Maggie's home, in case anyone had been lurking around there. Sam directed them to find the culprit – and soon, before he did.

The police reviewed the footage. They watched as a man walked up Chloe's path and placed the box on her doorstep. They couldn't see his face under the cap he wore, but at approximately the same time, a camera outside the trust picked up on another stranger. He lurked outside the trust office, looking in the windows before walking off. He tossed his cigarette butt onto the pavement as he left.

This second man was of a similar size and build to the man who'd visited Chloe's house. None of Chloe's friends recognised the man on the video. They now had to rule out Larry and Barker-Smith as the deliverer of the notes.

The police retrieved the cigarette butt from the sidewalk and sent it off to forensics. After a few days of waiting, they came up with a match.

The individual was flagged as high priority by the security services. The police would have called GCHQ, if GCHQ hadn't called the police station within five minutes of being alerted to the DNA match.

Club 26

'I think we've discovered who has the notebook. Barker-Smith asked me to look into a trust in Friars Meadow, a small town in Devon – and the Mayor of Totnes, Chloe Silverton,' said Hamilton.

'And …?' prompted Monroe.

'The trust has received well over a million in anonymous donations over the last year or so. If one of the people working at the trust found the case, they must have the notebook.'

'I want that fucking notebook,' Monroe said instantly.

'We need to tread carefully. I don't know yet who has the notebook. A Maggie Malloy opened the trust with fifty thousand pounds of her own money. It's more likely than not that she found it. She also worked at Provincial. God knows how she got the case open, though.'

'Find out who found the case, and what they did with the notebook. But for fuck's sake, be discreet,' said Monroe, through a haze of cigar smoke.

'Understood.'

Hamilton left Club 26. Finally, there was momentum. This fiasco was going to be over sooner rather than later. He headed back to his car. He had much to do.

Running Out of Time

July

A few days before poor Heathcliff was buried, Jonathan's team had their first lead in months relating to the investigation of the missing suitcase.

GCHQ had picked up a conversation between Barker-Smith and Major Hamilton. They had Barker-Smith's burner, thanks to Wickham. For months, the phone had been silent. But then, out of the blue, activity had started up again, with Barker-Smith needing to speak urgently with Major Hamilton about their agreement.

Hamilton agreed to meet Barker-Smith at the club. GCHQ had no operatives in the club, but their surveillance package was still in place. When Barker-Smith met with Hamilton, he handed him some documents. He asked if Hamilton's people would look into a trust and identify the Mayor of Totnes's involvement. He mentioned allegations of bribery and illegal funding.

GCHQ was not privy to the contents of the folder, so they were unsure if it related to Pandora. Either way, they needed to know what was inside it.

A week on, Jonathan walked out of number two, Marsham Street, after a meeting with the Home Office in Westminster. He raised his head towards the sun to feel its warmth – the bright sunlight was a stark contradiction to the dark and cold state of affairs he had just left. They knew the threat was still out there, and with this renewed activity, Jonathan was worried that Hamilton's team might have already located the missing suitcase.

During their meeting, one question kept being regurgitated around the table. What was this latest activity about? They agreed it was time to pull Barker-Smith in for questioning. Immunity from prosecution would be put on the table if necessary.

This didn't please Max or Jonathan. 'How many people will actually be arrested before all this is over?' Jonathan asked.

Max had to put his hand on Jonathan's arm to quieten him.

As Jonathan took in the fresh air – while waiting for their car back to Cheltenham to arrive – Max reminded him about decorum, and his lack of it. Jonathan watched as Londoners walked up and down the street, workers and tourists, oblivious to the problems they'd just discussed. How nice it would feel – to be so blissfully ignorant.

Jonathan checked his phone. There was a text from Angela: *Call urgently*.

He selected her name from his contacts and waited for her to respond.

'You wanted to know if anything ever came up about a Maggie Malloy,' said Angela.

'Yes, that's right,' said Jonathan, standing more erect.

Last month, he'd started digging into the trust. It was more out of curiosity than anything else. He simply wanted reassurance that she'd had no part in their investigation.

Jonathan barely knew Maggie, but from the moment he'd met her, he *still* hadn't been able to stop thinking about her. Romance had always taken the form of passing flings for Jonathan, but now he found himself questioning and lost in that thought.

'… killed Chloe Silverton's cat,' said Angela.

'Sorry, what did you say?' Jonathan pulled himself out of his reverie.

'Jonathan, the Butcher brothers were in Friars Meadow. They've been identified through DNA. One may have killed Mayor Silverton's cat. This can't be a coincidence. We have also picked up a conversation between Hamilton and Monroe – they think they know where the missing case is located. They mentioned Maggie Malloy and the trust,' said Angela.

'Send the conversations to my phone,' said Jonathan, as the car arrived to collect them.

On the drive back to work, Jonathan had his earplugs wedged tightly in his ears. He replayed the conversations several times. Barker-Smith was concerned about Mayor Silverton's popularity. He reminded Hamilton of their agreement, to which Hamilton said he would take care of things.

But the last conversation caught Jonathan's attention the most.

'I gave you that file over a week ago. You're not fobbing me off, are you?' said Barker-Smith.

'No, we're not. Did it not cross your mind to wonder where all that money came from?' That was Hamilton.

'No, they're donations,' replied Barker-Smith.

'Systematic donations totalling one million, in just over a year. Do the math,' said Hamilton.

The links clicked into place. 'Oh, fuck …'

'We'll take care of this from now on.' That was Hamilton again.

Barker-Smith then delicately pointed out that if it weren't for him, they wouldn't have a new lead. Barker-Smith also told Hamilton that Mayor Silverton's assistant, Maggie Malloy, had a dossier on him. Was it possible that she'd uncovered something about their operation?

Hamilton told Barker-Smith to relax. Everything he'd told them would be looked into, especially the trust and those who worked for it. He even mentioned how he'd been putting the Butcher brothers to use.

Jonathan knew how dangerous the Butcher brothers could be. He had to warn Maggie and the mayor, Chloe Silverton. He knew Barker-Smith was a leech but didn't know how far he would go to hold onto a seat, even one that had already been lost.

At least Jonathan knew now that the Butcher brothers were still in England, and last spotted in Devon.

Barker-Smith had mentioned a trust. Could he be referring to the Eve Merriweather Trust? After all, the only discernible link between Chloe and the trust was Maggie; she worked for both. Jonathan needed to figure out where Barker-Smith's lead came from, and why he was so concerned about the deposits.

Jonathan asked Angela to check their records and surveillance, to see if anyone from Friars Meadow had visited Barker-Smith's office or home, or called him in relation to Chloe Silverton, Maggie Malloy, or the Eve Merriweather Trust.

Did Barker-Smith have proof of corruption involving the trust and Chloe's campaign? Jonathan wasn't sure if it had anything to do with Pandora. If it didn't, it wasn't part of Jonathan's remit to investigate.

Jonathan looked out the car window. He needed to think. His mind raced back to the last time he'd seen Maggie. That Saturday, upon leaving Friars Meadow, he'd seen her out walking along the river. He could understand why – the countryside was beautiful. The rivers in Devon were obviously magnificent to trek along.

Jonathan's mind ticked off the facts. The Eve Merriweather Trust was small compared to most trusts. Maggie had been an employee at Provincial's Friars Meadow plant. The trust was opened legitimately with fifty thousand pounds from an inheritance. It had purchased a number of small to medium properties. What was its net worth?

A million-pound lightbulb just flicked on in Jonathan's head.

She couldn't have! It wasn't possible!

Oh, fuck, but she had.

Maggie had found the suitcase.

Jonathan sat upright in the car. He called Angela again and asked her to look into the financial records of the Eve Merriweather Trust, especially all the anonymous donations the trust had received since it opened. He stipulated that it was a priority.

For once in his life, he wanted to be wrong. Angela called back within ten minutes and gave him a rundown of the trust's financial figures, alongside the total amount of anonymous deposits.

Maggie had found the final suitcase and hidden the money in the trust. But how the hell had she opened the case?

He hoped Maggie still had the notebook. If he told Max about his suspicions, GCHQ would start a full investigation into Maggie and the trust. She would be arrested – he couldn't be that wrong about her.

If Jonathan said nothing, he would be withholding evidence of a crime. But if she was at the heart of Pandora, she would become a target for Hamilton and the Butcher brothers.

Barker-Smith would obviously do anything to be re-elected, but he would need evidence to accuse Chloe of corruption.

Was Maggie really a thief? Was Chloe? Were all her friends in on it?

Barker-Smith's file had led Hamilton directly to Maggie Malloy and Chloe Silverton. All those involved in the trust were in harm's way.

Jonathan needed to think. Max was tapping his arm. When Jonathan finally looked over at him, he realised he hadn't heard a word he was saying.

'Sorry, Max, could you repeat that?' Max had also been informed about the sightings in Friars Meadow.

'Listen, mate, this must be handled delicately,' said Max. 'This is our first lead in months. Tread carefully – Pandora's our priority, and any arrests are secondary. They know who has the suitcase. So, we better figure it out and get to them before Hamilton's people do. I want to see them arrested also, but the priority is Pandora.'

'If Hamilton and Monroe know who has the suitcase,' said Jonathan, 'it will put them at risk. If we get to them first, we can organise a sting operation and grab the Butcher brothers, Hamilton, and Monroe. So far, Monroe has kept in the shadows. We need to lure him out.' Jonathan sounded desperate.

'I know, but let's figure out who has that fucking case first,' said Max.

'I've been thinking about that,' said Jonathan.

Max knew that look on Jonathan's face – he needed to give him some space to think. So, he spent the rest of their journey quietly working on the day's cryptic crossword.

For the rest of their ride back to GCHQ, Jonathan started to formulate a plan. If it worked, it might just save Maggie and her friends. If it failed, he would put them directly in harm's way. Max mentioned that any arrests would be secondary to finding the case, which meant he had some wiggle room.

As they arrived back at the Doughnut, Jonathan asked Max a hypothetical question. Would they be willing to grant immunity to a couple of women for a lesser crime if they cooperated in securing Pandora, returning the money, and helping in the arrest of Monroe's people? Jonathan reminded Max of their immunity deal with Nicholas Wickham.

Max said he would consider it, depending on their involvement and cooperation.

'I need to speak with someone who might be able to confirm my suspicions,' he said.

Max trusted Jonathan's judgement completely and left it in his hands. Although, he warned Jonathan that he had until the end of the day to confirm his suspicions – Special Branch would be standing by.

Jonathan agreed and thanked his friend before heading off to his own car.

*   *   *

For Jonathan's sting operation to work, he would need Maggie and Chloe to cooperate. If his assumptions were correct about the trust's finances, it meant Maggie also has or had Pandora.

He doubted Maggie would be able to open Pandora. At the very least, she might have disposed of it. Either way, he needed to be sure. He had very little time. If Monroe's people were looking into the trust, they wouldn't waste any time on niceties. He had to warn Maggie and her friends of the danger.

Jonathan decided to speak with Chloe first. Then they could talk to Maggie together. If they agreed to cooperate, he might be able to secure them immunity. If they didn't, then it would be out of his hands.

That afternoon, he left Cheltenham for Friars Meadow. He estimated he'd arrive around 7 p.m. If there was no one at the trust's office, he would drive to Chloe's home.

It didn't take much research to find out where she lived. He didn't have time for subtlety. He would have to be direct and have his suspicions confirmed tonight.

Jonathan followed the M5 all the way down into Devon, as before. He had less than two hours to re-think his plan. It needed to be foolproof.

Angela called during his journey to confirm that one person had been seen a couple of times going into Barker-Smith's office from Friars Meadow: Larry Morecombe, ex-councillor of the town.

Jonathan now knew where the evidence had come from. There was nothing quite like revenge.

Cards on the Table

Once Jonathan arrived in town, he drove past the trust – which was closed – then to Chloe Silverton's home. She was not in either. Her neighbour suggested he try the pub, as she was spending a lot of time with the publican, Sam.

Jonathan drove to the pub and parked in the same spot. He walked up to the front door and held the handle for a moment. What if Maggie was in there? He knew that once he walked in, there was no turning back.

It was still light outside, but as he entered the warmly lit pub, the atmosphere was one of lively conversations. There was laughter over by the darts board and groups of people huddled together at their horseshoe tables. The clanking of glasses and music evaporating into background noise made for a spirited environment.

Jonathan surveyed the room but couldn't see Maggie or Chloe anywhere.

He walked up to the bar and asked the barman if he knew where Chloe Silverton was.

'Who wants to know?' came the reply.

'My name is Jonathan Swift.'

'If you're here to complain about the council, or ask for an interview, she's off the clock, so it can wait until tomorrow,' replied Sam.

'I'm not, but I need to talk to her and Maggie Malloy urgently,' said Jonathan.

'What about?' asked Sam, eyeing Jonathan more cautiously.

'It's a private matter.'

'Not from where I'm standing, it isn't,' said Sam.

'I believe Chloe Silverton and Maggie Malloy may be in danger. I would like to speak to them. I called in at her home, but she wasn't there,' said Jonathan.

'What kind of danger?' asked Sam, seriously.

'I'd rather discuss it with them.'

'I'd rather you discuss it with me first.'

This monologue could have gone on all night. Jonathan didn't have time for it. He had to dive in. 'I'm with the security services,' he said.

'You got ID?'

Jonathan produced his identification card.

Sam took a longer than necessary look. 'Listen,' he said. 'I care about both these women, especially Chloe. She's been threatened twice already. Are you here about that?' asked Sam.

'No. But I believe it could be connected. Please, I'm here to help them,' said Jonathan.

Sam stared at him for a moment. Then he asked one of the barmaids to take over for him.

'Come with me,' Sam said to Jonathan, as he came out from behind the bar. 'Where did you leave your car? I'll take you to Maggie's.'

'I'd rather speak with Chloe first,' said Jonathan.

'Chloe's at Maggie's – they play poker every Wednesday night,' said Sam, as they walked out of the pub.

'Thank you.'

The drive only took seven minutes. They exited Jonathan's car and walked up to Maggie's front door. As Jonathan traversed the path, he looked back at the town of Friars Meadow, spread out below him. The botanical gardens were beautiful from up high. He knew all the work done was thanks to the trust and Maggie – he was starting to understand why she'd done what she did with the money.

Sam knocked on the door and waited patiently for it to open. When it did, Jeremy was standing there.

'Hi, Jeremy, we're here to see Maggie and Chloe,' said Sam, stepping into the house.

'Who's he?' Jeremy nodded at Jonathan.

'Jonathan Swift,' he said.

'Got ID?' asked Jeremy.

'Not you too.'

'It's OK, Jeremy, he's with me,' interjected Sam.

'They're in the back room, playing poker,' said Jeremy, as he turned and walked back into the sitting room. 'They aren't scheduled to finish until 10 p.m.'

Sam smiled as he walked Jonathan through the house. He knocked on the door of the conservatory and heard a familiar voice.

'Someone better be bleeding,' yelled Morwenna.

Sam opened the door.

'Sorry to disturb, but you have a visitor.'

He stepped aside and Jonathan walked into the room.

Every mouth dropped to the floor.

Maggie slowly stood up. She couldn't believe what she was seeing: Jonathan standing right in front of her, in her conservatory. Initially, she had been flabbergasted when Julie told her he'd been at the pub, then she was piqued that he'd never come to see her.

'What are you doing here?' asked Maggie, as feelings of anxiety started to flutter in the pit of her stomach.

'I need to speak with you privately,' said Jonathan.

'Anything you have to say to Maggie you can say in front of all of us,' said Mrs McGuigan.

'It's personal.'

'We're all personal here,' said Morwenna.

Jonathan looked around the room. All the women were standing in a circle of defiance. They were clearly extremely loyal.

'I know where the money came from,' said Jonathan.

'What money?' asked Chloe

'The money in the trust.'

Everyone was still and quiet. They looked at each other, trying to read each other's thoughts.

'It was bequeathed to me,' said Maggie.

'I'm referring to all the deposits,' said Jonathan. 'But I'm not here to arrest you. That's not why I'm here.'

'What, then, are you after a cut?' asked Morwenna.

'No,' said Jonathan. Then he turned to face Maggie directly. 'I lied to you that afternoon in the bar. I don't work for the Chancellor of the Exchequer. That's what I tell people I'm not personally connected to. I work for the security services.'

Maggie was getting nervous. This was it – it was over.. It had been good while it had lasted. She could handle prison, as long as the government didn't undo every good thing she'd done.

Jonathan asked them to please sit down. 'I need to tell you a story,' he began. 'You're now a part of it, whether you like it or not. We need your help. But it could be dangerous. If you decide to help, the security services would be in a position to help you. But only if you cooperate.'

'Does it have to do with Barker-Smith?' enquired Chloe.

'Yes, it does,' said Jonathan.

'Go on,' said Chloe.

'I know the money came from the Provincial van heist,' he continued. Before they could defend themselves, he went on. 'I know you didn't hijack the van. However, those who did are still looking for the final case. They have killed three people so far. They're extremely dangerous. I know they killed your cat, Chloe, but that's nothing compared to what they'll do to the person who has that case. Barker-Smith works with those who want the case. He may have gotten his intelligence about your involvement from a certain Larry Morecombe. Barker-Smith passed this information on to his people to investigate – that'll lead them to you and to the trust, not to mention anyone else associated with it.'

'They'd do all this just for some money?' asked Julie.

'No, not just money,' said Jonathan, looking at Maggie. 'Please tell me you still have the black box that was inside the case.'

Everyone turned to look at Maggie, as they knew nothing about any box.

'Yes, I do,' said Maggie. Jonathan let out a sigh of relief.

'What do they have to do to rectify this?' asked Sam.

'I think I can offer you immunity, if we secure the black box and if you help us apprehend those responsible for the theft and murders.'

'All of us would need immunity,' said Maggie.

Maggie had dreaded this day – that her plans might come to an end. She wouldn't let her friends go down with her. Or worse, put them in danger.

But Jonathan could have her arrested, though he was choosing not to. Maggie realised for the first time just how important that black box must be. She instantly felt ashamed that she hadn't handed it in. It must be very important if the security services were still searching for it.

'What's in this black box, anyway? Diamonds?' asked Morwenna.

'I can't tell you that, but it's a matter of national security,' said Jonathan.

Maggie truly felt ashamed.

'If I help you,' she said, 'could you guarantee all my friends immunity? This was all my idea. If they need a scapegoat, it has to be me. Just me.' She was the one who had found the case and kept it.

This request brought a flood of loud protests.

Anaya asked her to say no more until she called Ernie Chandler.

'I know what you've been doing with the money. You've been giving it away through the trust,' said Jonathan.

Maggie's head was spinning. She felt she needed to tell this man everything. She hated the idea of him being ashamed of her, but she needed to think about her friends.

'Tell him, Maggie, it's OK. If it's to do with Barker-Smith, we have to stop him,' said Chloe.

For the next half hour, Maggie told Jonathan everything – from them losing their jobs, Eve committing suicide, and her accidently keeping the security keys, to finding the case in the river. She blurted it all out. By the end of the confession, Jonathan was smiling. Not because he'd enjoyed the story, but because of the sheer relief that she wasn't some devious criminal. It had never been about greed.

Jonathan told them he would speak with his superiors. If he could guarantee immunity for all of them, they would have to sign the Official Secrets Act, thus banning them from ever discussing what had and would take place.

Sam understood the seriousness of their situation and urged everyone to cooperate. When Jonathan asked where the black box was, Maggie took Jonathan to the window and pointed towards cupid sitting in his fountain. Jonathan needed to speak with his superiors, but he couldn't leave without securing Pandora. So, he and Sam agreed to stay the night and stand watch over it until it could be retrieved in the morning.

'What about Ernie, Alisha, and Mrs McGuigan?' asked Morwenna. 'They'll need immunity also. She's seventy if a day. You can't lock her up.'

'I can take care of myself, Morwenna. Jail doesn't frighten me. Just you try, sonny,' Mrs McGuigan said to Jonathan.

Jonathan asked how many other people were involved in the cover-up.

'Probably everybody in town by now,' said Morwenna.

Maggie told Jonathan about everyone who directly knew, but she agreed with Morwenna that half the town had their suspicions.

Jonathan smiled at the thought of an entire town cover-up. He excused himself from the room while he made a call to Max.

Once he hung up, he asked if he could have a moment alone with Maggie. She agreed, and they walked out of the room and into the kitchen together. While they were out of the room, Chloe called Ernie.

'Well, I think we have our "get out of jail free card",' said Morwenna.

'Yes, it appears so. But what will we have to do to earn it?' asked Anaya.

'Whatever it is, we can't let Maggie take all the blame,' said Julie.

'Either way, Barker-Smith is dangerous – we can confidently assume it was him who threatened Chloe, or else those Butcher brothers he mentioned,' said Sam.

They all nodded in agreement. Chloe told everyone present she would do whatever she had to in order to bring that son-of-a-bitch Barker-Smith to his knees.

Chloe then sat quietly while the rest talked. She loved being mayor and had much to lose if they were exposed. She still had so much to do. Would they let her keep her job? She didn't want to resign as mayor of Totnes or councillor of Friars Meadow. Chloe didn't want it to end. Not now.

*   *   *

'I don't want you to think I've been stalking you or anything like that,' Jonathan said, once they were in the kitchen. 'It wasn't until your name came up in our investigation. You hired a private detective to look into Barker-Smith. We had to get McIntyre to stop his investigation, as we had an operation in progress and couldn't risk any interference. I didn't even connect your name to who hired him until a colleague mentioned it. We were satisfied that you had nothing to do with the robbery.'

'It's OK, I understand,' Maggie replied. 'I was looking into Barker-Smith for Chloe – only, she wasn't even thinking of running for MP. Not at the next election anyway.' She paused to think for a moment before continuing. 'I know what I did was wrong,' she admitted. 'I should have handed the keys back to Provincial as soon as I realised I had them. But when I found the case, I took it as a sign. You know, to do something good with it. I was still so angry back then. If I handed the case in, nothing would have changed. I desperately wanted things to change. I don't want anyone to get hurt or arrested because of what I did. It was all my idea. If they need to string someone up, please just let it be me,' she pleaded. 'My friends have children. Chloe's now the mayor. They have more to lose than I do.'

'The final decision will be made by my superiors. But there is a lot at stake – I will fight your corner, Maggie. You will need to give the money back. But GCHQ's main priority is Pandora. Three people have been murdered because of that box,' Jonathan said.

'I understand, it's been in a safe place,' said Maggie. 'I've caused you a lot of stress, haven't I?'

'You kept us on our toes, there's no denying that,' Jonathan laughed.

The night ended when Maggie put down the phone to Ernie. He would review the documents that GCHQ needed signed in the morning. He said he had much to research before then.

After hanging up the phone, Maggie looked outside at the fountain. She felt guilty at keeping hidden such an important possession. If she had known, she would have turned it in immediately. She hoped the lives lost weren't due to her actions.

As Jonathan walked through Maggie's house that evening, he got to know the type of person she was by the warmth and personality that emanated from each room. As she headed off to bed, Jonathan spoke to her quietly in passing.

'I'm glad I met you that afternoon in the Rivoli Bar. I was truly sad at the thought of never seeing you again — I would have liked to have known you better.' Then he grinned and said, 'Maybe, when this is all over, we can have another drink.' They smiled at each other before Jonathan turned and walked back into the conservatory. Special Branch was sending a team, and while Sam stayed in the front of the house, Jonathan watched the back. He would keep both eyes on the fountain until they arrived.

In the morning, Max Evans arrived and presented Maggie and her friends with immunity papers. They were given to Ernie, who scrutinized them carefully.

Max was taken aback by how many people needed immunity. All of them had openly participated in the conspiracy, regardless of the consequences. He could see that Maggie obviously had loyal friends.

When Maggie asked Max what was to stop politicians or the police investigating the trust in future and wanting to make an example of them, he explained it to her like this: 'You've embarrassed them. It's as simple as that, Maggie. If they ever figure out what you've done, which I doubt they will, they'll see you've done what they've been incapable of doing. You spent money to make money. You created jobs and re-energised the economy in your town and around Totnes. That's why the Home Secretary has given you immunity. But if you step out of line again, they'll throw the book at you. Needless to say, you'll no longer be a part of the trust.'

Everyone signed the security papers without hesitation, and everyone agreed to Jonathan's plan equally fast. They listened intently as it became apparent to all in the room just how low down in the criminal chain they actually were.

The security services had removed Maggie's cupid from the fountain. When they dug up the earth beneath it, they uncovered a large suitcase. Sitting inside the case was a lone black metal box. Max placed Pandora in an official security case and handcuffed it to his wrist. He left without adieu and headed back to GCHQ with an armed escort.

To initiate Jonathan's plan, they needed Barker-Smith to believe that Maggie still had the black box. He knew they would have to tread carefully, but he needed to bait Barker-Smith into action. GCHQ had Pandora back; any arrests now would be a bonus. They could arrest Barker-Smith and Hamilton on what they had so far, but Jonathan wanted Monroe. Everything that had happened had been on his authority.

I'll Huff and I'll Puff

Larry Morecombe had been most helpful. On their first meeting, they discussed Chloe Silverton's popularity and her campaign plans. Barker-Smith had been appreciative for the heads up. He thanked Larry accordingly and offered to look after him once he was re-elected.

Larry asked Malcolm – as they were now on a first-name basis – if he would investigate the trust also. Barker-Smith agreed, but as he was too pre-occupied with removing his competition, he paid little attention to the goings on of a small-town trust. If he had, he would have made the connection between the trust and their missing suitcase.

Barker-Smith reassured Larry that he knew the right people to look into the trust's financial records and said he would be in touch.

Larry had asked Malcolm to be judicious, as the information came from a friend. Larry didn't want to implicate Thomas Carlyle in the corruption.

Larry was proud of his investigation. He hoped it would impress Malcolm enough for the MP to offer him a position on his staff.

Barker-Smith had called Major Hamilton to arrange a meeting. During that meeting, he handed Hamilton a folder containing details of possible money laundering. Could they see if there was a link between the trust and Chloe Silverton? Enough to end her career?

Barker-Smith didn't much like Larry. He knew why the man had been sacked as councillor, but he had been useful, and so he would find a dark corner to put him in, for now. Major Hamilton would deal with Chloe Silverton, then he would deal with Larry Morecombe.

Barker-Smith loathed the Butcher brothers. He feared Hamilton and regretted ever getting into bed with any of them. However, he had to think about his re-election.

This had all transpired over a week ago. After his last conversation with Hamilton, he realised what a fool he'd been. As Barker-Smith read through the paperwork on the Eve Merriweather Trust, the dates fitted. They wouldn't be pleased. He had risked a great deal in helping Hamilton and Monroe to get Bridget's notebook, and now he was starting to wonder if it had all been worth it.

Although Maggie and Chloe may have spent the money, they would still have the notebook – unless they'd disposed of it. Either way, they were Hamilton's problem now. If they knew what was on the notebook and what it was worth ... Well, that was another matter entirely. Monroe didn't like loose ends.

He knew Major Hamilton would use the services of the Butcher brothers again. That thought made his blood run cold.

They were disgusting human beings. The sooner this was over with, the better. Barker-Smith never thought for a moment that he would also be a liability.

*   *   *

A few days later, Elle Morecombe walked into the council's office in Totnes and asked a receptionist if she could speak with Chloe Silverton. When asked if she had an appointment, she answered no but stressed that she needed to speak with her urgently. The receptionist could see that Elle Morecombe was distressed.

In hushed tones, the receptionist called Chloe, and within five minutes, Elle Morecombe was in Chloe's office, sitting across from her.

'Thank you for seeing me at such short notice,' said Elle in a sombre voice.

'You're welcome, but I'm at a loss as to why.'

'My husband told me he had a new job offer in Totnes, for our MP Malcolm Barker-Smith. He seems to be quite satisfied with himself. A friend overheard him bragging in the pub the other day about ending your career. I believe he gave Malcolm Barker-Smith evidence of corruption.'

'That would fit. Someone entered Maggie's home and found documents regarding my campaign not long before I was threatened. I assure you, I'm not involved in any corruption. I've only received valid donations, and I never bribed anyone,' said Chloe. Then she added, 'You've taken a risk in telling me this, Elle.'

Elle Morecombe started to cry.

'I'm so sorry, Ms Silverton.'

'Chloe, please,' she said, as she rose from her chair and walked around her desk to hand Elle a tissue.

'I know it was my husband. He hated losing his job as councillor the way he did. I know he wasn't a good councillor. He let more people down than he helped. I'm sure this Barker-Smith will realise his worthlessness and drop him like a brick.'

'Thank you for telling me, Elle. I don't want to come between you and your husband. But he's aligning himself with dangerous people.' Chloe knew she couldn't tell her much about Barker-Smith because of the GCHQ investigation.

'When he became councillor, I was so pleased for him. I thought how good it would be to work side-by-side with him, looking after the community. But he didn't want my help – he never stuck his neck out for anyone. It was such a waste.'

'Serving the community isn't for everyone. I never thought I would love it as much as I do. And we could always use an extra pair of hands. You're not your husband,' Chloe affirmed.

'Thank you for saying so,' Elle sniffled. 'I'd like that. But I came here today to warn you – Larry's threats were not exaggerated. He believes you're going to get your comeuppance. He said Barker-Smith has evidence that can prove where your campaign funds came from. That Eve's trust has been laundering money and paying bribes on your behalf.' Elle wiped her nose with the tissue. 'You and your friends at the trust have done amazing things. You've injected life back into our town again. I never thought that possible. I knew Eve. She shouldn't have died the way she did, believing there was no hope left. Thomas Carlyle was her branch manager. I don't believe he helped Eve as he should have with her mortgage.'

'What do you mean?' asked Chloe.

'I don't have any proof, but I don't think he gave her sufficient advice on re-structuring her repayments. I don't know all the ins and outs, but he and my husband own a few of the foreclosure properties in town. Thomas organised the loans. A few other branch managers are doing it, also. They buy the foreclosure properties and then lease them until their value rises. It's disgusting. I believe Thomas Carlyle also gave my husband information on the trust's finances,' said Elle.

'He couldn't. The trust doesn't bank at Carlyle's bank,' said Chloe, becoming angry.

'I know. He called in a favour.'

This information made Chloe's face burn red. They sat quiet for a moment.

'Does your husband know you're here or how you feel?' asked Chloe gently.

'No, he's oblivious to anything that doesn't revolve around him,' said Elle.

'Good. Will you help us to set things right, then?'

'That's why I'm here.'

'And what will you do once we've done that, Elle?' asked Chloe.

Elle's face was set. 'Divorce the narcissistic bastard.'

*   *   *

Chloe passed on her conversation with Elle Morecombe to Jonathan's team at GCHQ, as previously agreed under the terms of their agreement.

Chloe knew the branch foreclosures did not fall under Jonathan's remit, but he'd said he would pass the information on to the appropriate authorities.

'Politicians love a corruption scandal that doesn't involve them,' said Jonathan.

'Thank you,' said Chloe dryly.

Now Jonathan knew who Barker-Smith had received his intelligence from. It was time to get the ball rolling. Hamilton would have fully investigated the trust by now, and its staff. GCHQ's only advantage was that Hamilton and his team didn't know they had Pandora.

As agreed, Chloe formally announced her candidacy for MP of Totnes at the next general election. She actually had no intention of running, but it would get Barker-Smith's attention. GCHQ needed him to take a bite. It was time to rid Devon of Malcolm Barker-Smith MP once and for all.

Jonathan had promised to deal with Thomas Carlyle and the others once their investigation was over. At the very least, he would lose his job. If these practices were widespread, there would have to be a full royal commission on banking practices.

Barker-Smith's evidence regarding the trust would be inadmissible in court, since it was obtained illegally. But it wouldn't stop others from investigating the trust in the future. There would always be risk of discovery. The trust needed to take appropriate steps to secure its future. Even though Maggie and her friends had their 'get out of jail free' cards, the trust did not.

Notwithstanding that, no one wanted the trust to close.

Chloe spoke to Maggie about it over dinner. They had to find a way to protect the trust. They had already taken steps to repay the money, as instructed. The sale of The Right Step to its employees had increased the trust's bank balance. But now, the trust's coffers were drastically reduced, though they still had numerous projects producing revenue. Yet, Maggie knew that the trustees would definitely have to scale down future activities. She'd done what she could.

No Turning Back

Early August

Lance Corporal Sean Butcher stood outside the Eve Merri-weather Trust on Highgrove Street. He could see two women inside. From their photos, he knew them to be Morwenna Stewart and Julie Hart. He took a good look – *not bad looking*, he thought. He hoped he didn't have to hurt either of them.

The Butcher brothers' assignment was to find out which one had discovered the missing case, and their odds were on Maggie Malloy. They were to search her home, and if there was nothing there, they would search the trust's office. Sean and his brother, Chris, could finally put this charade to bed and move forward with their business enterprise. If they couldn't find the case, they would have to conduct their search more vigorously. Then, they could get the hell out of Devon, and England, altogether.

The brothers weren't going down like Andrews. They had never met Monroe, only dealing with Hamilton. He had always been straight with them.

While Sean Butcher surveyed the trust, Chris Butcher drove up to Maggie's house. He knew she was in Totnes with Chloe that morning, so he wouldn't be disturbed. As he walked around the porch, checking the windows and doors, he failed to notice the two new motion sensor cameras high up in the trees, which automatically came on as he walked past. They each had a ninety-degree view in their respective directions. An identical pair were situated on the opposite side of the house.

By the time Chris Butcher had broken the lock on the back door and let himself in, the camera had triggered a message to Maggie's mobile, alerting her to a break-in.

Unfortunately, Maggie was having lunch with Chloe and a couple of her staff in a noisy restaurant and couldn't hear her mobile beep.

It wasn't until 2.10 p.m. that Maggie finally checked her mobile and saw the messages. She quickly dialled Jonathan and Sam and told them the alarm had gone off. Sam headed straight over to her house. He didn't wait for the police but instead stormed up the hill to confront anyone who might still be there.

But when he got there, it was empty. Jonathan, arriving shortly after Sam, accessed Maggie's computer to view the recorded video of the intruder.

Within ten minutes, Jonathan confirmed it was one of the Butcher brothers. He was long gone by the time Sam arrived, and her home had been ransacked.

He had obviously been looking for Pandora. Jonathan insisted Maggie grant them permanent access to her security system at home so they can be alerted immediately of any intruders.

Maggie raced home. As she walked through her home, surveying the damage, she couldn't hold back her tears. She felt dirty

and angry at the callous disregard he'd had for her life's possessions. Things had been smashed and thrown about in each room.

Sam gave her his shoulder to cry on, and insisted she not stay
there tonight. Jonathan sent a police forensic team to sweep the
house – he doubted they would find anything, but they needed to
proceed as they would for any home invasion.

Jonathan decided it was time to drop some breadcrumbs.

Everyone was called to an emergency meeting at the pub
after closing time.

Jonathan, Ernie, Mrs McGuigan, Sam, Maggie, Chloe, Julie,
Anaya, and Morwenna were all present. The Butcher brothers
would be apprehended – it was only a matter of time. But until
then, Maggie needed to stay with one of her friends.

Before everyone could offer, Mrs McGuigan spoke up:
'She'll stay with me.' That was the final word on the matter. If the
Butcher brothers were watching, they would assume she'd been
spooked by the break-in and would naturally stay with a friend.

In the pub, they discussed Jonathan's plan. They had to pro-
voke Barker-Smith into showing his hand. Jonathan needed Maggie to confront Barker-Smith about the trust and the missing case.

GCHQ had listening watches on all of its suspects. A new
agent had been stationed in Club 26, to listen in case talk about
the notebook picked up again.

*   *   *

That same evening, after a long and desperately needed bath at
Mrs McGuigan's, Maggie came downstairs feeling refreshed.
She was swiftly handed a glass of red wine.

'White wine just won't cut it tonight,' Mrs McGuigan promptly stated, taking a leaf out of Chloe's book. Mrs McGuigan then went back into the kitchen to fix dinner.

Maggie was beginning to realise just how dangerous their situation was. She had put her friends in danger – real danger. That was unforgivable. She picked up her mobile and called Jonathan. She needed to hear his voice – to be reassured that this was their best option.

'Don't worry, you'll be wired the whole time,' said Jonathan.

'But what if they frisk me?' she asked.

Jonathan laughed. 'Our technology is far more sophisticated than most people realise. I'm counting on them to check, but they won't find anything.'

On hearing his laugh, Maggie began to calm down. The warmth she felt wasn't from her bubble bath – nor from the red wine she held in her hand.

They said their goodbyes, and then Maggie took a deep breath and called Barker-Smith.

'Who?' he asked, feigning ignorance.

'My name is Maggie Malloy. I work for Chloe Silverton. I believe Larry Morecombe has been speaking to you about me and my trust.'

Larry couldn't confirm or deny their conversation, as Special Branch had picked him up earlier in the day and were holding him until their sting operation was over.

'I know Larry Morecombe gave you financial documents pertaining to the trust. Illegally obtained, I might add,' said Maggie.

'I'm sorry, I don't know what you're talking about,' said Barker-Smith.

'He was overheard boasting about it in the pub. He wants to hurt Chloe and spread lies of bribery and corruption,' continued Maggie.

'I don't know any Larry Morecombe,' Barker-Smith went on.

Maggie raised her voice. 'Oh yes, you do! He came to your office with information about Chloe's future campaign ideas. He was hoping to score a job with you. Someone broke into my house yesterday, and I know it was Larry or someone you hired. Stop threatening Chloe and leave the trust alone.'

'Or what, young lady?' For the first time, Maggie felt a chill run down her back. She heard evilness in his voice.

'If you don't stop, I'll go to the police. I have witnesses to Larry's drunken rant.'

'I wouldn't do that if I were you,' warned Barker-Smith.

'You try and stop me. I know he broke into my home and photographed documents in my drawer.'

'Stealing is a crime, Miss Malloy.'

'What are you talking about?' Maggie finally had Barker-Smith hooked on the line, and now she had to remain calm to reel him in. Jonathan was recording their conversation at GCHQ, and Maggie was doing well.

'I know where the deposits came from – the ones that you've been systematically depositing into your trust for over a year.'

'I, I don't know what you're talking about ...'

'Come now, Miss Malloy, yes you do. Don't be coy.' She could tell that Barker-Smith believed he was getting the upper hand.

'When did you find the case?'

'What case?'

'The Provincial security case. I'm not sure how you got the case open, but I'm not the one you need to worry about. The people I work for are extremely dangerous. They've killed for this case. The money doesn't interest them. They only want the steel box that was inside it.'

Maggie remained quiet for a moment.

'Please tell me you still have it,' continued Barker-Smith. Maggie paused for a moment, then spoke.

'I do.'

She could almost feel his smile through the phone. 'Good. Then the sooner you hand it over, the better for everyone involved. Mayor Silverton's cat was a small example of what these people are capable of,' said Barker-Smith.

'How do I know they'll leave me and Chloe alone once I give it to them?' asked Maggie, on cue.

'You don't. I suggest you try and offer up a deal of some sort. But Chloe Silverton will not be running for MP of Totnes. Do you understand?' said Barker-Smith firmly.

'Yes, you can have the stupid thing, it doesn't open anyway,' said Maggie, as rehearsed. She heard a sigh of relief on the other end of the line. So did GCHQ.

Barker-Smith said he would organise for someone to meet her and collect the box. Maggie refused, stating that she wanted assurance she would be left alone after she handed it over. Barker-Smith stated he wasn't a go-between but an MP. If she wanted assurances, she'd have to talk about that when she met with them.

All Barker-Smith would do was organise the rendezvous. The rest would be up to her. He wanted no part in the exchange, but he promised he would be in touch.

After this, he hung up.

Barker-Smith was genuinely relieved that Maggie Malloy wanted to meet with Hamilton and not him. He could finally wash his hands of the whole affair.

He didn't want to think of what Hamilton or the Butcher brothers might do to her.

*   *   *

'She has it,' said Malcolm.

'Thank god. Tell her you'll collect it in the morning,' said Hamilton.

'No, she won't go for that. She wants to meet you. She wants assurances she'll be left alone after the exchange. She's worried about her friend, Mayor Silverton, and the trust.'

'OK … Call her back and tell her I'll meet her tomorrow on the north side of the Totnes Bridge at 10 a.m.,' said Hamilton.

Barker-Smith called Maggie again, who agreed to his terms. He gave her the location and time, then hung up.

Mrs McGuigan came back into the living room.

'Dinner's ready!' she smiled. 'Is it all sorted?'

Maggie nodded, but she felt grim. 'It soon will be.'

*   *   *

'Maggie Malloy has it. Sean will meet with her tomorrow,' said Hamilton.

'Why not you? Why send one of the brothers?' asked Monroe.

'She wants assurances, so I doubt she'll have it on her. We'll see what she wants. We need to avoid any more bloodshed.'

'Get it done,' said Monroe, before he hung up.

*   *   *

The following day, Maggie sat on a seat by the river, admiring the view. The natural, hypnotic rhythm of the water relaxed her as she tried to stay calm.The water was reassuring until Sean Butcher sat down beside her.

Jonathan's surveillance team were not far away, hidden in the trees. When Jonathan saw one of the Butcher brothers approach, it put him on edge. He told his team to be ready. Jonathan didn't believe that the ex-soldier would try anything in public, but the man was unpredictable.

Sean Butcher leaned over and ran a scanner over Maggie. She felt a little surprised, but Jonathan had told her they would do this – to make sure she wasn't recording the conversation. Once he was satisfied, he spoke.

'Give me your mobile,' he demanded.

Maggie complied. He turned it off and removed the chip and battery.

'All we want is the black box. You can keep the money.'

'Are you in charge?' asked Maggie.

'No, but I work for those who are,' he replied.

'I want to speak to whoever is in charge. I want assurances from them,' said Maggie.

'That's not my concern. The only thing that should matter to you is handing over the box. We'll leave you alone once we have it.'

'Will you leave Chloe Silverton alone and allow her to run for MP?'

'That's not up to me. *Do you have it*?' His voice was rising, growing aggressive.

Maggie felt her heartbeat quicken, but she forced herself to remain strong. 'No not on me. I want a guarantee first. Leave me, Chloe, and the trust alone, and then I'll give you the stupid box. What's in it, anyway?' asked Maggie.

'Don't concern yourself with that. I don't think you know who you're dealing with. What happened to your friend's cat was nothing compared to what will be done to you and your friends if you don't hand it over.'

Maggie was getting frightened. She was out of her depth, but she had to finish the script. She took a deep breath.

'I've told you what I want – for you to get what you want. You need to speak with whoever you take your orders from and tell them my demands. I want assurances. In exchange, I'll hand over the box to your boss in person. That way, we'll both have something to lose if anyone breaks the agreement. So, don't send a patsy to meet with me.' Maggie grabbed back her phone. As she stood up, about to walk off, she turned and said: 'You have my number. Call me if we have a deal.'

Maggie slowly walked off, as instructed. Her brain told her to run quickly, but her legs said no – they were so stiff she thought they would snap.

Sean Butcher hated playing games. But this was not his call. He phoned Major Hamilton and relayed the conversation. Hamilton told him to stand by, but to be ready for the exchange.

Unbeknownst to Sean Butcher, underneath the seat was a scanner that was downloading every megabyte of data on his phone. GCHQ was now listening to Sean's conversation with Hamilton on his pay-as-you-go mobile. Now, and until Sean tossed his phone away, GCHQ could listen to all his conversations, and track his location. When the time was right, GCHQ would make the arrests. They knew the Butcher brothers would be at the exchange, and they would be able to arrest Hamilton and the brothers.

Maggie called Jonathan soon after she left the riverbank. Jonathan thanked her and told her the encounter had gone well. Now they just had to sit back and wait.

*   *   *

At Club 26, during lunch, Archibald Monroe asked James Hamilton if he trusted Miss Malloy. Hamilton couldn't give a definite answer but told Monroe that Miss Malloy hadn't had a criminal record up until the time she found the case.

'She only wants to protect her friends and the trust,' he said. 'The encryption box was locked, so she doesn't know what's in it. She's scared but wants a guarantee that she and her friends will not be harmed.'

He doubted that Mayor Silverton would challenge the seat of Totnes. Barker-Smith would not be happy if she did, but he had served his purpose, and had much to lose if he crossed them. He would be dealt with if he became a problem.

'What if we send someone else in my place?' asked Monroe.

'Not possible, Ms Malloy hired a private detective and knows about the link between Phoenix and Barker-Smith,' replied Hamilton.

Archibald Monroe was quiet for a moment while he weighed up his options.

'It's better to just agree to her terms,' said Hamilton. 'The encryption box is the most important card on the table. It will all be over with by this time tomorrow.'

'If she knows that Barker-Smith was working with us, we will need to pay her private detective a visit,' said Monroe.

'This is getting out of hand,' Hamilton protested. 'We don't need to draw any more attention to ourselves. She wants to talk with you. Once you give her assurances that she'll be left alone to run her trust, she'll hand over the box. Then it's finished with.'

Monroe knew there was too much at stake – he'd made promises himself. He agreed to meet with Miss Malloy.

'Once we've verified what's on the key, I want Maggie Malloy taken care of. Am I clear?' said Monroe.

'Yes,' said Hamilton. He got up to leave. He had someplace else he needed to be, and if all went according to plan tomorrow, his future would be secure.

Maggie received a text shortly after 2 p.m. with a time and place. She sent back a reply: *Agreed.*

They were to meet at the same location at 7 a.m. the next day.

*   *   *

Jonathan's team were in position on both sides of the river. GCHQ had communications covered, while Special Branch had officers completely surrounding the rendezvous site. An SO19 team were waiting to move in. They still had no sightings of the Butcher brothers but knew that they had to be nearby. Sean's mobile was nowhere near the rendezvous site; he must have left it behind.

All the players were coming together. Jonathan's only concern was for Maggie. She wasn't trained for this, and he'd put her life at risk once already. But now, he needed her to do it again.

Maggie fervently stated that she wanted to do it; she needed to atone for the theft. Plus, her friends' freedom was at stake.

Maggie was wearing a bullet-proof vest, given to her by Jonathan. It was lightweight but would stop almost anything. Jonathan didn't think Hamilton would dare have Maggie targeted out in the open – not with so many people around. If they did try anything, it would be once Maggie got back to her car, or possibly once she arrived home.

Jonathan watched Maggie from inside a black transit van. They had multiple cameras trained on her and the surrounding areas. He had reassured her that she would never be alone.

Maggie sat on a park bench. Her leg kept involuntarily tapping on the ground. It was five minutes past the allotted time; maybe it was a setup. Maybe they weren't coming.

Jonathan had given her the encryption box. The notebook was inside, but it could not be copied. Whoever came to collect the notebook would check its authenticity, but that's all they could do.

Max Evans had reluctantly agreed to this. They needed to apprehend Hamilton and the Butcher brothers, if or when they turned up. GCHQ placed a tracking chip inside the encoder as an extra measure. They had more men and women guarding it than the Prime Minister.

It was 7.15 p.m., and still no one appeared.

Then it was 7.30 a.m., and with no one in sight, Maggie held on a bit longer.

Finally, at nearly 8.00 a.m., Maggie got up and started to walk away. What had gone wrong? She felt vulnerable sitting there. It had been agreed that if no one turned up after an hour, she was to get up and leave. Maybe they were testing her.

As she started to walk along the path, a man approached her. Immediately, she knew this was it.

'Hello, young lady, will you walk with me?' the man said. She recognised his face from a list of suspects that Jonathan had shown her. He was Archibald Monroe, the managing director of Phoenix Security. Maggie was shocked – she'd expected Hamilton.

'I'm sorry I kept you waiting, young lady,' said Monroe.

'Why did you, then?' asked Maggie. 'I thought this was important to you.'

'I needed to make sure you were alone,' he replied. 'Do you have the device on you?'

'Yes.'

'Why don't we sit here under the bridge, and we'll confirm that,' he said.

This was a clever move by Archibald Monroe. They had walked from an open area to underneath the bridge arch next to the river. Hidden from view, Maggie was getting apprehensive – it was not going to plan. But she trusted Jonathan.

'When did you find the money, Maggie?' asked Monroe.

'When I was out walking along the river, in February last year,' she replied.

'And you used it to start a trust, correct?'

'I used my own money to start up the trust, but I topped it up with the money from the case.'

'You do know that if you speak about this to anyone, I will see to it that your friends will go to jail. You, on the other hand, will not get off so lightly,' threatened Monroe.

'I do. I want my friends kept out of it. They don't know about the box – only the money,' said Maggie.

'Really?'

Maggie realised quickly that she shouldn't have said this. It implied that no one knew she was here, talking to him.

'That's good. That means no one will gossip if they've had too much to drink,' said Monroe. 'Now, please give me the box.'

Maggie unzipped her grandfather's backpack and took out the black box. As she did so, a man walked up to them and stopped.

It was Hamilton. He unzipped his backpack and removed a device, which he attached to the black metal box. It started to scan the six locking mechanisms, and when it finished the box opened. Hamilton took the notebook out of the box and threw the box into the river. Then, he retrieved a small cable and computer from his backpack. He attached the cable to the notebook and waited while it confirmed what was on the device.

All three of them were silent for what seemed like a lifetime. Finally, Hamilton nodded to Monroe. It was the real deal.

'You're a smart young lady, Miss Malloy,' said Monroe.

As Monroe rose to leave, he turned to Maggie. 'You've kept your end of the bargain, so I'll keep mine. I hope we never see each other again. If we do, it will not be to your advantage.'

He nodded at her and left with Hamilton.

Maggie's heart was beating so loud that she thought they might hear it. She hadn't realised she'd been holding her breath.

She'd done it! It was finally over.

Once they were gone, she stood up, as instructed, and walked back towards her car. Her car was parked on the side of the road, beside a line of trees. She finally felt relieved when she saw her car up ahead.

But this feeling was short-lived when she noticed one of the Butcher brothers coming towards her.

He had a baseball cap on and sunglasses, but she recognised him from the video footage taken at her home. She started to panic. This was not in the script. She didn't know what to do. Stop? Run? What? If she turned and ran, he would know something was wrong. Her brain was racing – what was she going to do? She started to slow her pace. But, as she got to within fifty feet of him, two heavily armed SO19 officers appeared from nowhere and yelled for him to put his hands in the air.

His startled expression was visible only for a fraction of a second as he reached into his jacket and pulled out a gun. He aimed it at one of the SO19 officers, but the officer reacted immediately and fired first. Three bullets ripped through Christopher Butcher's chest and sent him flying backwards.

By the time the SO19 officers reached him, he was already dead.

SO19 quickly removed Maggie from the scene, in case the other Butcher brother was on the end of a sniper rifle.

While Christopher Butcher shot at the SO19 officers, a second unit descended on Major Hamilton and Archibald Monroe. The major, being more experienced, didn't follow in the same fashion as Chris Butcher. Seeing the amount of armour that SO19 were wearing, and knowing they never missed, he immediately surrendered and lifted his weapon high into the air.

Jonathan secured the key from Hamilton and had both of them arrested. The security cameras they'd installed underneath the bridge captured every word and every image of their conversation. Their arrests were rock solid.

Within minutes of their arrests, similar arrests were being made at the office of Malcolm Barker-Smith MP and at Club 26, where their surveillance team secured three other members who'd conspired with Archibald Monroe to purchase the software from him.

In the weeks and months to come, more arrests would be made in Friars Meadow. Thomas Carlyle and four other bank managers in the Totnes area were also arrested. Their charges included breaches of personal information and national banking practices.

Elle Morecombe said nothing as the police escorted her husband from their home. 'Call my lawyer!' he urged her desperately, as he was dragged from the house. Elle Morecombe would call a lawyer; her new lawyer, Ernie Chandler, asking him to start divorce proceedings. She took a bottle of wine from the fridge, sat down, and had a long, slow drink. She allowed a very slight smile to pull at the corner of her mouth.

*   *   *

Sean Butcher had seen everything through his sniper scope. His temper seething, he watched as SO19 gunned down his brother. He had no shot of protecting his twin, since there were too many of them.

He watched as they surrounded Maggie Malloy and escorted her into a car. *That bitch had set them up. How long had they known?* His anger grew as he kept staring at the body of his fallen brother.

He remained in his position for some time, watching the scene across the river. A tall man in a bullet-proof vest approached Chris' body. He gave several orders to the SO19 officers; he was obviously the man in charge.

Sean watched the man walk up to the car, where the Malloy woman was sheltered. She stepped out and hugged him. He stroked her face, then helped her back into the car and watched as she was sped away with a security officer.

Sean Butcher removed himself from the roof of the building. As he walked calmly back to his van, he repeated to himself, over and over, 'That fucker will pay.'

A Stitch in Time

Early September

Jonathan was becoming more and more apprehensive. There had been no sightings of Sean Butcher. No voice or facial recognition had been picked up by GCHQ. Max Evans pointed out the obvious – Sean Butcher had fled the country. But Jonathan knew he was still in Britain, biding his time. He would not leave until he sought retribution for the death of his brother. He knew him by reputation; Sean Butcher was still in England and wanted payback.

Max offered Maggie witness protection – and even a new identity – at least until Sean Butcher was found. But she categorically refused the offer. If Sean Butcher was coming for her, nothing would stop him. She couldn't live life by constantly looking over her shoulder, or worse, always afraid he would go after her friends while she hid.

'I can't leave Friars Meadow. It's my home. My life and my family are here,' said Maggie.

'I didn't know you had family in town,' said Max.

'My friends are my family.'

Max conceded, but he also feared for her. He saw how Jonathan was when he was with her. GCHQ and the police could not continue with round-the-clock protection for Maggie indefinitely. If Sean was out for revenge, he would bide his time and strike a week, a month, or even a year from now.

Maggie wanted to go home. Jonathan reluctantly agreed, but with stringent security measures.

By early September, Maggie was back home and working with Chloe at the council. Chloe was allowed to keep her position as mayor, but the Home Office stipulated that Maggie and Chloe could have nothing to do with the trust from this day forth.

They both agreed that their council work was rewarding enough. The government allowed the trust to continue with its depleted funds, especially after the Home Office received thousands of letters of complaint from residents in Friars Meadow and the surrounding towns in Totnes, all demanding the trust must be allowed to continue its work. The townspeople knew exactly who to write to, thanks to Ernie Chandler.

Subsequently, the trust was eight hundred thousand pounds lighter in funds. The shoe factory was now owned and operated by its employees and could not be touched. As agreed, a small portion of the factory's profits were donated back to the trust each month. This was then handed over to the Chancellor of the Exchequer until the full balance of the suitcase was paid back. As for the balance of the 'suitcase' money that was not deposited, Maggie and her friends decided to keep that piece of information to themselves.

The trustees made sure that there were enough funds to maintain the gardens and all other town initiatives. Julie and Morwenna took pay-cuts, but Sam covered their losses with shifts at the pub. Anaya declined her trustee salary, as her income as area nurse was ample enough – especially now that she was married to Dr Sharma, who himself had graciously donated funds to the trust.

Once all the commotion had settled down, everything got back to normal. Except, Maggie had trouble sleeping. She kept one eye open to every sound inside and outside of the house. Even the sounds of her mother's chimes, playing their tunes on the wind, now gave her the jitters. Creaking doors and shutters made for restless nights, but this was only part of the truth. She hadn't seen Jonathan for nearly a month. He had been working in Cheltenham while Maggie was in Friars Meadow, and she missed him.

*   *   *

On a fresh, crisp Monday morning, Maggie was driving to work. She drove down the same familiar road that snaked along the river, as she had done hundreds of times before.

The van appeared from nowhere – she didn't have time to react. It came up close behind her and rammed into the back of her car, time and time again, causing her to swerve. She couldn't slow down or pull over. If she did, she knew Sean Butcher would shoot her dead. Maggie couldn't outrun him – especially in heels. She tried to reach for her mobile, but then she had trouble controlling the car; she needed two hands on the wheel to prevent herself from running off the road.

She sped up. She knew these roads better than he did.

Maggie's eyes were wide open. Her hands were rigid on the steering wheel. It wasn't working – he was right behind her. As they came to a sharp turn, he sped up beside her and veered hard left, sending her car veering off the road and down a small ravine into the river below. Her airbag deployed, but her car tipped over and over and landed upside-down in the river. Water came in through the cracked windows. She had trouble getting her bearings as she tried to unfasten her seat belt. Her left leg throbbed, as did her head. She noticed blood swimming in the water around her.

But the frigid water kept her alert.

Maggie finally unclipped her seatbelt and landed upside down on the car roof. Pulling her left leg free, the pain was excruciating. She noticed the large gash in her thigh. The door was jammed, but she managed to unwind what was left of the window — it was just enough to crawl out. Dragging herself through the water, she collapsed on the other side of the river.

Her fear mounted now that she was out of the car. She couldn't run or walk; she had nowhere to go. She anxiously waited for Sean Butcher to shoot her at any second.

She lay down and started to cry. It couldn't end like this.

But the fatal bullet never came. She laid there for what felt like an eternity. After a time, help arrived in the form of a British postal van. By the time the ambulance arrived, she was delirious. In moments of ebbing consciousness, Maggie caught snippets of her journey to the hospital. She glimpsed doctors and nurses moving around her as pain shot through her thigh and head.

Then, bliss.

*   *   *

When Maggie woke several hours later, she found her friends standing around her in a private room at the Exeter Public Hospital. Jonathan had insisted she be kept isolated and safe. There was an armed SO19 officer stationed in the corridor outside her door in case Sean Butcher tried again.

While the twins and Harriet sat on the end of the bed, Anaya read her chart and talked to Julie, Morwenna, and Chloe. Seeing her friends around her, Maggie felt a false sense of safety. She knew that Sean Butcher was still out there. Why hadn't he killed her? Her thoughts were muddled, and she had a headache. Sean hated her enough to kill her but hadn't. Why was he playing with her? Had someone driven by?

She looked around the room at all the people who loved her most. Then, she saw Jonathan, and strangely she felt like the luckiest person in the world.

He walked up to the bed and sat beside her.

His warm smile filled her with the certain calmness that she only felt around him. After a few moments of fussing over her and a get-well kiss, Maggie's friends left the room to give them some time alone.

'He should have killed you. Why didn't he?' pondered Jonathan.

'I don't know. I thought I was going to die in the river,' said Maggie, hoarsely, trying not to cry.

'He's playing with you,' said Jonathan.

'To what purpose?'

'I don't know, yet.' Jonathan looked down at Maggie's bruised hand. He placed his own hand on top of it. 'I don't know what I would have done if he had killed you. I should have insisted you go into witness protection. I'm so sorry, Maggie.'

'I chose to stay at home. I can't live waiting for a bullet to come. I still have the motion sensors – they're watching over me, as well as Ernie, Mrs McGuigan, Chloe and Sam, and the others.' The warmth of his hand was comforting. She didn't want him to remove it.

Jonathan sat with Maggie for another fifteen minutes before he had to get back to work. He would use all the resources the security services had at their disposal to find Sean Butcher.

Jonathan spoke to the armed SO19 officer at the door for a minute before leaving. Maggie watched him go. She wanted to yell out to him to come back. Julie and Jeremy came back in, followed by Chloe, Anaya, Morwenna and her children. Morwenna said that she would take the children home; Mrs McGuigan had offered to look after them. Then, Morwenna would pop into Maggie's to get some of her personal items. This was allowed only if she was accompanied by an armed police escort.

'Do you think that cute one outside would escort me?' smiled Morwenna.

Morwenna kissed Maggie on the forehead and left with Fin, Alfie, and Harriet, who left Maggie her Paddington Bear for comfort. Maggie felt like crying. She didn't know whether it was from fear or happiness.

Maggie told Chloe, Anaya, and Julie what Jonathan had said about Sean Butcher. They couldn't understand why Sean hadn't killed her.

'Maybe he wasn't after you, but someone else,' Jeremy offered.

'What do you mean, sweetheart?' asked Julie.

'It was Jonathan's operation that got his brother killed. Maybe he wants Jonathan killed, and couldn't find him, so he put you in the hospital to draw him out,' Jeremy reasoned matter-of-factly. He had overheard their earlier conversation but had sat quietly reading a book, feigning disinterest.

'Oh my god,' said Maggie. 'What if he's here at the hospital now? Jonathan's walking outside into a trap!'

'Not if we can help it,' said Chloe. She ran from the room and straight to the SO19 officer. As Chloe talked to the police officer, Julie pulled out her mobile. The only phone number that GCHQ had given out during the investigation was Angela Milford's. Maggie's mobile was at the bottom of the river, and she didn't know Jonathan's mobile number by heart. Julie dialled Angela's mobile and waited for what seemed like an eternity.

'Angela Milford speaking.'

Julie blurted out everything that had just taken place.

'Thank you.'

The phone went dead on the other end. The SO19 officer was already running down the corridor and heading for the stairwell. If he could get down to the ground level quickly, he could catch up with Jonathan before he exited the hospital.

Maggie held Anaya's hand tightly. Her only thought repeated itself on loop: *Not again, please God, not again.*

*   *   *

Jonathan walked out of the lift on the ground level while trying to dial Angela's mobile. It was engaged. He tried her desk landline. He left her a voice message with instructions. He tried her mobile again. *Engaged.* He needed to get back to the office.

As he walked out of the hospital and into the car park, he tried dialling Max's mobile. But it was also engaged, so he left him a message.

He reached into his pocket for his keys. He was walking fast; he had no time to lose. He needed to find Sean Butcher; this had to end. Unprofessionally, he wasn't paying attention to his surroundings. His mind was on Maggie. He didn't see Sean climb out of a parked car on the edge of the car park until it was too late.

Sean's right hand and arm went across his chest, reaching inside his jacket. As Jonathan unlocked his car, he closed in on the man who'd orchestrated the death of his brother.

Sean had a silencer attached to his pistol. He would walk up behind him, shoot him in the head, and leave him sitting in his car.

Sean aimed his gun at the back of Jonathan's head.

Then a bullet ripped through his skull, entering through his right temple. Sean Butcher was dead before he hit the ground.

Jonathan spun around and jumped back against his car as he saw Sean Butcher lying in a pool of his own blood. It was *déjà vu* for Jonathan, looking down at the second Butcher brother.

The SO19 officer raced up beside him. They exchanged a silent nod. Jonathan's phone rang. He listened as an irate Angela warned him of a potential attack.

Hedging Your Bets

October

'*Fucking MI5*,' yelled Max.

More than one analyst heard the ranting of Max Evans as he stormed out of his office and walked down the Street to Jonathan's office.

'You're not going to fucking believe this,' said Max.

'I probably will, but surprise me anyway,' said Jonathan.

'James Hamilton is now the new managing director of Phoenix Security.'

'*What?*'

'He's been working with MI5 ever since we discovered what was on the notebook. It seems our cousins in London didn't believe we could find the stolen software, so they hedged their bets and recruited Hamilton — in exchange for not only immunity, but a seat on the fucking board,' said Max as he slowly calmed down and stopped pacing the floor in front of Jonathan.

'You know, it was a smart idea to have someone on the inside. It's probably why Hamilton urged Monroe to be at the meet in person. That would ensure Hamilton secured Monroe's job after the dust settled. We only ever had Hamilton's involvement, not Monroe's. Hamilton will be an MI5 stooge for the rest of his working life. They'll have him and Phoenix Security in their pockets.'

'Yeah, I know. But I'm pissed off that I didn't think of it.'

'We have Monroe for the conspiracy to commit murder and espionage. The Butcher brothers are dead, and Malcolm Barker-Smith has been dealt with,' said Jonathan.

'True ... Fuck it, I'm off to the gym, I need to let off some steam,' said Max, as he walked towards the door. Then, as if he'd had a sudden thought, he turned back. 'Oh, by the way, what about Maggie Malloy? How is she?' enquired Max.

'She's good, I believe. I haven't seen her for a while. She's getting on with her life,' said Jonathan, sounding despondent.

'Well, what are you waiting for? Get down there and visit her! I wouldn't let her get away if I were you. She's a keeper,' smiled Max, as he tapped his knuckles on the door before leaving the room. Jonathan watched Max leave his office, knowing that he was absolutely right.

Cleaning House

Archibald Monroe pleaded guilty for conspiring to commit robbery and murder. He took the plea bargain that his QC had urged him to consider.

Barker-Smith had been found guilty of conspiracy and subsequently suffered a mental breakdown, stating that he was too ill to stand trial – as all good politicians do. This charade didn't last long, and he was subsequently sentenced to five years.

The government had set up a review of the banking practices in Totnes. Through this inquiry, many people came forward with testimonies of wrongdoing. It was going to be a long commission, and people were seeking compensation.

Thomas Carlyle was unceremoniously sacked, along with a number of other branch managers. Both he and Larry Morecombe would be charged with a number of offences. Since they were both in the midst of divorce proceedings, they were sharing a rental property in Friars Meadow until it was sold.

Mayor Silverton was true to her word and implemented the same initiatives that had flourished in Friars Meadow all around Totnes. The logging would commence the next year. It was going to be a prosperous year for Totnes.

Sarah, Morwenna's daughter, had started working full-time for Chloe at the council as her aide. She still found time to drive the mobile library twice a week and would be starting university the next year. Chloe continued to see a future politician growing inside Sarah and made it her priority to see that she flourished.

Maggie and her friends had grown even closer because of their adventure and ordeal. They nurtured a sincere appreciation for the meaning of friendship. For Maggie, they weren't just her friends, but her family – a very large extended family.

When Maggie looked back on the woman she had once been, she realised that all her anxieties and fears had been a kaleido-scope of emotions she'd had trouble expressing. They had been boxed up, just like Pandora. Maggie was free to explore a whole new chapter in her life, full of confidence and love.

She needed to be brave and to tell Jonathan how she felt.

Maggie would have done just that if Jonathan hadn't turned up on her doorstep that cold October evening.

Come All Ye Faithful

December

Christmas was once again upon the town of Friars Meadow. The colourful Christmas decorations were pride and place all over town. They certainly gave the Ritz a run for its money. The lights lit up the snowy night sky and sparkled as delicate snowflakes fell over them, illuminating all their beautiful colours.

Maggie and her friends were at the pub on Christmas Eve, drinking too much, eating too much, and singing in their most strained, flamboyant voices.

Everyone was present. Anaya, her new husband Theo, and her two daughters were there. One of her daughters, Maya, was presently working behind the bar, while Sarita was accompanied by her boyfriend.

Chloe, Matthew, and Sam were together, as Sam had taken the night off. He was spending more nights with his new fiancé.

When Sam proposed to Chloe at the beginning of December, it was an offer she couldn't refuse. He presented her with a gift box, decorated with an overly large red ribbon and bow on it. When she opened it, a beautiful white kitten was staring up at her. Around its neck was a ribbon with a diamond ring attached to it. A note inside the box said, *two for one offer*. Chloe laughed, cried, and said yes all at the same time.

Meanwhile, Morwenna's kids were excited about tonight's visitor. Her children had negotiated the opening of one present before bed, and Fin and Alfie wanted to get home to bed absurdly early. Morwenna wasn't going to look a gift horse in the mouth. She still had some wrapping to do.

Julie and Jeremy were at the pub with her parents. Julie had enrolled at university and would be studying law. Ernie offered to take her on as his intern, considering how busy he'd been these last few years. This was a relief to Alisha, who had been run off her feet – although she loved every hectic minute of it.

It was no surprise the anyone, Ernie escorted Alisha, his legal secretary and now office manager, to the Christmas Eve celebrations. Their friendship had grown over the last few years, and Ernie cursed himself for being so blind.

Mrs McGuigan and Elle Morecombe walked to the pub together that evening. Mrs McGuigan had taken Elle on as her new lodger. They would be spending Christmas dinner with Chloe, Sam, and Matthew. Elle's divorce had gone through, and her house had been sold. She wasn't afraid of her future – in fact, she was excited about it. She had bought a small cottage outside of town and was planning a holiday abroad. She'd even invited Mrs McGuigan to join her. Elle had also taken Chloe up on her offer and would commence working at the Totnes Council after her travels.

Meanwhile, in the pub, Jeremy was propelling a thousand questions at Jonathan. He now knew what he wanted to become when he grew up – a spook. Jonathan managed to avoid answering most questions, thanks to the secrecy act. At the same time, he made a mental note to keep an eye on Jeremy over the next few years. His intelligence was clearly off the charts. If Jeremy still wanted to join the security services once he finished university, Jonathan wanted to make sure GCHQ got first dibs before MI5 could get their hands on him.

They all raised a toast to the happy couple – Sam and Chloe. Maggie and Jonathan smiled and joined in the cheers. Sam started to cry, telling everyone that he was the luckiest man in the world.

Maggie couldn't recall a happier Christmas. She leaned back against Jonathan's shoulder and listened as the whole pub sang another Christmas carol.

Snow could be seen gently falling outside the windows. Maggie snuggled into Jonathan's chest. He put his arms around her, and Maggie smiled the smile of a truly happy woman. She knew in her heart that she could live anywhere on Earth with this man in her arms.

And shortly, she would.

Acknowledgments

This story came to me many years ago. Like any good plot, the writing process of this work has grown and developed over the years to the book which you now read. In 2021, it won the Readers' Favorite's Honorable Mention Award for adult fiction adventure, and I am humbled by the support it received.

This was my first published book in adult fiction, and I have since had the opportunity to embark on a new adventure, publishing a children's novel called *The Interlopers*.

While this is being written, I have two more novels in the editing stages, which hopefully will be published in the new year. Thank you, dear readers, for making my dreams a reality and for joining Maggie and friends on this adventure.

Last, but not least, what is a heist without excellent co-conspirators? I would like to thank the team at Aurora House for all their help in making this book possible, and my loved ones who support my every plot no matter the twists.

About the Author

Completing a Bachelor of Arts, majoring in Creative Writing and Literature, brought out Paula Welch's passion for writing, and she hasn't looked back.

Paula has now written two novels, *The Interlopers* and *A River of Fortune*, and is currently working on her next two.

You are holding Paula's refreshed debut into adult fiction, *A River of Fortune*. A tale of suspense, intrigue, romance, and an amazing heist.

After this read, to add to your collection, be sure to look out for *The Interlopers*, Paula's first young adult novel, which she has centred around the wonders of space and the ideas of what is actually 'out there'. As Paula says, 'It never hurts to dream, because one day your dreams may come true.'

Keep up with Paula's latest news at www.paulawelch.com.au